Alaska Firestorm

The Blazing Hearts Wildfire Series

LoLo Paige

The Blazing Hearts Wildfire Series
Burned by love...healed by fire.

Alaska Spark – Book One
Alaska Inferno – Book Two
Alaska Blaze – Book Three
Alaska Firestorm – Book Four
Alaska Flame – Novella

IN ALASKA'S UNTAMED wilderness, fearless women battle raging infernos and their own inner demons. This action-packed romantic suspense series follows brave wildland firefighters navigating a world where flames and desire burn equally fierce. Working alongside daring smokejumpers and seasoned incident commanders, these heroines face danger at every turn in the Land of the Midnight Sun. Each standalone book delivers medium steam, pulse-pounding suspense, and the raw beauty of Alaska. Ready for your next favorite trope? You've found it!

Workplace romances
Alpha male protectors
Strong female firefighters
Friends to lovers, enemies to lovers, friendship alliances
First responders in small towns
Romantic suspense in Alaska's spectacular settings
Life or death stakes fighting catastrophic wildfires
Sabotage and danger

Wildland Fire Terms

AFS: Alaska Fire Service, located at Fort Wainwright, in Fairbanks, Alaska. The Alaska Fire Service is a branch of the U.S. Bureau of Land Management that takes the lead on wildland fire suppression for the northern half of Alaska.

After Action Review: A discussion of what went right and wrong while fighting a fire, resulting in lessons learned and how they'll be applied in the future.

Alphalicious: One who takes charge with a confidence that others find attractive.

Anchor point: The point where firefighters begin fireline construction.

BLM: U.S. Bureau of Land Management, in the U.S. Department of the Interior, who employs federal firefighters in several states.

BOLO: Be on the Look-Out. A term mostly used in law enforcement but also used in fire.

Containment: A fire is contained when it's surrounded by a fireline, where trees and brush are removed, robbing the flames of fuel. Fires can jump containment if wind-driven.

DOF: State of Alaska, Division of Forestry. Lead agency for wildland fire suppression for the southern half of Alaska.

Demobe: Short for demobilization, when crews and individuals are released from a fire.

Flank: The two side boundaries of a fire roughly parallel to the main direction of spread.

Head: The leading edge and most rapidly spreading part of a fire.

Incident Command System: A standardized on-scene emergency management system all entities use without jurisdictional boundaries. The IC, or Incident Commander, oversees all of it.

JBER: (pronounced J-Bear) Joint Base Elmendorf–Richardson is a United States military facility in Anchorage, Alaska. It's a consolidation of the United States Air Force's Elmendorf Air Force Base and the United States Army's Fort Richardson.

Mop-up: The process firefighters use to extinguish and remove burning debris after an area has burned. Firefighters often cold-trail soil, feeling for still burning hot spots.

NIFC: The National Interagency Fire Center in Boise, Idaho, consists of nine federal and state agencies who establish wildland fire policy. They also provide nationwide logistical support with people and equipment for wildland firefighting.

Pulaski: A long-handled chopping and trenching tool used in fireline construction. The tool has an ax blade on one side and a hoe-like blade on the other.

Chapter 1

Big Lake, Alaska

Ripley Beecher fought the controls of the air tanker that bucked with another violent pocket of turbulence, nearly wrenching the yoke from her white-knuckled grip. The familiar burn of terror and determination mingled—a cocktail she'd grown addicted to over the years. Boiling air from beneath them tossed the twenty-ton aircraft like a child's toy. It was all she could do to maintain control.

"Dammit!" she hissed through clenched teeth. Sweat beaded beneath her flight helmet, sliding down her temples. "Hold steady, girl." She talked more to aircraft than she did most people. At least the planes listened.

The altimeter spun downward. Waving treetops of tall Alaska spruce rushed up to meet them, crowns igniting like thousands of torches. Trees that had witnessed countless seasons during their stay on earth were now gone, decades of growth reduced to ash in minutes.

"Left engine's running hot," First Officer Loman called from the co-pilot seat, his usual mansplaining replaced by supportive urgency. "Oil pressure dropping."

"I see that." Ripley didn't waste breath on anything but essentials. The metallic taste of fear coated her tongue—not for herself, but for the homeowners below. The pressure was on—if she didn't complete this drop, an entire subdivision would be lost to the insatiable red monster.

Her radio crackled to life. "Tanker One-Six-Zero, this is the Big Lake incident commander," said a deep voice. "We're tracking your approach to the drop. Those downdrafts are brutal today."

"Copy that, Big Lake. Can you give us an update?"

"Winds have shifted to the northeast. There's crowning and spotting ahead of the main front. Evacuation is underway, but we need that fire retardant drop ASAP. Bird Dog, our spotter plane, will lead you to the drop point," rumbled the voice, steady as granite.

A squawk on the radio signaled the arrival of her escort. "Tanker One-Six-Zero, this is Bird Dog. We have you on visual. Follow me in."

"Copy, Bird Dog. On your six," she replied, maneuvering the large air tanker into position behind the smaller plane, gauging their distance by airspeed. She followed the blinking lights through the smoke while scanning the terrain.

The evacuation scene below twisted her stomach—cars, pets, and people fleeing for their lives. She'd been one of those people racing away from the Malibu fires with nothing but the clothes on her back, after abandoning her stuck car in panicked traffic over a year ago.

The tanker lurched sideways, tossing Ripley's covered coffee mug across the cockpit. Loman made an expert catch before it hit the floor.

"Steady as she goes," he said, without missing a beat. "One thousand feet, slow to drop speed."

As they approached the drop zone, Ripley's focus narrowed to a laser point. Every sense was on high alert, her muscles tense and ready. The violent turbulence buffeted the plane, but her hands stayed firm and measured on the controls.

Her jaw tightened at the deteriorating situation. "Big Lake, how do you want the drops—two at thirteen hundred gallons each or one with a full salvo load?" She glimpsed the emergency lights flashing on roadways below, evacuating homeowners. They needed minutes. She could give them those minutes. Lives and property hung in the balance.

"I need the full monty, or we'll lose these homes. Maintain fifteen hundred feet AGL until you reach the drop zone. Winds are nasty. Use caution," replied the incident commander. His Sam Elliott voice could convince her to drop slurry inside a tornado.

"Understood. Tanker One-Six-Zero inbound at fifteen hundred above ground level." Tall smoke plumes came into view, resembling a nuclear blast mushroom cloud rather than smoke from an uncontrolled wildfire.

The person coming through her headset betrayed none of the anxiety he must be experiencing on the ground. He struck her as someone who never lost his cool.

A violent updraft caught the plane in another sickening lurch, and warning alarms screamed through the flight deck. The computerized voice nagged with robotic indifference: "TERRAIN, TERRAIN. PULL UP, PULL UP."

"I know, I know! I can't pull up now, dammit!" she sassed the computer, wrestling with the fire-driven winds. At least the computer didn't care if she cussed it.

Loman's knuckles whitened on the gate controls. "If you're committed to dropping this load, you better do it soon, Captain."

"Hold tight." Ripley gritted her teeth; her focus narrowed to the single task of lining up the approach. The weight of responsibility pressed down like an anvil. Seconds mattered. It was tricky to dip low enough to hit her mark while ensuring accuracy without jeopardizing safety.

The Bird Dog spotter plane danced and weaved like a drunken dragonfly, its pilot fighting the same treacherous air currents. "Think you should abort, One-Six-Zero. Full deterioration. Pull up!" shouted the spotter pilot.

Then she saw why, and a chill shot up her spine despite the convective heat. In their path was a wall of flame corkscrewing upward in a vicious firenado—a tornado, only with fire.

"No! Anything but this!" she sputtered. The sight of spinning flames seized her chest as the column of fire towered higher than their altitude, sucking Blazebuster toward its deadly vortex. As Ripley throttled up speed, the left engine temperature gauge flashed red.

"Left engine's overheating!" Loman called out.

"Got it!" She stayed steady despite the sheer terror that rocked her insides. "Negative on the abort, Bird Dog! Making this drop."

"Copy that." The spotter plane sprayed a smoke trail to mark the drop zone, showing Ripley exactly where to place the retardant.

Ripley wrenched the yoke back, coaxing Blazebuster's nose up. Pride and stubbornness warred inside her—she'd rather die than present weakness to the firefighters on the ground—they were counting on her.

The intense winds threatened to roll them inverted. Every instinct screamed to bank away from the firenado, but that would ruin the drop angle. Ripley held steady, sweat pooling on her lower back, neck hairs standing on end.

"Tanker One-Six-Zero, conditions rapidly deteriorating," stated the incident commander in his steady voice. "Fire behavior poses a risk to aircraft. Advise to abort." He was giving her an out.

She wasn't having it. She could do this. "Negative. Proceeding with the drop. Bird Dog, I'm staying on approach."

"Copy that, One-Six-Zero," responded the spotter pilot. "Hold her steady. This air is lethal."

"We can't fly any lower, or we won't pull out of it," warned Loman, his tension apparent.

"Another hundred feet. Come on, girl," she coaxed the tanker, itching to dump the payload sloshing in her tanks.

The firenado sent a blast of hot air radiating outward. Blazebuster suddenly dropped, and spruce trees stretched upward like grasping fingers.

"Holy shit!" Loman gasped as the treetops rushed toward them.

She could damn near count the needles on the tree branches, and her stomach dropped with the altitude—the sickening sensation of free fall. For a heart-stopping second, the tanker dipped dangerously close to the tall spruce. Then a sickening *thwack-thwack-thwack* echoed through the fuselage as it dipped too low—spruce tops smacking the undercarriage. Warning lights flashed, and the left engine temperature climbed higher.

Ripley locked onto her drop target. "NOW!"

Loman punched the release, and the aircraft bucked upward as two thousand six hundred gallons of red slurry streamed from its belly. Ripley eyed the monitor to make sure the drop hit the target. Hard to gauge with smoke mixed in with the retardant. Tall flames consumed everything in their path while thick smoke billowed into the sky, lit beneath by a hellish glow.

She hauled back on the controls, fighting to gain altitude with one struggling engine. Her heart banged her chest so violently she wondered if Loman could hear it over the alarms.

"Come on, girl, get your ass up to altitude!" How many times had she muttered these words when she'd dropped slurry on the Pacific Palisades and Eaton Canyon fires in California? "Just a little more lift. Come on, girl." She gritted her teeth so hard she thought they'd crack.

Like a reluctant phoenix, the aircraft clawed its way upward, engines screaming.

Five hundred feet. Six hundred. Eight hundred.

The warning alarms fell silent, save for the steady ping of the malfunctioning engine indicator. The crew persevered, along with Blazebuster. They'd live to fight fire another day.

Loman shot her an affirming glance. "Good flying there, Tex. That turbulence sucked."

"So what's new?" she murmured, blowing out air. "She did good, though." Pride and relief mingled after doing the impossible yet again.

"How's that left engine?" Loman shot her a concerned side-eye.

"Still running." She eyed the indicator. "Blazebuster thinks she's a logger the way she sawed off those treetops." She banked the plane toward the Palmer air field.

"We should outfit Blazebuster with chainsaws under her belly," joked Loman.

Blazebuster's radio sprang to life with that melodious voice. "One-Six-Zero, saw you bucking those winds. Perfect placement, a thing of beauty. You saved an untold number of homes and bought us valuable time."

"Not sure how beautiful it was, but glad we nailed it." She blew out a relieved breath. "Left engine's compromised, so returning to Palmer Air Base." The incident commander's compliment felt good. She'd take it.

"That was some flying. I remember Blazebuster from the Pacific Palisades last January."

His reference startled her. "You worked on the California fires?"

"You mean hell on earth? Yeah," he rumbled back. "Have a safe landing."

His reference carried weight—someone who understood the nightmare of those catastrophes—the reason she'd fled three thousand miles north. The shared memory created an unexpected bridge across twenty-four hundred air miles and countless scorched acres. Three weeks in Alaska, and she'd already encountered a firefighter who'd witnessed the same California hellscape.

"Copy that. One-Six-Zero clear." She was curious as heck about the man attached to that voice. Mister Unflappable, the kind whose blood pressure never budged, no matter what.

"Palmer Air Base to Tanker One-Six-Zero," radioed another voice. "We're aware of your engine. Emergency crews standing by. You're cleared for landing on Runway Two."

"Copy that, Palmer," she responded, running through emergency landing procedures with Loman.

For once, her first officer didn't mansplain aircraft operations to her. Instead, he worked silently through the checklist, his way of approving how she'd handled the drop.

She missed the bewitching voice of the Big Lake incident commander, wishing he hadn't gone silent.

Stop pining for a male voice you heard for less than ten minutes. You're pathetic, Beecher.

As the Palmer runway came into view, her grip on the controls relaxed—the familiar centering calm that always followed a high-adrenaline drop, the quiet after the battle.

The rush of survival after a dangerous drop was her addiction, her drug of choice. It wasn't her first close call, and it certainly wouldn't be her last. The adrenaline crash would come later, once she was alone... the trembling hands, the hollow exhaustion, always checking herself: had she been brave or stupid, and how much risk was too much?

As she guided Blazebuster's descent to the runway, she took pride in her chosen career: the danger, the thrill, and the satisfaction of making a difference. The solitary life of an aerial firefighter suited her perfectly, despite the loneliness that sometimes ached inside of her. No room for romance or serious relationships in her life.

Fire is my faithful companion, and danger is my constant lover.

She keyed her mic. "Palmer Tower, Tanker One-Six-Zero on final approach. Left engine at critical temperature."

As the runway rushed up to meet her, she thought this was just another day in the books, another deadly fire, and another time she'd cheated death. She liked to joke with friends that each flight was just one more day at the office.

If they only knew.

Chapter 2

Tanner

Tanner Westlake squinted against the morning sun, pleased that the mud drop had slowed the fire enough for crews to get a containment line around it. The Big Lake fire had raged for hours, but the drop had made all the difference.

"Damn, that was some flying."

He had coordinated countless drops, but this pilot's precision in turbulent conditions was a thing of beauty. The aircraft had swooped low, released a perfect stream of red slurry exactly where he'd needed it, and saved an entire subdivision of homes.

When the fire subsided, he decided to take a quick drive out to the Palmer Air Base.

He wanted to... no, he *had* to meet that tanker pilot.

The one-hour drive from Big Lake to the air base gave him time to reflect on the morning's events. He'd known conditions were bad when he sent the tanker crew, had factored that aspect into his decision to drop one full load instead of two half loads. He just hadn't known *how* bad. But the tanker pilot hadn't hesitated, even when he'd counseled recall. Her skill had impressed the hell out of him. He'd rarely seen such accuracy under pressure, while navigating severe turbulence.

When the Alaska Fire Service said they were sending him their best, a new hire from the lower forty-eight, they hadn't been kidding. Not a lot of pilots could have handled that drop, and she'd made it seem like a seamless maneuver. He'd observed her dropping slurry on the deadly Los Angeles fires back in January, and he'd been curious to meet her ever since. In his view, tanker pilots were the *real* heroes of wildland firefighting because they put their lives on the line with every drop.

As Tanner pulled into the air base, he spotted Tanker One-Six-Zero next to a sizeable hangar. His gaze tracked like magnetic north to a shapely figure in a sage-green Nomex flight suit. She had her back to him as he got out of his truck and approached. She was talking animatedly with a plane mechanic.

"I'm telling you, that left engine was running hot," she said, hands on her hips. "We need to check it before my next run."

"I'll get right on it," replied the mechanic, striding out to Tanker One-Six-Zero.

As Tanner approached, the pilot turned. Her reddish-blonde hair was pulled back into a long ponytail, save for a few loose tendrils. He was captivated by her statuesque pose, one arm curved around a white helmet.

"You must be the one." He stopped in front of her, smiling, careful to keep his distance.

"You mean the one who nags plane mechanics? And you are...?" She lowered her aviation shades, sapphire eyes darting to the name tag on his yellow Nomex shirt.

He extended his hand. "Tanner Westlake, incident commander for the Big Lake fire."

"The man with the voice. Hello." Her grip was firm as she assessed him. "Ripley Beecher. Nice to meet you, Mr. Westlake. What brings you out here to Palmer?"

"First off, Mr. Westlake is my dad. Call me Tanner." He flashed her a toothy grin, much wider than he intended. "I wanted to meet the person who made that impressive drop in those intense wind conditions. That, and I'd like your input on strategy."

Her brows lifted in surprise. "Just doing my job. How's the line holding?"

"You bought us the time we needed. However, I have concerns about our overall strategy with so many structures in the area." He had no actual concerns, so he'd made up an excuse to keep talking with her.

"Is that right?" Ripley appeared curious. "What might those be?"

Tanner hesitated as he eyed a skinny blond man striding toward them. "Do you have time to discuss it over a quick coffee?" He pinched a mosquito from the side of his neck, as if picking lint.

"Don't you have to be back in the action?"

"I have the Aurora Hotshot Crew from the Alaska Fire Service monitoring fire behavior until I get back," he rushed to say.

The blond guy stood next to Ripley and dipped a nod at Tanner. "Ready for some breakfast while the mechanic checks out our engine?"

Ripley ignored his question to introduce them. "This is Tanner Westlake. He's the IC of the Big Lake fire. Mr. West—I mean Tanner—this is Nubs Loman, my first officer."

Loman's brows shot up. "Good to meet you. Yours was the voice on the radio."

"Guilty." Tanner shook his hand. "From what I could tell, you're with a good flyer."

"You don't have to tell me," said Loman, nodding. "Beecher has proven herself repeatedly."

Ripley swiveled her head to Loman with raised brows. "What I do isn't a matter of proving myself. It's a matter of getting the job done," she said sweetly.

Tanner sensed tension between the two as she added, "The IC liked our drop."

"She's good, isn't she?" Loman put an arm around her shoulder as if claiming her for his own. "I'm lucky to be her first officer." He said it in a hands-off manner, which amused Tanner.

Ripley rolled out of her first officer's grasp. "Mr. Westlake—I mean Tanner, liked our drop and wants to talk about attack strategy, but he's pushed for time. Let's get a coffee." She headed inside the building, leaving the two men to follow.

Tanner caught Loman's frown and knew it for what it was. *One of those possessive types*, he thought to himself. His instinct told him this woman didn't tolerate being controlled... by anyone.

They made their way to the air ops break room, where Tanner poured coffee into three styrofoam cups.

He handed one to Ripley. "I'm thinking of focusing on the left flank. The forecast has the wind changing direction later this afternoon. If we don't get ahead of it, we'll lose our containment line. How did it look from your vantage point?" His head motioned skyward.

"From what I observed, the right flank is where you should focus your containment efforts. If that goes, you'll lose the town of Big Lake," replied Ripley.

Tanner pried his gaze away from her flushed lips as she casually leaned against the counter, sipping her coffee.

"We could lose subdivisions if we hit the right. Bird Dog tells us we need to get that left flank first."

"The fire is burning too fast on the right. I can hit that one easy with Blazebuster once we refuel and get that left engine fixed." She glanced at Loman, who nodded.

Tanner gave her a closemouthed smile. "Good name for an air tanker."

"I gave it the name," said Loman proudly through his Tom Cruise smile.

Ripley chuckled. "He did, actually. I can't take credit for that one."

Tanner regarded Loman. "What do you think, the left or right flank?"

"I'd say hit the left first," seconded Loman. "Although both need containment as fast as possible."

"I disagree." She gave Tanner a direct look. "The rate of spread is faster on the right flank, which is closer to the town of Big Lake. I can hit one flank with a full load or hit them both equally with half loads. Up to you."

"Good point." He pretended to consider.

"It's hard to tell from the ground," she pointed out. "Why don't you go up with Bird Dog or have someone take you on a recon flight?"

Tanner knew all that. He tried shaking off the guilt for cooking up this conversation to talk to her. A devious smile tugged at his lips—he'd already had someone fly a recon drone over the fire, but he skipped that minor detail.

His cell phone sounded. Tara O'Connor, the Aurora Hotshot Crew supervisor.

He tapped to answer. "What's up, Tara?"

"Strong wind shift, sooner than predicted. We have a major flare-up on the right flank. She's running fast. Can you order a slurry drop to hit it?"

He raised his brows, looking at Ripley. "Consider it done. I'm on my way there now."

"Copy that, see you soon," said Tara, ending the call.

Tanner slid his phone into the pocket of his yellow Nomex shirt. "Turns out you were right. My hotshot supervisor says we need a drop on the right flank."

"I won't say I told you so, but I've flown fire a long time. I know what I'm talking about." When her gaze locked with his, he didn't give a flip who'd been right.

"I'm on it." Ripley fed coins into a vending machine to get a breakfast roll. "Grab a bear claw, Loman. We don't have time for breakfast." She nabbed a roll, downed her coffee, and tossed her cup into the trash.

"Good to meet you, Mr. Westlake—I mean Tanner. Maybe we'll meet up on other fires."

He hoped so. He wouldn't mind seeing her again—hell, he'd love to hit on her—but not during work. That kind of thing was frowned upon.

Tanner lifted the radio from his shoulder holster and keyed it. "Aurora Hotshots, do you copy?"

Tara responded. "Copy. Good news?"

"Affirmative. Tanker One-Six-Zero is en route, ETA in fifteen."

"Copy that," said Tara.

"Westlake clear." Tanner smiled at Ripley. "Aurora Crew has been notified. Be careful up there." This was a given, but he always said it, anyway. He walked out with Ripley and Loman to their aircraft.

She paused at the base of the aircraft's stairs. "Try not to worry, Mr. Incident Commander. We've got this." She gave him a half smile and climbed into the cockpit, while Loman boarded the other side.

Tanner backed away as the Dash 8-400AT engines fired up. Ripley gave him a wave, then taxied and lifted off toward Big Lake. He strode to his truck, admiring her poise and self-assurance. Although he'd driven out here expressly to meet this pilot, he reminded himself this was only business.

Right. Keep telling yourself that, Westlake.

When Ripley's voice came over his radio, confirming a successful drop on the right flank and seconded by Tara, he breathed relief.

"Good work, One-Six-Zero," he spoke into his radio. "It's been a pleasure working with you."

"Glad to be of service," she replied. "Till next time. One-Six-Zero clear."

"IC clear," he drawled back.

Till next time? He kind of liked the sound of that.

Wildland fire was a small world, so he figured they'd probably run into each other down the line. He wouldn't mind seeing this feisty, skilled pilot again.

He wouldn't mind at all.

Chapter 3

R*ipley*

Later that afternoon, Ripley stood on the tarmac at the BLM Alaska Fire Service base in Fairbanks, watching as the ground crew swarmed around her air tanker. The Big Lake fire had been mostly contained, but the memory of those intense hours lingered, along with thoughts of the incident commander she'd met.

She rubbed her tense shoulder and shoved away the image of Tanner Westlake's amiable smile and calm demeanor. It wasn't like her to dwell on someone she'd barely met, especially during a busy fire season, but their brief interaction took up more real estate in her mind than she cared to admit: he was amazingly alphalicious.

"I've seen that deep-in-thought look before." Mel Faraday's voice broke through her reverie. The seasoned helicopter pilot strolled up to her, his weathered face creased with a familiar smile. He adjusted his Alaska Fire Service baseball cap.

Since she was fairly new to the Alaska wildland fire community, Ripley figured honesty was a good start—to a degree, at least. "Just thinking about the Big Lake firefight. What do you know about the IC?"

Mel's eyebrows rose. "Tanner Westlake? He has a proven reputation as one of the best fire behavior specialists and is also one of those WUI guys. Everyone thinks highly of him."

"Ah, a WUI expert." She pronounced it 'wooey,' the same as those who were familiar with the wildland urban/rural interface. "He seems... I don't know, different," she mused, pleased that fire behavior was also in her wheelhouse.

"How so?" Mel rolled his toothpick to the other side of his mouth.

"He strikes me as one of those cool-under-pressure types. Someone who doesn't get rattled when things go sideways. At least he seemed that way on the radio. And pretty much the same when I met him in person."

"You met him?" Mel peered at her curiously.

"He came out to Palmer Air Base and talked to us when we landed," she explained. "Asked my opinion on strategy for slurry drops. IC's don't normally do that. They tell *you* where to place the drops."

Mel watched a Twin Otter plane touch down. "He's also a renowned smokejumper and has incident commanded his share of fires. Even on the East Coast."

"Where is he based?" she asked with an air of nonchalance.

"The Missoula Smokejumper Base," said Mel, eyeing her.

Disappointment poked her that he wasn't based in Alaska. Now she was curious. "Does he still jump fire?"

"Not since he became a WUI expert. He worked the Southern California fires earlier this year," explained Mel.

"He mentioned that. Those were horrific fires. Half the time, we couldn't even fly because of the Santa Anas. People lost their lives, and so many others lost their homes." Recalling those experiences still chilled her to the bone.

Mel nodded somberly. "Yeah, those winds were deadly for flying fires. I'm glad you took my suggestion to transfer to

Fairbanks. You seemed extremely stressed after California. I figured coming up north might do you some good."

"California was tough. Flying fires where Dad's plane went down, was..." Ripley thought further back to another dreadful fire a few years ago, one that had wrought personal devastation. With a small shake of her head, she snapped to the present.

"So, back to Westlake. He listened to my input when we disagreed on the attack strategy. Some incident commanders don't listen to anyone," she said plaintively.

"This guy must have made an impression." Mel grinned. "It's okay to be impressed, Ripley. Doesn't make you any less of a badass."

"I have a reputation to uphold." She straightened herself with dignity. "Pilots have a badass mystique."

"Your dad used to say that."

"And he taught it to me," she replied.

Mel had been her dad's best buddy and had become like a second father to her over the years. She'd turned to him more than once for advice, feeling close to her dad whenever she was with Mel. She trusted him completely.

"For some reason, I can't get Westlake out of my head. That's not like me—I meet tons of people in wildland fire. You know me. I don't let personal relationships interfere with my job."

"That's a good policy to have. Can't say I haven't been tempted to indulge in a romance myself on occasion. Just don't let it distract you up there." He pointed at the sky.

"I don't plan on indulging in a romance," she said quickly.

He rolled his toothpick to the other side. "You never know, you could bump into Westlake somewhere down the line. Fire is a small world."

"Don't you dare let on to anyone that I wanted to know about him," she cautioned.

"My lips are sealed." Mel pretended to zip them shut. "You and I have both worked with people in wildland fire who've gotten involved. It's only natural to be attracted to those who work in our same insane world. After all, this is where we spend most of our time."

Ben, the lead mechanic, approached with a clipboard. "Captain Beecher? We found the issue with the left engine. Looks like something hit it."

"Blazebuster thought she was a chainsaw." She rolled her eyes as if the tanker had a mind of its own. "She took out some treetops."

The mechanic shrugged. "Don't worry. We'll get the engine fixed."

"Thanks. Keep me posted." She sighed, envisioning the mountains of paperwork she'd have to complete explaining the damage. StormAir, her company contractor, owned the air tankers, and they were sticklers about anything that happened to their aircraft.

She turned to Mel. "Can I borrow your truck? I'm going to run into town for a massage."

"Keep your phone handy," he replied, tossing her the keys. "Lightning storms in the forecast for Southcentral Alaska and the Interior."

"Thanks, Mel." Her hand unconsciously went to her shoulder, feeling the knots of tension. The turbulence from the Big Lake fire had done a number on her muscles.

The drive into Fairbanks gave her time to rationalize her interest in Tanner as strictly professional admiration. He'd scored points with her having worked the California fires she had—she recalled his velvety voice on the radio when dropping slurry in those hellacious Santa Ana winds. Her colleagues had praised her for her cool head in all the chaos, but back then she was too busy to wonder who the man was attached to that voice.

Yet, as she lay on the massage table an hour later and the tension ebbed from her muscles, she drifted to the image of Tanner's steady gaze and his deep drawl on her radio—harboring on—dare she think it?

Sexy? Yes, sexy. Oh, my God!

Red flags spiked all over her brain.

Nope, don't think that way about people you work with.

She thought about her love life. What love life? She almost laughed out loud. It didn't exist, and it hadn't, since forever. She hadn't been on a date since her cousin's wedding last year, when the bride had set her up with a software engineer, a stoner so narcissistic his selfies had selfies.

Ripley grimaced as the massage therapist worked out a stubborn knot, and she made a new resolve to lock these thoughts or feelings, or whatever the heck they were in her vault and throw away the key. Mel was right; she couldn't afford the distraction. She was recognized as one of the best, and that had to be enough.

After her father died, Ripley's mother had been so torn up she was medicated for weeks on end. She was never the same and eventually died of a broken heart. Ripley resolved never to love so deeply that losing them would destroy her. Love always ended in pain.

Losing Dad had been devastating, but losing her mother ten months later nearly broke her. When she lost Allison too, something snapped, and she learned to compartmentalize her grief. It worked most of the time... until she glimpsed a rainbow during flight and choked back the tears.

She dressed and left the spa, relishing her relaxation. The masseuse had done a terrific job of kneading her aching muscles. As she drove back to Fort Wainwright and the fire base, her phone buzzed. She picked it up and glanced at the text from the plane mechanic.

Captain Beecher, the left engine is salvageable. We need to replace a couple of components, then Blazebuster will be good to go.

She loved seeing the word 'Captain' after all the required hours and the years it took for her to become an aerial firefighter. Her father would have been proud of his only daughter.

Ripley grinned at the text, then texted her reply.

Whatever the hot-looking incident commander had stirred up in her, the sky was where she truly belonged. She knew that as sure as the sun rose in the east.

For now, her aerial firefighting career would have to be enough.

Chapter 4

R*ipley*
The shrill siren of her cell phone jerked her awake. She fumbled for the device on her nightstand, her heart waking up before she did. A call at three a.m. could only mean one thing.

"Beecher," she rasped, trying to sound alert.

"Ripley, it's Dave Doss," said her immediate supervisor. "We have a situation down in Anchorage. When can you be ready to fly?"

She was already out of bed, stepping into her flight suit. "Fifteen minutes. How bad is it?"

"The wildfire's moving fast through heavy spruce and birch. The fire's extreme heat is creating pyro-cumulus clouds, and it's one mile from residential and business structures. You've been specifically requested as the tanker pilot for this one."

"I have?" Her brows rose in surprise. "Is my left engine fixed?"

"Yep. The mechanic has it running in tip-top shape. They replaced some parts and are re-fueling your tanker as we speak," replied Doss.

"Good. On my way." She ended the call and zipped up her Nomex flight suit. She glimpsed herself in the mirror and blue eyes stared back. She twisted her strawberry-blonde hair into a tight bun to keep it out of the way.

At age thirty-nine, adrenaline still pulsed through her the same as when she'd experienced her first fire call over a decade ago in California. As she laced up her boots, her gaze dropped to the photo on her dresser. Allison's smile still haunted her. She'd lost her bestie from flight school two years after her parents, and not a day went by that grief didn't invade her thoughts. God had robbed her three times, and it was damn hard not to be embittered.

Ripley grabbed her day pack with her aviation gear and headed out the door into Alaska's cool summer dawn, which came early this time of year. Fires burned across the state, casting a pallor of smoke over everything, turning the sun into a red rubber ball. She'd requested a shuttle from the Alaska Fire Service to pick her up and take her to Fort Wainwright just outside of Fairbanks.

She took advantage of the ride over to tick off the tasks she had to do once she arrived at the hangar. She'd get her fire briefing from Dave Doss. By the time she pulled into the parking lot, she was fully in the zone.

The base buzzed with activity. Despite the early hour, the busy fire season demanded round-the-clock action—radio chatter mixed with the sounds of ground crews loading equipment, while aircraft engines and helicopter rotors echoed across the airfield.

Blazebuster stood ready outside its hangar. Ripley exited the van and swung her pack over her shoulder. She'd piloted the Dash 8-400AT ever since the FAA had certified the air tanker two years ago. StormAir's Canadian fleet also supported Cal Fire, so she was familiar with its maneuverability. This tanker could operate on short runways and high elevations, while carrying more fuel than similar-sized tankers.

"Beecher!" Doss waved her over to the briefing area. "Good to see you. We have a critical suppression level down in Anchorage."

"I figured as much when you told me the location. What's the latest?"

Doss pointed to his hand-held map. "The fire started around midnight in dense woods in East Anchorage. It's spreading fast in the dry, beetle-killed spruce. We must prevent it from reaching the Anchorage Hillside, which has several subdivisions. You'll report to the incident commander, Tanner Westlake."

"Westlake?" It popped out like she'd just won the lottery, and Doss gave her an odd look.

"You know him?" he asked.

"Not really, just dropped slurry on the Big Lake fire," she said dismissively as her pulse kicked up a notch.

She'd gulped at the mention of Westlake. Since he was based in Montana, she hadn't expected to see him in Alaska again. She wasn't exactly disappointed to learn he was the incident commander, either.

"When you get to Anchorage, a shuttle will take you to the ICC, the incident command center on Lake Otis Boulevard. From there, you'll receive your fire assignments. Have a safe flight down." Doss hurried off to brief other staff.

Ripley smiled at Mel, who strolled up with Nubs Loman. "Now there's double trouble," she teased.

"You're sure in a good mood today." Loman flashed his flirtatious smile.

"I'm always in a good mood," she tossed back.

Nubs Loman was a shameless flirt, but also a damn good first officer and co-pilot. His ground-based flirtations were harmless enough but, in the cockpit, he was all business and knew his job.

Mel rolled his ever-present toothpick to the other side of his mouth with a lopsided grin. "I have a sneaking suspicion why."

"That's enough, Faraday." Ripley gave him a firm stare. "If you out me about what we talked about, I'll toss you out of Blazebuster with the next load of slurry."

Loman gave her a quizzical look. "What's that all about?"

"Nothing. Nubs, why don't you get some coffee while I chat with Mel," she suggested.

Loman nodded and headed inside the hangar to do just that.

Ripley gave Mel a look that would stop a bulldozer. "Did you know that Westlake—"

Mel beat her to the punch. "Name requested you to fly this fire," he finished with a sly grin. "You must have made an impression on him as well. I don't believe in coincidences. Keep an open mind when you work with him. You never know what can happen."

She placed her hands on her hips. "What's that supposed to mean?"

He held up his hand. "Just keep an open mind. There's a reason things happen the way they do. I'm flying Juliet down to do water drops. See you in Anchorage, Captain Beecher." Mel pointed two fingers at his own eyes, then at Ripley's, reminding her to stay alert. He moved to his helicopter to get Juliet ready to fly south.

A mechanic approached and handed Ripley a clipboard. "Pre-flight checks are complete. She's fueled and ready to go."

Ripley scanned the flight log and signed it. Satisfied, she handed it back. "Thanks, Ben. Let's hope Blazebuster behaves today." She turned to her first officer, who appeared with two coffees in to-go cups. "Ready, Loman?"

"Yes, ma'am." As a veteran, he always saluted her military style, and she dipped her chin in a respectful nod, accepting the coffee he handed her.

They strolled toward their plane, excitement brewing inside her, at the sight of the Dash 8-400AT standing proudly, its red and white paint gleaming in the sunlight. She did her walk-around inspection, running her fingers along the smooth, metallic fuselage, grounding herself before taking control of the aircraft.

"Alright, Blazebuster," she murmured. "Help me slay the dragons."

Loman was in the co-pilot's seat as Ripley climbed in and started her pre-flight routine. She checked every switch and setting, then reached for her aeronautical map. She plugged in the latitude and longitude coordinates and thought of Allison. God, how she missed her.

"Please watch over me up there," she silently whispered to her best friend.

The plane's radio sprang to life. "Tanker One-Six-Zero, this is the Wainwright Tower. You're cleared for takeoff on runway two-zero. Winds are fifteen knots, gusting at twenty."

Ripley keyed her mic. "Copy that, Tower. Tanker One-Six-Zero, rolling."

She fired up the engine, spinning both propellers. A shot of adrenaline sped through her at the steady vibration of the plane springing to life.

She eased the aircraft into reverse and waited for the pushback tug to attach and back them up at the required distance. The tug operator gave her a thumbs-up to indicate she had control of the aircraft. She moved the lever into the forward position.

Loman tapped some adjustments on the dash, then nodded. "All set."

Ripley guided the aircraft to the left until it straddled the thick white and orange line on the runway, then she throttled forward, loving the rising whistle of the engines as they whizzed the props into action. The engines steadied their hum, and the ground fell away as the rush of nothingness gave her the sensation of floating. It didn't take long to rise above the smoky haze, where the azure sky was always a welcoming sight.

"These engines are surprisingly quiet," Loman commented once they'd reached altitude. Every flight was the same routine—he'd mention how loud the aircraft was that he'd co-piloted for the U.S. Air Force at JBER in Anchorage. Next would come the plane's history.

He didn't disappoint. "Did you know that the Dash 8-400AT is a variant of the Bombardier Dash 8-400, specifically modified for use as a large air tanker?" said Loman into the hot mic on his headset.

Let's see, how many times has he told me this? Must be the fiftieth.

She smiled anyway, giving him an imperceptible nod as she stared at the blue sky.

His voice streamed into her headphones. "This turboprop airliner was modified for aerial firefighting because it's well-suited for low speed, high-precision flight operations required in firefighting missions. But then, you know that, right?"

It always seemed like he was testing her knowledge, as if she were lacking. She knew it was because she was a female tanker pilot, but she wasn't offended by it. Some guys had a difficult time adjusting to the fact females piloted air tankers. Aerial firefighting was thought of as the 'elite of the elite' in the hierarchy of firefighting. She took pride in that aspect, ignoring those who doubted her capabilities because of her gender. She knew when to pick her battles.

And she didn't let it get in the way of her job.

Chapter 5

T*anner*

The rhythmic ticking of the wall clock irritated Tanner, mocking his restlessness. He leaned back in his chair, staring at the ceiling of his office behind the visitor's center at the Missoula Smokejumper Base. Instead of focusing on the stack of reports piled on his desk, his mind kept drifting back to Alaska, to the Big Lake fire... and *her*.

Ripley. Her name was as fierce and unconventional as she was. He recalled their brief encounter, envisioning her determined stride and the glow in her eyes when they discussed strategy. What impressed him the most was the skill with which she'd maneuvered that large air tanker. Tanner had worked with countless pilots over the years, but this one had made an indelible impression.

Was it because of her looks? If he was honest with himself, he had to admit she was a beauty. A wry smile tugged his lips as he recalled their disagreement on attack strategy. She'd stood her ground, and he liked that. He couldn't deny the powerful attraction he'd felt while talking with her.

His smile faded as his cell phone lit up with another message from Melissa, his ex-wife. Even after the divorce, she was still clingy and dependent. Their marriage had crumbled under the weight of her constant need for attention. Wildland firefighting was hard on marriages, and his had become another failed statistic. He sighed and tugged his eyebrow hairs with his thumb and forefinger, a nervous habit he'd picked up in his smokejumper days.

A sharp knock on his office door jolted him from his thoughts. "Come in."

A fire dispatcher poked his head in. "Sorry to interrupt, but we just got word of a major wildfire threatening the city of Anchorage. The State of Alaska Division of Forestry and Fire Protection has jurisdiction for this one, and they've requested you specifically because you're a WUI guy. You'll also be working with Marc Stover, the Anchorage Fire Department Wildfire Division Chief. He's a legend up there."

"Anchorage? That can't be good. When I was up there, all I heard was how dry everything was." He did a quick mental scan of the surrounding topography.

The dispatcher showed Tanner the report on his digital tablet. "The fire's spreading rapidly, threatening several residential areas. They're worried about the Anchorage Hillside neighborhoods and the east side of the city if it's not contained soon. Also, today is summer solstice, with lots of festivals going on, so the timing isn't great."

Tanner scanned the report, his brow furrowing. The combination of unusually dry conditions, high winds, and the urban-wildland interface could turn this situation into a nightmare, unless swift action was taken.

"Sir, the State of Alaska Division of Forestry wants you to incident command this one," said the dispatcher. "Here's the resource request." He handed him the clipboard.

Tanner stood. "Get my overhead team ready. Looks like we're heading north."

He collected his gear, along with his always-on-the-ready fire pack. His mind raced, considering strategies, resources needed, and the potential challenges of working with multiple local, state, and federal agencies. He'd be a fed co-commanding a state-run incident, so he'd better get up to speed on the State's way of doing things.

An hour later, Tanner and his overhead team boarded a Horizon Air flight to Seattle, where they would then board an Alaska Airlines jet for the three-and-a-half-hour flight to Anchorage. As the Embraer 175 commuter jet lifted off from Johnson-Bell Field at the Missoula airport, he relaxed into his seat. He pulled out his digital tablet to review the latest fire updates. The flames had already consumed twenty acres east of town in the lower Hillside neighborhoods, with no sign of slowing.

His jaw clenched as he studied the map. This fire was a whole different beast compared to Big Lake. The proximity to Anchorage added layers of complexity: evacuation logistics, protecting critical infrastructure, and coordinating with local authorities, just to name a few. The media's attention would be intense.

Nothing he hadn't dealt with before. Not like the Pacific Palisades in L.A., which was the worst he'd ever experienced. Anchorage was a smaller city, but that didn't mean the fire threat was any less deadly. He took advantage of his time in the air to line up his organizational ducks and form his incident command team. He'd already requested Alaskan smokejumper, Ryan O'Connor for his Air Attack supervisor; he'd jumped fires with him before. He'd also been impressed by the efficiency of the

Aurora Interagency Hotshot Crew on the Big Lake fire, so he listed them on his resource request form as well.

He closed his eyes and took a deep breath. This was what he was trained for: urban-rural interface fires that threatened life and property. He loved the challenge of these high-stakes wildfires, where his job was preventing them from becoming structural fires.

Tanner's thoughts drifted to the tanker pilot. He decided to add Ripley Beecher to the requested resource list, knowing air tanker pilots were in high demand not only in Alaska, but also in the lower forty-eight. Even if he was lucky enough to get her for this fire, he knew how important it was for him to keep things professional.

Once the fire season ended, well... he'd see about that.

He'd thrown himself into his fire career after the divorce, convincing himself he was content alone. He dated occasionally but spent so much time away from home that meaningful relationships were impossible. One time he'd gotten serious with a California actress filming in Montana, but she'd been smitten with his smokejumper status rather than with him.

Tanner had just nodded off when the voice came over the intercom announcing their descent into Anchorage. He shook himself awake, then sat up in his seat, preparing to switch his mind into incident commander mode. As the plane broke through the clouds and flew across Cook Inlet, he caught his first glimpse of the fire.

The scale of the blaze was staggering. Tanner's heart raced at the smoke column rising higher than the Chugach peaks, tinged orange by flames below. Even from this distance, he could tell this was no ordinary wildfire—this was the sort of conflagration that could devastate a community. Everyone in Anchorage must be on edge. This would be one hell of a firefight.

As the plane touched down, his phone chirped a text message confirming a shuttle was waiting outside baggage claim to take him to the command center.

Tanner gathered his duffle and fire pack from the conveyor belt, then climbed into a large red SUV, with the State of Alaska Department of Forestry & Fire on the side. He greeted the uniformed driver and made idle conversation on the ride to the command center.

The smoke plume became more onerous as they pulled into the parking lot of the middle school, that served as an incident command center on Lake Otis Boulevard. The lot was full of first responder trucks from every local, state, and federal agency under the sun.

As he strode toward the front doors, he glanced at the ominous charcoal sky, hoping he could get a handle on this fire pretty damn quick. He entered the hive of coordinated chaos that was the ICC. Maps covered the walls, radio chatter filled the air, and harried-looking fire staff moved purposefully between tables labeled Situations, Planning, and Media.

"Westlake! Glad you're here." Ryan approached, extending his hand. "Hell of a welcome back to Alaska, huh?"

"Good to see you again, Ryno." Tanner invoked Ryan's nickname, shaking his hand firmly with a backslap.

"No one's called me that in a while," laughed Ryan. "Follow me, and I'll get you up to speed."

"Let's do it," said Tanner. "Always good to see a fellow jumper."

Ryan led him to the map table where several agency heads had gathered from the Anchorage Fire Department, the State of Alaska Forestry Division, and the U.S. Bureau of Land Management. He made introductions, and Tanner made it a point to match faces with the nametags.

"Here's the skinny in a nutshell," explained Ryan, pointing to a map. "Fire started just after midnight in dense spruce east of Elmore Road. Ignition source unknown. What we know for certain is that the fuel loads are extreme, humidity is at record lows, and the urban-wildland interface is threatened."

Tanner studied the map, tracing the fire's perimeter with his finger, noting its proximity to the residential areas. "Current resources?"

"Three hotshot crews, including the Aurora Interagency Hotshots, eight Type II hand crews, fifteen engines, and two bulldozers," explained Ryan. "We have two large air tankers operating out of Ted Stevens International Airport for drops on forest lands and three helicopters for water drops on the wetlands, since chemical retardant isn't allowed in wetlands."

"Should be enough," Tanner said grimly, already seeing the gaps in coverage. "But I don't like the rate of spread."

"Which is why we called you, since you've managed these kinds of complex incidents before," explained Ryan.

Tanner nodded, understanding the unspoken expectation. This wasn't just about fighting a fire. This was about protecting a city, managing evacuations, and navigating the complex politics that came with high-stakes decisions.

"I'd like to do a recon. Do you have a pilot who can take me up?"

"The tanker pilot you requested is here, and I understand she's also certified to fly small planes," responded Ryan. "After the morning briefing, I'll introduce you to the troops."

"Thanks." Tanner took a deep breath to calm his nerves, already forming a plan to convince Alaska's largest city to have faith in his ability to control this fire before bad things happen.

And he also had the good fortune to score a flight with a pilot whose judgment he trusted. He loved life's glorious surprises.

Chapter 6

R*ipley*

As the air tanker neared Anchorage, Ripley spotted the thick smoke plume rising to the left. She was instructed to land at Ted Stevens International Airport, the designated tanker base for the Elmore fire instead of the usual Palmer base. Ryan had arranged for slurry tanks and aviation fuel to support the air tankers, and the international airport was closer and well-equipped to handle firefighting aircraft.

She landed Blazebuster on the main runway with air traffic control guidance, then taxied to the back forty near the cargo carriers and freight operations.

A shuttle van waited to transport Ripley and Loman to the Incident Command Center. The shuttle driver deposited them with their gear, and upon entering the middle school that served as the ICC, Ripley scanned the room for familiar faces. She spotted Mel, who'd flown Juliet, his Bell helicopter, from Fairbanks. She noted the MEDIA sign in one corner with several reporters speaking into mics.

Mel was talking with an AFS helitack crew, and Ryan was busy with Air Attack staff. As she waited to talk to Ryan, she stood looking around—and then saw him staring.

Tanner's gaze locked onto hers, and for an Anchorage second, everything faded to a muffled background. Ripley had a jolt of she-wasn't-sure-what upon seeing him again. Just as he started toward her, Ryan rushed up to escort him to the front of the multi-purpose room, which served as the ICC's briefing room.

Ryan picked up a mic. "Time to begin this morning's briefing, so everyone can get into the field. I'd like to introduce the new incident commander, Tanner Westlake. He comes to us from Missoula, Montana, with a wealth of experience fighting fires in the wildland-urban interface. Tanner?" Ryan passed him the mic and stepped aside.

"Thanks, Ryan," he began. "I understand firefighters from the Anchorage Fire Department Wildfire Division have been fighting the Elmore fire since it broke out after midnight. We'll relieve them with state and federal crews to give them a chance to rest. Thank you, Marc Stover. I look forward to working with you." Tanner nodded at the AFD wildfire chief, who smiled and nodded back. He kept his talk short and sweet, emphasizing the importance of coordination between the agencies to contain this fire.

He ended by announcing, "Aviation folks, meet me in the back room for our air attack briefing." He cast a glance at Ripley, Loman, and Mel as several reporters rushed up, shouting questions.

Tanner held up his hand in a stop motion. "When I finish with my staff, I'll be happy to answer your inquiries." He strode to the back conference room as reporters continued shouting questions. When his staff was inside, he closed the door.

He glanced at the maps tacked to the walls, and large desktop monitors for tracking aviation operations. Tanner motioned everyone to sit at a long conference table.

"Thank you all for being here." Tanner dipped a quick nod at Ripley. "Your direct report is Ryan O'Connor, our air attack supervisor, whom most of you are familiar with."

"Welcome to the crazy, everyone," joked Ryan. "Ripley Beecher and Nubs Loman, welcome. We're glad you're here. This won't take long, as we need to get you airborne. You'll report to me, but when you're on direct attack, you report to Tanner. Hope that's not too confusing."

Ripley smiled. "Not for me. I'm used to reporting to multiple people on a fire."

"Good. Let's get started. The AFD Wildfire Division has been trying to hold it, but we need mud drops to slow the head, which is moving toward neighborhoods." Ryan looked at Ripley. "As you are aware, we don't drop chemical retardant on wetland areas. I'll make sure you have a map with those boundaries. The fire is burning in flammable beetle-killed spruce in stands so dense a moose can't even walk through it."

Ripley stared at the map with the fire's perimeter, mentally plotting her flight path and drop zones. "Thanks for the briefing. We'll head back to the airport."

"I took the liberty of calling the airport ground crew to load your tanker with slurry," said Ryan. "Blazebuster, right? I saw her up in Fairbanks before I left. She's a beauty."

"She sure is." Ripley was proud of the planes she flew, especially this one—it responded to her touch like a caring friend.

"Also, we've leased a Cessna at Merrill Field for recon flights. Tanner will fill you in. Excuse me, have to run. Good meeting you." Ryan dashed out the door.

When Loman excused himself for the little boys' room, Tanner slipped into his chair. "Fancy meeting you here."

"Well, it seems you requested me. Didn't expect you to come back so soon from Montana." Ripley raised an eyebrow. "Couldn't let you have all the fun, could I?"

"Thanks for signing on with us. I liked your work at Big Lake." His smile widened, then he became serious. "Ryan said you'd take me up for a recon flight. You're certified to fly a Cessna, right?"

Ripley blinked in surprise. "I learned on one. Why do I think you already knew that? You don't want one of the recon pilots?"

Tanner shook his head. "I need someone who understands fire behavior and can assess conditions."

"Okay." She appreciated the offbeat compliment.

"Mel Faraday is coming too," said Tanner. "He needs to see what we're up against when he makes his water drops where the fire is burning the wetland areas. And to note locations of water sources, transmission lines, and cell towers."

Ripley smiled. "I know Mel from way back. He talked me into transferring here from California."

"Small world. Fantastic," he said, eyeing Loman approaching them.

"Ripley is taking me to fly a recon," Tanner informed him.

"Thought we were doing a slurry run." Loman gave her a questioning look.

She shrugged. "Won't take long. Why don't you go to the airport and get Blazebuster prepped, and I'll see you there?"

Loman appeared annoyed, but that wasn't her problem. Not when the incident commander had asked her to take him up.

"See you later, then," muttered Loman.

Tanner drove Ripley and Mel to Merrill Field, five minutes from the ICC. He parked, and they all strolled toward a waiting Cessna. Ripley climbed in and settled into the pilot seat, beginning her usual pre-flight checks. Since this was the same model of plane her dad taught her to fly, it was like coming home again. Mel climbed into the back seat, and Tanner rode shotgun.

All three put on headsets with hot mics. Ripley checked with Merrill Field tower, who gave her clearance for takeoff. Because of the fire, Anchorage air traffic controllers were re-routing planes away from the East Anchorage air space to allow for firefighting aircraft.

"Ready for liftoff?" she said into her hot mic, eyeing a smoke plume she'd have to navigate around.

"Copy that," Tanner's deep timbre rumbled into her ears.

She taxied the Cessna to the runway and lifted off, banking toward the mountains. The scale of the fire quickly became apparent. What appeared daunting from the ground was truly staggering from the air. The fire weather turbulence increased as they flew closer.

"This blaze has grown in a short amount of time," said Tanner.

Ripley's hands steadied on the controls. "This isn't large enough yet to pose visual problems, but if we don't get mud on it soon, it will. Not to mention the entire city having to go under a health alert."

"You got that right," Mel muttered from the back seat as the plane crabbed to the left, then right. "Flames are moving fast. Winds aren't helping."

Tanner leaned forward. "Too fast. Ripley, can you take us over the right flank on the eastern side?"

She banked the plane, flying low, careful to stay clear of the smoke plume, when movement on the ground caught her eye.

Ripley pointed to a clearing. "Look! Two people are moving away from the point of origin!" Their erratic movements struck her as odd.

"They don't move like frightened civilians," drawled Tanner, peering through his side window.

"Sure don't. Their movements seem deliberate," intoned Mel from the back seat. "No one but the fire staff should be beyond the roadblocks."

The figures broke into a run, disappearing into the dense forest.

"They saw us checking them out," said Ripley. "You want me to circle the area?"

"Nah. Now that they know we saw them, they'll stay out of sight." Tanner tapped Ryan's number on his cell phone. "Hey Ryno, I don't want this on the radio. Send APD to the roadblock on Elmore Street, next to where the fire started. We need a fire investigator to identify the point of origin. Just saw two people where they aren't supposed to be, moving through blackened ground. We're on our way back. Thanks, Ryno." He nodded and ended the call.

"Ryan is notifying APD and is also finding a wildland fire investigator to help us out," reported Tanner.

Ripley glanced at him. "Why do you call him Ryno?"

"When I first worked with him, there were three guys named Ryan on our smokejumper squad, and we needed to tell them apart. Everyone called him Ryno because he tackled fire like a charging rhinoceros." Tanner grinned out the window as he recalled the memory.

Ripley flew to the east side of the fire, where the head moved through beetle kill. "Here you go. We need to hit this with slurry first."

Tanner studied the landscape below. "Okay, I've seen all I needed to see. I have a better sense of the topography to form an attack plan. I don't like all this beetle kill. Chief Stover told me the State and Municipal fire crews have been doing fuels reduction on the Hillside, but there's still plenty left to fuel wildfires. Ripley, let's get you back so you can drop slurry."

As Ripley flew toward Merrill Field, they all peered at the ground below, searching for the mysterious figures they'd seen moving through the burned ground. No sign of them.

"I was afraid of this," murmured Tanner. "The municipal fire guys suspected it could have been a deliberate set."

Silence fell as the implication of 'deliberate' sank in.

"If so, better catch them before they can set more," said Mel.

Ripley took a deep breath. She didn't want to think about a worsening situation. This was enough of a challenge with these wind gusts whipping the beetle-killed spruce, making it even more of a tinderbox.

Tanner tapped his cell again and put Ryan on speaker. "Ryno, how soon can you get that wildland fire investigator here? The one you said was so good?"

"Jon Silva," responded Ryan. "He's also a good friend. I'll see if he's available. He's based in Nevada, but I can get him to come up to help us out. He supervised the Aurora Crew back when they were a regular handline crew. He ran into health problems, so he quit firefighting to do investigations instead."

"Great. See if you can get him up here ASAP."

"Will do. See you soon."

Ripley stole a glance at the furrowed brow of the incident commander, who seemed lost in thought. She stayed quiet as she made her final approach into Merrill Field.

The fire below threatened to devour everything in its path. And if it was the result of foul play, she was damn well going to do her part to help uncover the truth.

Ripley pushed all other thoughts aside, focusing on the next task at hand, which was to take Blazebuster on the first slurry drop. Whatever mysteries lay behind this inferno, she hoped the police and this Jon Silva person would solve them.

The battle for Anchorage had just begun, and Ripley intended to give it everything she had.

Chapter 7

Tanner

His eyes darn near crossed after studying the Bureau of Land Management Master Title Plats, showing land status ownership, topographic maps, and satellite imagery of the Anchorage Hillside. The afternoon sun slanted through the windows of the ICC, casting shadows across the active room. He twisted his eyebrow, trying to focus.

"Tanner?" A voice cut through his concentration, and he spotted Tara, supervisor of the Aurora Hotshot Crew, and Ryan's better half.

"Hey, how goes the battle?" he asked, stretching his arms. "What do you see as our biggest challenge?"

Tara leaned over the map, her brow furrowing. "The density of the timber. We need heavy equipment to create an effective fuel break. Two people on our crew are certified to run dozers. Kenzie Quinn, who is on a firefighter exchange with us from Australia, and Tupa, originally from Anchorage."

Tanner nodded. He'd worked with hotshot crews before, but the Aurora Hotshots had a reputation for being one of the best in Alaska. "How quickly can you get a dozer in there?"

"I need a couple hours to mobilize before we can actively cut a line," replied Tara.

"I'll take care of that for you." Tanner reached for his cell as someone knocked on his open door.

A tall blond man with a broad chest poked his head in. "Tanner Westlake?"

Tara broke out in a smile. "Hey, Cohen, so the state turned you loose to work with us plebes in the big city?" she joked, motioning at Tanner. "Cohen Tremblay, this is Tanner Westlake, our IC from Missoula. Cohen is from British Columbia. He trained and qualified the Aurora Crew as an interagency hotshot crew last year up in Talkeetna."

Tanner extended his hand, and Cohen shook it. "I've heard all good things," said Cohen with a toothy smile. "They tell me you and I are working this one together."

"Is your wife with you?" asked Tara.

Cohen gave her a lopsided grin. "Raynie is out there hugging everyone on your crew." He glanced at Tanner. "We both worked with the Aurora Crew last year. Kind of how we met."

Tanner returned a knowing smile. "I hear that happens now and then during a fire."

"Now I work for the State of Alaska Division of Forestry, so I'm your state counterpart. Normally, I'm based in Palmer with the Pioneer Hotshots, but since I have command experience, they figured I'd be an asset down here."

"Good timing," said Tanner. "Tara needs the two dozers to cut a line through that beetle kill. I assume the State has fire contracts in place for heavy equipment?"

"Yes, we do. Let me know anything else you need. They told me I'd be your night shift IC." Cohen whipped out his cell and moved off.

"I'm taking my crew to Elmore Road to relieve the AFD Wildfire crew," said Tara. "Stop out when you get a minute, and I'll explain what we're doing. Oh, and Ryan told me to give you these." She placed a set of truck keys on the table. "It's the white crew cab parked at the end of the lot with Alaska Fire Service on the door. See you later."

"Thanks, appreciate it," replied Tanner as Tara headed out the door.

His radio sprang to life with Ripley's voice. "Air attack, this is Tanker One-Six-Zero. Our ETA for the first drop is in twenty minutes."

"Copy that, Tanker One-Six-Zero," replied Ryan. "Thanks for the update. IC, did you copy?"

"Sure did," Tanner drawled into his radio.

"There's a good observation point you can drive up to up at Stuckagain Heights," suggested Ryan. "Follow your GPS to get up there on Basher Road. You'll need to put your truck into four-wheel drive. Unless you want to take an ATV, all-terrain vehicle."

"Thanks. I'll head up to see what's happening in real time."

"Sounds good. All clear." Ryan exited the transmission.

USING THE TRUCK'S GPS, Tanner turned onto Campbell Airstrip Road, then Basher Drive, shifting into four-wheel-drive to maneuver the steep road to the Stuckagain trailhead. Once there, he had a sweeping view of the fire's eastern front. Ominous smoke loomed over the Chugach Range neighborhoods, their picturesque charm overshadowed by the flames that threatened them.

Acrid smoke hit his nostrils as he stepped out of the cab. Below him, the ravenous orange beast devoured everything in its path, hungry for more. The fire's head tossed burning debris in front of it, causing spot fires. Flames crowned through the dense spruce, leaping from tree to tree.

He climbed back into the truck and drove to where the Aurora Hotshot Crew dozed a defensive line along the eastern flank. Tara had relieved the city firefighters, and the Aurora Hotshots were kicking serious ass. She came over to talk to him.

"We'll make better headway with aerial support," said Tara. "Crown fires are moving too fast for the ground crews."

Tanner checked his watch. "Aerial support is inbound. Show me where you'd like it targeted," offered Tanner, pulling a map up on his digital tablet. Even though he was confident where Beecher should place the drop, he liked input from crew bosses on the ground.

Tara pointed to the map where the fire was making its most aggressive push. "Right here. If we can slow the head for our dozers to get a fireline in before the wind shift, that would be ideal."

Tanner scanned the sky and spotted the smaller Bird Dog aircraft assigned to guide the incoming tanker. Minutes later, the larger silhouette of the Dash 8-400AT appeared, its distinctive shape unmistakable against the smoke-filled horizon.

"Tanker One-Six-Zero, this is the IC. Do you copy?" he radioed, strange anticipation waving through him.

A brief pause, then Ripley replied. "Copy, IC."

"I sent you the target coordinates," he informed her.

"Thanks, I have them on my monitor," she replied. Hearing her on the radio sent a ridiculous rush through him. *Focus, Westlake.*

"Bird Dog will guide you in. Drop a full load to slow the head enough for ground crews to establish a dozer line."

"Copy that," responded Ripley. "Target in sight. Beginning approach."

Tanner watched as Bird Dog guided Ripley's aircraft into position and let out a smoke trail to mark the drop zone. As she lined up for the drop, Tanner held his breath. He always did when tankers released slurry. What tanker pilots did was flat-out dangerous. Wind conditions could be tricky, with thermals from the fire creating unexpected turbulence.

Ripley held her course steady as slurry cascaded from the aircraft's belly, creating a red cloud along the fire's leading edge where flames advanced toward unburned fuels.

"Tanker One-Six-Zero, you nailed it," said the pilot of the spotter plane as it pulled away.

"Good. Returning to base for reload. Let us know if you need another," Ripley said easily as the tanker banked and headed back to the airport.

"Copy that. Clear." Tanner was delighted the drop had made the desired progress.

Tara cheered. "We have our window, sports fans. Get those dozers busy!"

The Aurora Hotshots sprang into action with saw teams clearing pathways for both dozers. Hand crews followed, using Pulaskis to widen and clean the line. Both Cat D8 bulldozers roared to life, blades carving the forest floor to create a mineral soil barrier to contain the advancing flames.

Tanner's instinct was to pitch in and help, but he reminded himself he wasn't fighting the flames this time. You can take the boy out of the firefight, but you can't take the firefight out of the boy.

He pulled out his cell to call his co-commander. "Cohen, the combined air and ground attack has positive results. The eastern flank has slowed, giving Tara's crew a window to doze a line."

"Terrific," replied Cohen. "Hopefully, with the cooler evening temperatures and higher humidity, the fire will lie down, and we can get the rest of it contained with the night crews. You should get some sleep. They have us bunking at the Greatland Suites, an extended stay hotel in Midtown. I'll remain at the ICC until you're back in the morning."

"Thanks, I'll take you up on that." He was tapped out and could use some shuteye. He ended the call and keyed his radio. "Aurora, what's your progress?"

"Going faster than expected," replied Tara. "We've made almost two miles of a fuel break."

"Good. Cohen assigned another hotshot crew to relieve you for the night. We'll reassess in the morning."

"Get some sleep," said Tara.

"We can sleep when we're dead, right?" he joked. "You know as well as I do, no one sleeps during fire season. See you in the morning."

He wondered how Ripley was doing as he climbed into his truck, and unsurprisingly, found himself heading toward the Ted Stevens Anchorage International Airport. It was routine for an IC to check in with Air Attack... but if he was being honest, it was more of a magnetic pull to a certain tanker pilot that drew him now.

Tanner parked next to the hangar and spotted Ripley standing beside her aircraft, deep in conversation with a mechanic. Even in the unflattering glare of the floodlights, with her wrinkled flight suit and messy ponytail, she was striking.

He waited for her to finish her conversation. "Nice flying today, Beecher."

She turned, surprised. "Westlake. Didn't expect to see you here. Thought you'd be buried in paperwork."

"Thought I'd check in with Air Attack before calling it a night," he replied, aiming for nonchalance. "Your drops made a difference on the eastern flank. Tara's crew got their dozer line established."

"Glad it helped, but the Aurora Hotshots are the ones doing the heavy lifting. All I did was fly the plane."

He noticed how lovingly she ran her hand over the name painted on the side of the fuselage.

"Any issues with Blazebuster?"

"Left engine ran a little hot on the last run, but the mechanic thinks it's just a sensor issue. It took some damage in the Big Lake fire, but the mechanics in Fairbanks made some adjustments to fix it."

"Good to hear." He hesitated before adding, "Where are you staying? They have most of us at the Greatland Suites, so that's where I'm headed—in case you need a ride."

"I was just going to have the mechanic run me to the hotel. I'm staying at Greatland as well." Ripley hesitated just long enough to make him wonder if he'd overstepped. "Thanks. I'll take you up on that."

Chapter 8

Ripley

As they drove through the traffic in Alaska's endless summer daylight, where midnight seemed like mid-afternoon, Ripley took in the sights and sounds of Anchorage, not sure why she suddenly felt shy. Westlake was handsome as hell, but he was still her boss.

"Thanks for the ride. You didn't have to, you know."

"That's why I did it." He braked for a light. "How long have you been with the Alaska Fire Service?"

"About three weeks," she replied, looking at a moose grazing in Earthquake Park as they turned onto Northern Lights Boulevard. "Transferred up from California at the end of May."

"Can't blame you for that." He slowed for another moose, which couldn't decide whether to cross the street.

"Wildlife in Anchorage. Love it," she commented. "Fires burn just as hot here as they do in the lower forty-eight." She peered at the Chugach Range looming behind the billowing smoke as they drove toward it. "Can't beat the scenery from the cockpit, though. Especially Mount Denali."

"I thought Missoula's mountains were big. But when I come up here, they're anthills in comparison." Tanner smiled, with a shared appreciation for Alaska's wild beauty.

"Do you fly much?" she asked. "Besides having jumped out of perfectly good airplanes?"

"I'm not a pilot, if that's what you mean. Landed a Twin Otter once when the pilot had a heart attack. Other than that, no."

"That must have been fun," she joked. "You should come up sometime when I make a drop. It's fun to watch the Phos-chek stream out on the instrument panel monitor."

"Think Loman would mind?" His remark surprised her.

"Why would he mind?" She snorted. "And anyway, he has no say. He thinks he does, though."

"I have a feeling Nubs really likes you," said Tanner.

"Likes me?" She laughed. "What are you, a high school sophomore? Hardly. He's flirtatious by nature, that's about it. He's a good co-pilot, though."

"How did he come by Nubs? Can't imagine that's his real name."

She chuckled. "His real name is Bryce Loman. He always talked about his dad and grandpa, who made him work his fingers to the nubs on their sawmill in Moose Pass, Alaska. The name stuck." She tilted her head. "Everyone who works on fire has a nickname. What's yours?"

He wrinkled his face. "It's not very complimentary. Smokejumper buddies assigned it to me when I was in my twenties."

"Now you have to tell me. Come on, out with it," she challenged, folding her arms.

He hesitated. "Understand that I was a lot younger." He let out an annoyed sigh. "Wolfman."

She guffawed, choking on subsequent laughter. "Let me guess. You either chased wolves or women."

He only smiled.

Ripley bobbed her head. "Uh, huh. I get it now."

"I don't do that anymore," he refuted. "The nickname wore off when I got married."

Her eyes immediately went to his ring finger, but it was empty.

"What's yours?" he asked.

"Blazebuster, after my plane," she said proudly.

"Appropriate, I like it," he said approvingly. "Are you hungry?"

"Starving," she admitted. "I could eat a moose."

He chuckled. "Well, I can't promise moose, but how about the best grilled halibut sandwich in Anchorage?"

"I'm there." She studied his solid profile, noticing the way his forearms flexed as he gripped the steering wheel.

"Is Momma O's in Spenard okay with you? I heard it's a local favorite."

She nodded, grateful for the distraction from her wandering thoughts. "Sounds great."

Tanner turned into a compact parking lot, and they went inside to place their orders for halibut sandwiches and fries. They took their food to go and climbed back into the truck, the delicious aroma filling the cab. His hand brushed hers as he handed her the food. She noticed him watching as she unwrapped her sandwich.

"Mmm," she hummed after taking a bite. "This is amazing."

He grinned. "Told you. Best in Anchorage."

As they ate, their conversation flowed easily, chatting about the fires they'd worked. He told her about his life in Montana and his love for the outdoors. She shared stories of flying and dreams of running her own aviation company someday.

"How'd you end up as an aerial firefighter?" He wiped his mouth with a napkin.

"I fell in love with flying, then discovered I loved firefighting, too. I worked on a hotshot crew for a few seasons, then thought about applying to smokejumper school. The thought of jumping out of planes freaked me out, so I learned how to fly tankers."

"I know you need a shit ton of ground firefighting hours before you can fight fire in the air. Must take a lot of dedication and patience."

"You're telling me," she said. "The hours were insane. Didn't leave room for anything else in my life."

"Not even for relationships?" He hesitated. "Are you involved with anyone?"

Ripley knew where this conversation was going, and she wasn't sure she wanted it to. Was this another fire guy who wanted an easy lay between shifts? She figured staying vague about it was the best tactic. "Oh, you know, now and then. You?"

He quieted. "Not anymore. I'm divorced."

"Oh. That must have sucked." This bit of news made her brighten.

He made a dismissive motion. "You know how firefighting is with relationships. I'm always gone, especially since fire seasons have become year-round now."

She understood all too well. "Yeah, I've seen my share of marriages end in this business. Not to mention the mental health issues that go with the job. And the lack of good pay and benefits—at least for federal firefighters. Don't get me started..." She grinned at him.

After they finished eating, Tanner drove to their hotel, and Ripley sensed a bit of tension simmering between them. When he parked and killed the engine, neither moved. Her gaze dropped to his lips, then back up to his pools of gray.

She eyed him cautiously. "You know, I wasn't sure what to make of you at the Palmer Air Base. At first, I figured you for another by-the-book incident commander who doesn't listen to the people doing the actual work. I was wrong."

He raised an eyebrow. "Why do you say that?"

She met his gaze. "Because you actually listen to your people, yet you multi-task with the big picture and the gory little details."

"Thanks, I guess? High praise from someone who views everything from ten thousand feet."

"My higher perspective gives me clarity." She opened her door and stepped out.

They walked into the hotel together, keeping a professional distance as they crossed the lobby where several firefighters lounged in front of a TV. At the elevator, Ripley pressed the button for the second floor while Tanner selected the fourth.

"0700 briefing tomorrow?" she asked as the doors slid open on her floor.

"Yep. I'll give you a ride over if you like."

Her heart tugged a little at his offer. "Thanks, but Air Attack has a van scheduled for pilots heading to the ICC for the morning briefing."

"Great. I'll make sure the coffee is on. I hear Anchorage is known for its delicious coffee."

"I heard that, too." She stepped into the hallway and turned to face him. "Thanks for the ride... Wolfman."

He gave her an eyeroll. "I shouldn't have told you that," he lamented, holding her gaze longer than was necessary.

She hauled her fire pack inside her hotel room and made herself at home. As she showered, her thoughts drifted to Westlake and his rumbling voice and calm manner. He was amazingly attractive, with a pleasant personality.

Nope, nope, and nope. You're here to do a job. Focus. Don't get attached.

Tomorrow would bring new fire behavior, shifting winds, and more critical decisions. She needed to be rested and ready.

Hopefully, they'd get this fire contained sooner rather than later.

Chapter 9

Tanner

Once at the ICC the next morning, Tanner immersed himself in reports and weather forecasts, piecing together the fire's behavior. Maps spread before him like a battlefield, each contour line and wind forecast a potential enemy in this firefight.

As the sun lifted higher over the Chugach mountains, he made his rounds at the front lines. First, he checked in with Tara and the Aurora Hotshots for a status report before this morning's fire briefing, where he'd met with Cohen and Marc Stover, the AFD Wildfire Chief.

A mile past the roadblock on Elmore Road, Tanner flashed his fire ID, then stepped into the charred landscape, the pungent smell of burned timber hitting his nostrils. The ground was still warm beneath his boots as he spotted Tara, her bright yellow hard-hat standing out among the blackened trees.

"Morning, Tanner," Tara called out, her cheeks smudged with soot.

"How's it going?" he asked, scrutinizing the dozer line they'd built.

"I got clearance from Cohen to move the Aurora Hotshots to the left flank to doze another line to prevent flames from burning uphill to the residences," explained Tara, pointing. "There's a fuel break the state and AFD Wildfire crews built this spring a hundred feet on both sides of Campbell Airstrip Road.

We're using their break as an anchor to extend the line across the Hillside."

"Federal agencies don't allow dozers, or chemical retardant drops in the wetlands," explained Tanner. "Make sure you keep the dozer line outside of the wetland's boundary. I've ordered water drops for flames within the boundary, but the main part of the fire is so far outside of the wetlands. I'm working within interagency agreements and emergency protocols for these sensitive areas."

Tara motioned in the direction where the crew worked. "Kenzie and Tupa have been working non-stop with the two dozers, making sure to stay out of the wetlands. We have a three-mile fuel break on the right flank, with this road as an anchor point."

A woman climbed off her dozer and extended her hand. "G'day, I'm Kenzie Quinn. Pleased to meet you."

Tanner shook her gloved hand. "Thanks for all the hard work you're doing."

"Digging the uphill line is tricky because of the slope gradient," said Kenzie with her Aussie accent. "We're trying not to tip the dozers over."

Tara smiled at her crew member. "Kenzie comes to us on a firefighter exchange with Canberra in Australia. This is her third year with us."

Tanner's phone buzzed, and Ryan's name flashed.

"What's up, Ryno?" he answered, stepping away from the women.

"We have a situation at the ICC. Agency heads are breathing down my neck, wanting to know why you aren't here. Not only that, but protesters are also outside hassling fire staff."

"Oh, boy." Irritation flashed through him. "Tell them the IC is completing his on-the-ground assessment and I'll be there in ten or fifteen."

"What about the protestors?" asked Ryan.

"I'll handle that when I get there. What are they protesting? Let me guess—dropping retardant."

"You got it," said Ryan. "They don't like us turning their beloved city greenbelts red."

Tanner squeezed the bridge of his nose. "This is the part where we're the bad guys. Never mind that we're doing it to protect the city."

"Yes, unfortunately. See you when you get here," replied Ryan.

Tanner ended the call, frustration bubbling. The never-ending push and pull between laws and regulations and what had to be done in an emergency to save lives and property was exhausting. But it was part of the job. This is why they'd hired him—because he was good at it.

When he pulled into the ICC parking lot, he took a deep breath and stepped out of his truck. He put on his sunglasses and pulled down his baseball cap, then strode through the gauntlet of shouting protesters, holding up signs with photos of dead birds and other wildlife. Never mind that the photos weren't from this fire.

An older, bearded man peered at Tanner's hard-hat with "Incident Commander" emblazoned on the front. "Hey! How can you let our forest ecosystems be destroyed?"

A woman cried out, "What you're doing is wrong!"

Another long-haired man with a red beard to match stepped in front of him. "You're killing wildlife habitat with retardant chemicals! How can you sleep at night?"

Rather than enter a debate with an antagonistic crowd, something he'd made the mistake of doing on lower forty-eight fires, he dipped a courteous nod and stepped inside the ICC. Two security guards stood inside the double front doors to ensure no one without a fire ID entered the building. Tanner made a note to have his fire information officer do a press release explaining how and why they were using the Phos-chek retardant, and its impacts on vegetation.

Cohen spotted him and nodded acknowledgment. He stepped up onto the wooden platform and spoke into a mic. "Ladies and gentlemen, we're starting our morning briefing."

Tanner stood next to his state counterpart. "Good morning, everyone," he began, calm but authoritative. "Here's the current status of the Elmore fire. It's contained on the right flank, using Elmore Road as a natural barrier, and so far, it hasn't jumped the line. We have a three-mile dozer line between the head of the fire and the Shadowing Spruce neighborhood, a quarter of a mile from the fire's head."

"What if the dozer line doesn't hold? And what if burning debris is tossed on the other side of the fuel break?" asked a reporter, digital tablet in hand.

"What about the left flank, closest to the Hillside residences?" asked a Channel 2 news reporter, standing next to her cameraman, who aimed his camera at Tanner and Cohen.

"We're dozing a fuel break on that side as well. We're also laying down water drops and slurry on the green side of the fuel break to stop flames in case they jump the break." Tanner drew the strategy on a whiteboard, explaining the air attack and the importance of the crucial dozer lines.

"What if the fire jumps the lines?" someone shot at him.

"Our priority is preventing the fire from reaching the Chugach Foothills neighborhoods," emphasized Tanner. "Once we have seventy-five percent containment, we can put out the fire, weather permitting."

Agency officials and reporters nodded, satisfied for the time being. Experience told Tanner the reprieve would be short-lived.

In this job, you were only as good as your last decision.

When the briefing ended, he stayed glued to the radio, listening to Ryan coordinate the ongoing air attack, as the head of the fire kicked up in the afternoon. His pulse sped up at hearing Ripley, confident and steady as she maneuvered Blazebuster into position.

"Tanker One-Six-Zero, you're clear for the drop at the head," radioed Ryan. "Winds are steady from the northwest. Bird Dog will lead you in."

"Copy that, Air Attack. Beginning my run now," said Ripley.

Tanner picked up binoculars and glassed out the window of the back meeting room. He could make out Bird Dog, then the larger air tanker swooping low over the treetops, its belly opening to release a cascade of red slurry. With Ripley making the drop, it bordered on erotic.

Whoa, now that's a stretch. Knock it off, you hardly know her. He chided himself for letting his mind go to the gutter.

The day blurred into a series of briefings, interviews, and explanatory phone calls. The fire investigation had begun with Jon Silva, the investigator sent by the National Interagency Fire

Center in Boise, along with the State Fire Marshal. Cohen introduced him to Tanner.

The fire investigator extended his hand. "Hello, Tanner. Jon Silva, your wildland fire investigator."

"Good to see you. What do you have for us?" Tanner asked, shaking his hand.

"We think it may be a deliberate set."

Tanner's stomach soured. "You're sure?"

"When you called in the two people you saw while flying over the start area, APD sent officers to check and found this." Silva showed Tanner a series of photographs. "Multiple points of origin with traces of accelerant. And this." He held up an evidence bag containing a charred cigarette lighter with an intricate design etched into the metal.

"Custom-made," Silva explained. "One of a kind. Whoever did this wasn't trying to cover their tracks. They wanted us to know it was deliberate. I'm taking it to the crime lab to see if we can get prints."

Tanner stared at the innocent-looking lighter with a mash-up of anger and disbelief. Someone had intentionally put thousands of lives and hundreds of thousands of dollars of property at risk. The thought made his blood boil. Great, now he had arsonists to complicate this firefight.

"Any leads?" asked Tanner.

Silva shook his head. "Not yet. But we'll find them."

After Silva left, Tanner sank into his chair, tugging at his eyebrow. The fire was no longer a natural disaster. It had morphed into a crime scene—a deliberate act of destruction that threatened Alaska's largest city. He gazed out the window at the smoky sky. They would contain this fire and find whoever was responsible—they had to, or the deliberate sets would most likely continue.

And God help them when they were found.

Chapter 10

R*ipley*

Ripley sat in the front row of the crowded room for the afternoon briefing, her gaze fixed on Tanner as he discussed firefighting strategy. She did her best to maintain neutrality, but her heart did the pitty-pat thing every time Tanner's gaze swept over her.

She cursed herself for reacting like this.

"The Turnagain wind is pushing the fire south-southeast," Tanner was saying. "We'll focus our aerial attacks on the head of the fire while the ground crews reinforce our containment lines."

A barrage of questions followed, and she observed Tanner field them with ease, his responses clear and concise. When he didn't know something, he admitted it without hesitation, saying he'd find the answer. She marveled at his ability to put everyone at ease. His easygoing charm seemed to diffuse the tension in the room.

His eyes met Ripley's briefly, and she smiled and looked away—but not before Mel caught the exchange as he sat next to her. He elbowed her, and she elbowed him back, giving him an eyeroll.

Now she regretted sharing her thoughts about Westlake; Mel was having way too much fun teasing her. It wasn't *her* fault Tanner was easy on the eyes. What was she supposed to do, put a sack over his head so she wouldn't stare at him?

"Aviation folks, meet me in the back conference room," directed Tanner as he wrapped up the briefing.

Once everyone was assembled, he got right to it. "The fire's running again. We have a Turnagain wind that's kicked up, gusting to thirty. Flying is challenging in these conditions. We need the drops, but don't risk it if you feel you can't."

No sooner had those words left Tanner's mouth than a report came over the radio: the fire had jumped the left flank and was running uphill, threatening a neighborhood. Everyone in the room tensed.

"Damn," Tanner muttered, his face grim. He looked at Ripley. "I know it's no fun negotiating thirty-knot winds, but we need a drop on the left flank ASAP. You up for it? Thirty-five knots are pushing it for an aerial attack."

Ripley answered with a nod. "I've flown drop missions in stronger winds. If it's too much, I'll let you know."

"Let's get you and Loman in the air before it does."

The shuttle van sped Ripley and Loman to the Anchorage airport, where they raced to Blazebuster. Each did their pre-flight checks while Bird Dog lifted off first. As Ripley took off, she glimpsed the orange glow of the fire crawling uphill, growing taller by the second.

The turbulence slammed them almost immediately. Blazebuster bucked and veered sideways in the strong air currents shooting out of Turnagain Arm, as the wind followed the Chugach Range. Ripley's knuckles were firm on the yoke as she worked to steady the air tanker.

"Coming up on the drop zone," Loman called out. "There's Bird Dog."

Ripley let Loman do all the coordination with the spotter plane in front of them.

She lined up for a final approach to the target, the howling winds buffeting them, threatening to blow them off course. The spotter plane let out a trail of smoke: X marks the spot.

"Steady," she muttered. "Here's the target! Four, three, two, one... Release!"

Loman opened the gates, and the slurry flew. Blazebuster shot upward, suddenly freed of its heavy load. Ripley wrestled with the controls to compensate, her heart in her throat as they bounced through the turbulence.

She steadied the aircraft back to horizontal, but as they were climbing away, she heard panicked radio chatter. Her blood ran cold as she listened: some of the slurry had dropped onto moving vehicles, covering their windshields and causing them to crash into each other.

Her breath caught in her throat—her job was to save lives, not endanger them. The thought that she might have caused injuries or death tossed her out of kilter.

"Damn," said Loman. "How did *that* happen? We were well away from traffic areas."

"What the hell?" she practically shrieked. "Traffic was supposed to be cleared in this area!"

Tanner's voice came over the com. "Tanker One-Six-Zero, I'll meet you at the airport."

"Copy," she replied.

That can't be good.

The flight back to the airport was silent, and Ripley's hands shook as they touched down. She'd flown in dicey conditions before, but this was the first time she'd caused vehicle accidents.

She prayed the drivers were okay and there were no kids in the cars.

As she and Loman climbed down from the cockpit, Ripley spotted Tanner's truck pulling up, and apprehension coursed through her. She'd assured him she could handle the conditions. She had, mostly, but she had zero control over the drastic wind conditions that may have blown her slurry off the mark.

Tanner leaned against his truck as Ripley and Loman approached.

She threw her arms up in the air. "The damn wind knocked us off course as we opened the gates. Are the drivers okay?"

"Don't know yet, but don't worry. I'll handle it. Your drop slowed the fire, and our crews are working on it."

She shook her head. "Still, I feel bad about it. Those Turnagain winds were intense."

Tanner gave Ripley a direct look. "Can I have a word?"

"Uh, sure." She glanced at Loman, who hesitated. He seemed reluctant to leave them alone.

Ripley sensed Loman viewed Tanner as competition. Apparently, his workplace flirtations ran deeper than she thought.

"I'll leave you to it, then." Loman pointed at Ripley. "Let me know if you need anything. I'll treat you to dinner tonight, and we can talk about it." He gave Tanner an annoyed look, then strolled toward the waiting shuttle van parked next to their hangar.

"Thanks, Nubs, but I'm pretty tired," she called after him. "Think I'll go back to the hotel and call it a night."

"Loman, tell the shuttle driver I'm giving Beecher a ride," hollered Tanner.

Loman stopped as if to respond, then nodded and continued walking.

"I think he wanted you to go with him," said Tanner, as they watched him head to the van.

"I'd rather go with—" she started, when Tanner's cell interrupted.

He tapped it to answer. "Cohen, what's the word on the drivers? Uh-huh. Right. Okay. See you in the morning after your night shift." He ended the call.

"No word on their conditions yet. Apparently, the press is hyping the vehicle accidents, spinning it to sound like we were careless with our drop. It's even hit national news," relayed Tanner.

"What? That's insane!" Ripley had expected backlash, but saying it was carelessness on her part pissed her off. She tamped it down, not wanting to lose her shit in front of her boss.

He shook his head. "I've had this happen on lower forty-eight fires. Don't worry, I'll handle it."

Several notifications pinged her cell. "My phone's already blowing up."

"Let me see it." Tanner snapped his fingers and held out his hand.

"Why?"

"Your phone. Give it to me." He gestured impatiently with his fingers.

"But why?"

"Don't question your fire boss. Just do it," he said in a firm tone.

She slapped it into his palm harder than she'd intended, her stress getting the best of her.

He powered off her cell and handed it back. "There. See how easy that was? Deal with it in the morning. Ryan and our fire information officer will handle the media and other inquiries."

"I need to know if those drivers are okay. This was my fault. I was at the controls and ordered Loman to release the slurry. I caused extra problems that you don't have the time for. You have enough to deal with..." She trailed off, unable to keep the tremor from her voice.

"Stop second-guessing yourself." Tanner pulled her into a hug, and the unexpected warmth of his embrace caught her off guard.

Instead of resisting, she allowed herself this vulnerability while carefully holding herself in check. She let him comfort her because she hadn't the willpower to push him away.

"I wanted to start off on the right foot in Alaska." She eased herself away from him. "Thanks for... understanding."

"Everyone needs a hug now and then. Even if it's from your boss." He jangled his keys. "Come on, I'll drive you to the hotel."

She didn't argue. There would be investigations, reports to file, and repercussions for the damaged cars and the drivers' injuries. She would have to fill out paperwork for StormAir.

All of that could wait until morning.

THEY STOPPED FOR A combo pizza, which they both inhaled. Then Tanner walked Ripley up to her room.

She fished her key card from her pocket, pausing at her door. "Thank you for... for calming me so I didn't lose my shit. Keep me posted on the condition of the drivers. I don't care how late it is. Oh, wait, you turned off my phone." She wasn't on her game, and it annoyed her.

"I did that for several reasons."

"And what might those be?" she asked in a weak voice.

He took a step closer, sending shivers of delight through her. Her mind blanked.

"You and I both know in our line of work, we don't have the luxury of time." There was that damn Sam Elliot voice again that fluttered her insides.

"For, uh... for what?" She sensed an undeniable magnetism building between them and knew where this was heading, warring with herself whether to stop it.

"We steal every second we can." He closed the gap, cupping her cheek, his face close to hers.

Her heartbeat skyrocketed because she knew what was coming. For the love of God, he was her incident commander. Impropriety complaints flashed through her mind. She had a stellar reputation and couldn't afford any of that.

Just as she was about to step back, an annoyed voice made her jump. "Well, well. What do we have here?"

She instinctively backed away from Tanner, her cheeks heating.

Loman sauntered toward them, smirking. "Didn't realize we were mixing business with pleasure on this assignment, Beecher."

His accusation, piled on top of everything else, frosted her cookies. "It's not what it looks like!"

"Oh, I think it's exactly what it looks like." Loman's tone dripped with innuendo. "Thought you were tired." He shot her a look that was anything but friendly before disappearing into his room, the door slamming shut behind him.

An awkward silence dropped, and mortification washed over her. "I'm sorry," she lamented, shaking her head.

"Nothing to be sorry for. It was my doing. I was out of line," Tanner said quietly. "I should go."

Ripley nodded. "Yes. Early start tomorrow and all that."

"Right." He hesitated. "Hey, I'm sorry if I—"

She held up her hand. "No apologies. Really. We're both spun up after today. Loman has been hitting on me since we began working together in Fairbanks. I assumed he was only flirting." She took an uneven breath. "That's what I get for assuming. He knows I'm not interested, but he's like a persistent mosquito. He won't stop trying."

"Well, anyone with a brain can see that," snorted Tanner.

She lifted her chin. "This... I mean, we... we need to keep things professional." Her cheeks filled with heat, irritating herself with confusion. She was attracted to him, but it wouldn't be right. Wrong place, wrong time, and wrong situation.

His head bobbed up and down. "We're professionals. I'm all about that."

She tilted her head, her eyes narrowing. "You're making fun of me, aren't you? Oh, that's right, you're also a smokejumper. Therefore, you're a professional bullshitter."

"I'm not bullshitting. I'm serious." He sounded sincere. But how would she know? She hardly knew him.

"Okay, let's put this behind us." She motioned to herself, then at him. "You're my boss, so we both know this would be a conflict of interest."

Keep telling yourself that, Beecher.

"Copy that." He gave her a close-mouthed smile. "Like I said, I was out of line. Won't happen again. Goodnight, Captain

Beecher." And with that, he ducked out and headed for the stairwell.

"Goodnight... Wolfman!" she called after him.

"What did I tell you about that?" he called over his shoulder before disappearing through the stairway door.

She swiped her key card, relieved to be in the privacy of her room. As the door closed behind her, Ripley leaned against it, trying to calm the storm of emotions ricocheting inside her.

What had she been thinking? Getting involved with someone in the fire world—especially her boss—could jeopardize her career. Yet his closeness, and how perfectly their bodies fit when he embraced her, was impossible to ignore. Romance was a luxury she couldn't afford. Besides, there was no room for involvement in her busy schedule.

Her heartbeat finally quieted. If Loman hadn't shown up, Tanner would have kissed her. The attraction between them was without question, but not while they worked together. And like the fires they fought, trying to contain this one would be like playing whack-a-mole with an alligator.

She was too tired to sort this, so she took a shower, letting the stress of the day disappear down the drain with the swirling water. She finished up, dried herself off, and slipped between the sheets. Whenever she closed her eyes, she saw fire retardant coating burning, crashing cars, and she tossed and turned.

But what bothered her most was the ghost of a kiss that almost happened.

Chapter 11

T*anner*

As Tanner lay on the bed in his hotel room, fiddling with his eyebrow, he couldn't believe his nerve. He'd wrapped his arms around Ripley on the tarmac, then tried to kiss her? It was like she had him under a spell.

What were you thinking, you bonehead?

She had tapped into his empathy, and he'd responded in a way he thought might help. He knew what it was like to mess up on a fire when things happened that were out of his control. He only wanted to reassure her, then he was drawn to her like magnetic north.

At least Ripley had the courage to let herself be human. He admired her stoic, stalwart personality and her willingness to be honest about her emotions. He wished he could do that but viewed it as a weakness in himself. He maintained a strong alpha male persona for this career he'd chosen. It was an unwritten rule with fire people to keep a stiff upper lip, no matter what.

His phone sounded, and Cohen filled him in on the condition of the vehicle occupants: a mom with a ten-year-old girl in an SUV, and an older couple in a compact sedan. All were okay, with minor injuries. He thanked Cohen and tapped Ripley's number—then remembered he'd shut off her phone.

He debated before going to her room down on the second floor. Tapping lightly, he waited, then the door opened a crack with the chain lock in place.

Ripley peeked out with bleary eyes. "Oh, um, Westlake. Why are you here?"

"I have info for you. Can I come in?"

"Um… yeah, sure." She slid the chain lock off and opened the door.

She had on a low-cut T-shirt that hit her thighs. His eyes darted to her legs, then trailed back up. She wasn't wearing a bra.

Oh, brother, I'm in trouble.

He'd better make this quick before his little buddy stood up and saluted.

"Cohen just called to say the drivers survived the crash, and they're all okay," he informed her.

"Oh, thank goodness." Ripley's eyes widened. "How many?"

"Four. A mom and young daughter in one car, and a couple in another. They were all treated at Providence Hospital for minor injuries but were released." He offered her a reassuring smile. "You said to let you know, no matter how late it was."

She stumbled back with a sigh of relief. "I was so worried, I couldn't sleep. I kept thinking, what would I do if…" She shook her head.

The raw emotion in her voice and the way her eyes glistened shattered his restraint. In one swift move, he scooped her into his arms and kissed her until she went limp.

She pulled back breathless; her eyes the size of two moons. "We agreed this wasn't a good idea."

"No, we said it wasn't professional. There's a difference," he countered, his gaze fixed on her.

"Not when I'm half dressed in my hotel room, and you're standing there all hot and handsome..." She gave him a perplexed look.

"Hot and handsome?" As far as Tanner was concerned, that was a green light. "I don't give a damn what people think. How can it be a bad idea if we both feel the same way?"

"Well, that's being presumptuous, isn't it?" Ripley lifted a brow. "How do you know I feel the same way?"

"I see it in your eyes." He cradled her face, peering into her baby blues. "I see it during the briefings whenever you look at me."

"What? I do not! I don't look at you in any special way at work!" she protested, pulling his hands away.

"Liar. You're blushing." He took her by the wrist and drew her into him, kissing her again.

She made a feeble attempt to fight him off, but he only deepened the kiss, loving the feel of her... losing himself in the taste of her. When he'd held her at the airport, he'd wanted to strip that damn flight suit off her right there on the tarmac. He wanted nothing more than to fling her onto the bed. Instead, he broke the kiss, wondering if she felt his heartbeat thumping against her chest.

He forced himself to back away. "We'd better go to bed."

She glanced at the bed and stiffened with a deer-in-the-headlights look.

He chortled. "I meant go to our separate beds in our separate rooms. What do you think I am, a sex-crazed animal?"

She folded her arms with both brows raised. "Well, I don't know. Are you?"

"Trying hard not to be." He was doing his best to control himself. "When this fire is over, I'll likely morph into wolf mode. For now, we both need sleep. Morning comes early in this neck of the woods."

"What is it you do in wolf mode?" She eyed him cautiously. "Are you one of those guys that has a fling on every fire? Or a boss who exchanges high performance ratings for you-know-what?"

"Hell, no! You think that's what this is?" It came out stronger than he intended, fueled by his uncharted territory of navigating a fire romance. "Honest to God, this is a first."

She gave him a doubtful look. "Uh, huh. Well, if you breathe one word of this little tête-à-tête, I'll strap you to Blazebuster's wing and fly you through the flames. I don't need accusations of getting special favors for a roll in the sheets with the boss."

This time, he was the one with wide eyes. "Aye, aye, Captain. It's in the vault."

"Alrighty, then." She opened the door and motioned him to leave with a look that belied her words.

Why do I have the feeling she doesn't want me to go?

He leaned in for another taste of her lips. "Kiss me, then go fly tomorrow."

"See, now you're getting greedy." She pointed to the hallway. "Go."

"Good night. Make good choices," he teased.

"I plan on it." She closed the door, and he heard her fall back against it.

He paused long enough to hear her murmur a 'whew' and a 'holy shit' before ambling up to his room. He'd win her over... maybe not today, but when this fire ended, she wouldn't stand a chance.

Not when I enter my wolf mode.

THE NEXT MORNING, THE winds had subsided, but experience told Tanner this was the calm before the storm. He pored over weather reports and fire behavior models, determined to stay at least two steps ahead.

Tara called him on his cell. A family of five were trapped in their home, surrounded by encroaching flames. Without hesitation, Tanner sprang into action, coordinating ground crews and air support. He hopped into the truck and drove past the roadblock on Elmore Road to monitor the situation, radio in hand.

Ryan had instructed Tanker One-Six-Zero to make the drops. From his position on the ground, Tanner watched as Ripley maneuvered Blazebuster through the smoke-filled sky. She made the salvo drop, which doused the flames, giving the Aurora Hotshots the opening they needed to reach the trapped family.

Tanner held his breath as he listened to Tara and her crew race through suffocating heat and blinding smoke to extricate each of the five people, then leading them into the burned black. Fire didn't burn twice, so the black was safe.

"Aurora to IC, do you copy?" Tara's voice wiggled, out of breath.

"Copy. Are they out?" asked Tanner.

"Affirmative. Rego is leading them through the black and out to Elmore Road."

"Good job, Tara. Thank you for that."

"Copy. We'll stay to spray the house. We have a hose lay hooked up to a water tender truck, so we're trying to save the home," said Tara, panting.

"Okay, safety at all costs," Tanner reminded her. "I'm sending more hotshot crews to help you guys out to contain the line again."

Tara keyed two clicks to sign off, and Tanner noticed Blazebuster flying back to Anchorage airport. He eyed the large insignia on the side of the plane: a flame encircled in red with a red diagonal bar crossing out the fire. The insignia reminded him of the logo from the *Ghostbusters* movie, and he chuckled. Ripley had done it again. He radioed Ryan to take charge at the ICC because he had an errand to run.

Tanner sped across Anchorage and down Northern Lights Boulevard to the airport. He waited for Ripley to taxi to her parking spot next to the hangar, so the ground crew could get Blazebuster ready for its next mission.

Instead of waiting in his truck, Tanner got out and flashed his fire ID to security posted at the chain-link gate. He entered and strode across the tarmac toward the air tanker as her pilot cut the engines.

Chapter 12

Ripley

When she'd awakened earlier that morning, Ripley's mind had instantly flooded with thoughts of last night's unexpected closeness to Tanner Westlake.

"What was I thinking? I kissed my flipping fire boss!" she'd groaned out while blow-drying her hair and putting it into a sleek long ponytail. She'd tugged a few tendrils loose to frame each side of her face, then chided herself for primping for a fire shift—which she'd never done in her entire flipping life.

Ryan had phoned as she was zipping up her Nomex flight suit, telling her to get into the air, as a family had been trapped in their home. The fire had jumped the line, pushed by the early morning winds. Racing time, she and Loman had climbed into Blazebuster to lay slurry for the Aurora Hotshots to get the trapped family out.

After the drop, she'd landed and taxied toward the hangar, pleasantly surprised to see Tanner's truck parked next to it when she cut the engines and climbed down from the cockpit.

"Your boyfriend is here," said Loman, an edge to his words. He exited the aircraft and strode off toward the hangar, shaking his head.

"He isn't my boyfriend!" she fired after him, removing her helmet and shaking out her hair in exasperation. She noticed

Loman walked past Tanner without speaking. He'd been awfully quiet during their flight, only speaking when he had to.

After Loman entered the hangar, Tanner got out of his truck and marched toward her, removing his hard-hat. In front of God and everybody, he swept her into a passionate kiss right on the tarmac. Apparently, the adrenaline of the morning's events had overwhelmed all sense of his propriety.

She pulled back in protest, trying to catch her breath.

"I don't give two shits whether this is appropriate," he burst out. "We're both adults. I won't sneak around, pretending I don't have feelings for you."

"But how can you? We hardly know each other! It's only been—"

He cut her off with another kiss. She responded with such fervor that the world fell away from them. He spoke against her lips. "You and I have too much in common. We fight fire, but we shouldn't fight this."

"I have a career to consider, since we've clearly blown by the getting-to-know-you colleague stage."

"I'll be careful from now on. But you just saved a shitload of lives and I had to do this." He brushed back the tendrils that she'd deliberately liberated from her ponytail.

"You've become that wolf you talked about." She laughed. "I know our time is limited, but let's slow down this dog team. You're sledding a bit too fast for me."

"You're a pilot, used to traveling 450 miles per hour. How can this be too fast?" he teased, stepping back. "I wanted to show you my appreciation for your fast, efficient response today."

"A simple thank you or an 'atta girl' would have done the trick. Or better yet, an 'excellent' on my performance evaluation." Her justification sounded lame after he'd kissed the hell out of her.

"We have to hop over to the afternoon fire briefing. Come on, I'll give you a ride."

Dazed, Ripley got into Tanner's pickup, and he switched the ignition. The radio blared, and he turned up the volume to listen to a news report praising the tanker pilot for saving a trapped family.

"What did I tell you? One day we're the bad guys, and the next we're the good guys. This replaced yesterday's report about the vehicles. The yin and the yang of firefighting."

"It wasn't me that saved the day. It was Blazebuster," she deflected.

"My point is, please don't worry about the slurry drop on those vehicles. Everyone is fine. The media are singing your praises after saving the trapped family."

She shrugged. "I'm not in this for glory or recognition. I'm here to do a job. Protecting lives and properties are a given."

When they arrived at the ICC, Tanner immediately engaged in a discussion with a cluster of agency heads in the afternoon fire briefing. Ripley admired how easily he flexed from one minute to the next. She wished she could bend like that.

She sat next to Tara in the front row of folding chairs. Tara leaned sideways and squeezed her arm. "Thank you for helping us yesterday and today, especially. Your drops made all the difference for us to get a line in and get that family out."

"So glad it all worked out," responded Ripley. So, this was Ryan O'Connor's wife. She was drop-dead gorgeous, even in her green and yellow Nomex and baseball cap with her dark auburn ponytail streaming out the back of it.

Tanner stepped to the front podium and outlined his strategy for bombarding the fire's head with slurry and extending the dozer line. Agency representatives voiced concerns with competing priorities, and Ripley watched as Tanner navigated the bureaucratic minefield with patience and skill.

After the meeting dispersed, Ripley waited until most everyone had left, then jerked her head toward the empty conference room. Tanner followed her in, and she closed the door.

"We need to talk. About last night and this morning..."

Tanner's expression was solid. "I won't apologize. It is what it is."

"You realize this is about optics, right? We must stay neutral on the job. You and I both know it won't be good if others find out. Everyone probably knows by now, since Loman saw us in the hallway last night."

"We were just talking," he said matter-of-factly.

Standing this close to him wobbled her knees, and she involuntarily stepped back, throwing up her usual resistance. "I think we should hold off, at least until after this fire ends." If only she could stop thinking about those damn kisses that had rocked her world.

"I suppose you're right," he said with a lopsided smile. He was placating her.

"I know I am. Let's cool it for now. Agreed?" This attraction was perilous, and she'd convinced herself that distance was the best choice.

"Sure," he replied.

She didn't believe him.

Someone knocked on the door, and they dashed away from each other. Ryan poked his head in. "Tanner, Marc Stover, the AFD Wildfire Chief would like a word."

"On my way." He turned to Ripley. "How about we discuss this later?"

"There's nothing more to discuss." She said it more abruptly than intended, hating that she was the heavy. "I'd better get back to the airport."

She brushed past him and hurried out the door, cussing herself for getting distracted by this incredibly attractive man. Her sense of duty wrestled with the newfound desire for meaningful intimacy. If only she'd met Tanner at a solstice festival or on a Colorado ski slope—anywhere but on a fire where he was her boss.

For now, they each had a job to do. Lives and homes hung in the balance, and Ripley was determined to give her all to the firefight. As she headed outside to catch the shuttle back to the airport, she squared her shoulders, shoving thoughts of Tanner's kisses out of her mind.

Fire didn't care about her personal life, and she didn't have time for one, anyway. Not until the last ember was extinguished and the city of Anchorage was safe.

Only then would she allow herself to think about what she wanted.

Chapter 13

Tanner

The conference room in the rear of the ICC closed in on Tanner as he waited for the fire investigation meeting. He couldn't recall when he'd last slept the entire night—maybe Tuesday? Wednesday? The days blurred together as they always did on a project fire.

Jon Silva breezed in with two people. "Hey Tanner, how's it going? This is Detective Lydia Martinez with the Anchorage Police Department, and Alaska State Trooper Neil Iverson." He motioned to Tanner. "This is Tanner Westlake, the incident commander."

"Good to meet you. Have a seat." Tanner nodded toward the conference table.

"We have something to show you." Silva spread out photos on the table. He tapped one. "The lab results are conclusive. The residue we found contains traces of petroleum distillate mixed with what appears to be homemade napalm—gasoline combined with styrofoam to create a gel-like substance that burns longer and hotter than gasoline alone."

"Homemade napalm?" Tanner leaned forward, squinting at the images. The blackened remnants of what appeared to be a plastic container were barely recognizable.

"And there's this," Silva continued, sliding another photo toward him. "The custom lighter we recovered matches the ignition pattern of multiple points of origin—a coordinated effort to ensure the fire would spread rapidly."

"We're looking at deliberate intent, with premeditation. Not some random kids playing with matches," said Detective Martinez.

Tanner let out a heavy sigh. "So, we're looking at arson."

The officers both nodded.

"Wait'll the media gets wind of this. Whoever did this obviously planned for it. They chose a location with heavy fuel loads, challenging access for responders, and maximum potential for spread toward populated areas," said Silva.

Trooper Iverson cleared his throat. "The intent was clear—to endanger lives and property."

Tanner blew out air. "Where do we go from here?"

"Since this is now a crime investigation, we're searching for the perpetrators," replied Martinez. "We want to interview your air crew. I understand one of your pilots..." the detective glanced down at her phone, "a woman named Ripley Beecher reportedly spotted individuals fleeing the scene?"

"Yes, she did. I'll arrange a meeting," said Tanner.

THIRTY MINUTES LATER, Ripley and Mel sat on the same side of the table with Cohen and Tanner, across from the investigators. Ripley recounted what she'd seen during their reconnaissance flight.

"Two figures moved away from the point of origin," she explained, her hands illustrating the direction. "It wasn't random—they were walking around in the black, then took off when they saw our Cessna."

"Can you describe them?" Martinez pressed.

Ripley shook her head. "We were too high for any details. One was wearing blue, and the other wore something pink. Either clothing or maybe a backpack."

"Male? Female?"

"I couldn't tell. It happened too fast," responded Ripley.

"We all saw the same thing," Tanner pointed out. "But as Ripley said, they disappeared before we could get any other details."

Mel seconded. "I also saw two people moving with purpose, not in the manner of panicked civilians."

Detective Martinez closed her notebook. "Thanks, everyone, for your cooperation. We'll be in touch if we need anything else."

Everyone rose from the table. "Beecher, got a minute?" Tanner said in a neutral voice as the rest disappeared out the door. He closed the door behind them, then took the chair next to her.

Ripley shook her head. "I wish we could have given them more to go on."

"We saw what we saw," Tanner shrugged.

Ripley's frustration was palpable. "Two people may have deliberately set a fire to endanger a city, and all I can tell them is 'one wore blue, one had pink'?"

"You gave them a direction to look. That's more than they had before." He noticed her staring blankly at the wall, apparently processing the interview.

She turned to him. "I wish I could give them a better description. Hard to get detail from a plane."

"Don't beat yourself up. You told them what you could." He leaned toward her. "You're doing amazing work out there. You made that rescue possible yesterday, buying time for the crews to evacuate a family. I'm still in awe of the drop you made during that firenado in the Big Lake fire."

"Oh, that," she teased. "Just doing my job."

Tanner shook his head. "Most pilots wouldn't have attempted drops in either of those conditions."

She gave him a dubious look. "Are you complimenting my flying, or saying I'm a risk-taker?"

"A little of both, I guess." He followed up with a yawn.

"Have you been getting enough sleep?" She appeared genuinely concerned, which warmed his heart.

He made a dismissive wave. "I'll sleep when this fire is out."

"That's not how it works, and you know it. You need to rest," she chided.

"There's too much to do."

"None of it will get done if you collapse from fatigue." She patted his arm. "You incident commanders burn out because you think you're indispensable. That's what all of those other people out there are for." She nodded at the door.

"Thanks for the reminder." Her touch sent a pleasurable sensation through his exhausted body. He fantasized about lying naked on a beach somewhere with her.

"Hey, earth to Tanner, come back here."

He snapped back to the present. "What about you? You've seen a lot of action these past few days."

"I got seven hours last night," she countered. "I'm required to. FAA regulations."

"I'm fine. Nothing another cup of coffee won't fix." He rubbed his eyes.

"Take a breather and let Ryan handle things, since Cohen has to sleep from his night shift. That's why you have a command team. You're no good to anyone if you have a foggy brain," she pointed out.

"Fine," he conceded. "I'll sit here and chill. Scout's honor." He held up three fingers.

"You were a Boy Scout?"

"Yeah, but got kicked out for not extinguishing a campfire. It burned a few acres. Ten acres, actually."

"And now you're spending the rest of your life making up for it," she teased.

"Something like that." He liked the subtle scent of her shampoo, the rise and fall of her breath, and the way she tucked the loose tendrils from her ponytail behind her ears.

His radio jumped to life. "IC, this is Ryan. The fire jumped the line on the northeast corner, and its running toward a subdivision. The Aurora Hotshots are responding."

Tanner keyed his radio. "Copy that. I'm on my way." He turned to Ripley. "Duty calls. You'd better get to the airport."

She nodded. "See you on the radio, Commander."

He gave her a suggestive look. "Kiss me and fly."

"Sure, buddy." She spun him around and gave him a light shove as they left the room. "Right here in front of God and everybody."

As he hopped into his truck, longing and responsibility waged a conflict inside him. What he wouldn't give for this fire to be out. Whatever these feelings were he had for Ripley, he was sure this wasn't a temporary fling, nor was it merely physical... although that was a winning point. It felt more like a kinship of shared purpose and mutual respect. Nothing like his marriage.

He adjusted his focus back to his responsibilities. He had a city to protect. And somewhere out there, arsonists to catch.

Everything else would have to wait.

Chapter 14

R*ipley*
The smoke had thickened, reducing visibility and making each slurry drop a challenge to find holes in the smoke.

"Tanker One-Six-Zero, this is Air Attack. Do you copy?" Ryan's voice streamed into her headset.

"Copy, Air Attack," Ripley responded, navigating a thermal updraft.

"We need you to split your load. First target is the uphill spread at coordinates I'm sending to your onboard computer. Then hit the head," instructed Ryan.

Ripley glanced at the coordinates appearing on her display. "ETA is three minutes to the first drop." She eyed Bird Dog, lining up in front of her to mark the target. She maintained plenty of distance behind him.

Loman input the coordinates into their navigation system. "Winds are shifting again. Could get dicey."

"When isn't it?" Ripley muttered, lining up the aircraft for their first target.

Bird Dog's blinking lights guided her through the smoke toward the uphill flames. Ripley focused on the instruments before her and the fire below.

"Tanker One-Six-Zero, it's a go for the drop," the Bird Dog pilot called. "Winds holding at fifteen knots, gusting at twenty."

"Twenty knots. No wonder this fire is running." She spoke calmly, despite the adrenaline charging through her veins. "Starting my run."

Ripley eased Blazebuster lower, the aircraft bucking against the thermal currents rising from the fire. She studied where Bird Dog sprayed smoke to mark the drop zone.

"Almost there," said Loman, eyeing the target coordinates. "Okay, now!" He opened the gate for the first half of their load.

The red slurry was released smoothly, creating a line between the advancing flames and the unburned green. Ripley pulled up, banking away from the smoke column.

"Nice, Tanker One-Six-Zero," Ryan confirmed on the radio. "Proceed to the second target."

As they approached the fire's head, a subtle vibration shook the aircraft, not caused by turbulence.

"Not again," groaned Ripley. "The mechanic said he fixed the problem." She grimaced at the gauge. "Let's do this second drop and head back to the airport."

"Tanker One-Six-Zero, you're clear for the drop," radioed Ryan.

The second half of their load hit exactly where needed, strengthening the barrier between the fire and the homes beyond. Ripley could almost hear the cheer from the ground crews as she pulled up and away.

"Engine temperature's still climbing," Loman noted, his finger tapping the gauge.

She keyed her mic. "Air Attack, this is Tanker One-Six-Zero. We have a potential issue with our left engine. Returning to base."

"Copy that, One-Six-Zero. Make sure it gets checked out," responded Ryan.

As they turned toward Anchorage International, Tanner came through the radio. "Tanker One-Six-Zero, what's the status with your engine?" His concern was loud and clear.

"Just a hot engine. Nothing critical," she assured him. "But I'd rather not push our luck."

"Roger that. Keep me posted." His relief was subtle but unmistakable. "The drops are helping the hotshot crew's progress with containment, and Marc Stover has the Anchorage Fire Department's wildfire division pitching in to help. We've evacuated two of the neighborhoods on the Hillside as a precautionary measure."

"Good to hear," Ripley replied, managing a small smile. "The coordination between agencies has been impressive."

"It has," agreed Tanner. "Almost makes my job easy."

The flight back to the airport was tense, with Ripley monitoring the engine temperature while Loman coordinated with the tower for their approach. By the time they touched down, she was sweating, despite the cockpit's air conditioning. She had to get this engine fixed once and for all.

A ground crew waited as they taxied to a stop. The lead mechanic, a burly man named Frank, approached as Ripley climbed down from the cockpit.

"Heard you've got engine trouble. Same one?"

She nodded, her legs weak as she jumped onto solid ground. The adrenaline crash combined with hours of intense concentration left her feeling drained... and frustrated.

"This engine keeps acting up, and the mechanics who've inspected it say they've fixed it," said Ripley.

He shrugged. "Could be anything from a cooling system issue to a mechanical failure. We'll check it out."

"Keep me posted." Suppressing a yawn, she held up her phone. "Here's my cell number."

He noted it. "I'll call you with an update."

The thought of a hot shower and getting prone for a while was too tempting to resist. As she trudged toward the waiting shuttle, her phone buzzed with a text from Tanner.

Dinner? You must be starving. I know I am.

She debated, her thumb hovering over the screen. After lecturing him about cooling things off, she should turn down the invitation. But warring with herself was a bitch, and apparently, she was a hypocrite. She gave herself an eyeroll as she tapped a reply.

What do you have in mind?

His response came quickly: *Takeout from a sushi place. My room?*

Ripley bit her lip, considering. The thought of a crowded restaurant right now didn't appeal to her. A meal in his hotel room was harmless... wasn't it?

Need a shower first. How about seven?

Tanner replied: *Room 412. The food will be waiting when you get here.*

Ripley pocketed her phone, a disordered mix of anticipation and apprehension swirling inside her as she boarded the van. She berated herself for blurring the lines with her fire boss while working for him. But when this fire ended, they'd each return to their respective bases in two different states. No harm done.

Besides, he was someone she enjoyed spending time with. A temporary fling was erotic to her way of thinking, as long as she didn't get attached.

In her hotel room, she stood under the hot spray until her skin turned pink, washing away grime and tension. Stepping out, she wiped the foggy mirror and winced. Dark circles shadowed her eyes—thirty-nine years old and feeling decades older.

She blow-dried her hair, then pulled on clean jeans and a soft, form-fitting T-shirt. No makeup. She never packed makeup for a fire—why would she want to look good for the flames? If Tanner was expecting anything else, he was in for disappointment.

She rode the elevator up to the fourth floor, then knocked on Tanner's door.

He opened it, damp chestnut hair flopping over his forehead in a sexy vibe. He was barefoot in a faded gray Missoula Smokejumpers T-shirt and jeans. He stepped aside to let her in. "Perfect timing. Door Dash just delivered two bento boxes from a Japanese sushi place."

Her mouth watered at the smell of delicious food.

"Yakitori chicken or teriyaki steak strips?" He lifted the lids from two takeout boxes on the small coffee table.

"I'd eat cardboard if it had soy sauce on it," she admitted, sinking onto the loveseat, poised to dive in. "I'll take the chicken."

Tanner laughed. "That bad, huh?"

They ate in companionable silence, her body relaxing as the food worked its magic.

"What did you find out about the engine trouble?" he asked, working chopsticks into his rice.

She wiped her hands on a napkin. "Frank's checking it out. I should hear from him soon."

"Two days ago, we were looking at a potential disaster. Now we've got it nearly boxed in."

She confirmed with a brief nod. "The crews have done amazing work."

"So have you." The way his eyes roved over her made her breath catch in her throat.

She couldn't help but go with the flow. "You know, I wasn't sure about you at first."

He raised a brow. "Oh? I'm afraid to ask."

She met his gaze. "I'm not saying it's a bad thing. Just that you've turned out to be as crazy as the rest of us—you just hide it better behind that cool, calm demeanor while you work yourself to exhaustion. And you always come up smiling," she added.

"Being crazy is a compliment?"

"In this business? Absolutely." She finished her meal and sat back on the loveseat. "That was delicious."

Tanner finished his, then slid his arm along the back of the loveseat, resting it on her shoulders. The weight of it was comforting, and she embraced his heat. After all, they'd already kissed.

He clicked the TV remote, and *Big Bang Theory* appeared.

"I love this show!" She relaxed into him, lulling herself into a half-sleep.

"Hey," he rumbled against her ear. "You falling asleep on me?"

She straightened, blinking. "Oh, sorry. Been a long day."

"Don't apologize." He brushed the hair from her forehead, his fingers lingering on her cheek.

Her pulse shot up. She should thank him for dinner and go back to her room.

Professional distance be damned, he's too comfortable.

She leaned into his touch, turning her head to look at him.

"Ripley," he murmured, her name a question on his lips.

She answered by closing the distance, her mouth finding his in a kiss that started gentle but quickly deepened. Tanner's arm tightened around her, drawing her closer as he turned sideways to cradle her face with his other hand. Unlike their first kiss—this one was slower, more deliberate. Ripley turned into him, her hands sliding up his chest to curl around his shoulders.

Tanner's lips were warm, his stubble rough beneath her fingers. He tasted like steak mixed with something uniquely him. She was half in his lap, her legs draped across his. His hand slid down her neck, leaving a trail of warmth. When his fingers reached the bottom of her T-shirt, he hesitated, breaking the kiss to look at her.

"Can I?" he breathed.

Everything in Ripley wanted to scream yes. The feel of his hands on her skin and the solid warmth of his body were intoxicating. Before she could answer, Tanner's hand slipped beneath her shirt, his fingers warm against her bare skin. She gasped as his hand slid higher, lightly over her ribs, to the edge of her bra.

It would be so easy to give in, to lose herself in him. But as his thumb edged under her bra and brushed the underside of her breast, reality came crashing back. No matter how much she wanted this, they were in the middle of a firefight, and he was her incident commander.

Ripley caught his wrist, stilling his movement. "We should stop," she groaned out, not wanting him to stop at all.

He paused, his breath coming fast, withdrawing his hand. "You're right. I'm sorry if I—"

Ripley interrupted. "I want it too. But as my boss, this could get—"

"Complicated?" he finished for her.

"Exactly."

The air became charged with unresolved tension, and she struggled to regain composure. "I don't do this on fires. I know some people do, but I don't," she confessed.

Tanner grinned. "What, turn down advances from hot and handsome incident commanders? Your words, not mine. You're the one who said it."

"Oops." She bit her lip, cheeks flaming. "I let one slip. How embarrassing."

"Not for me," he drawled in his Montana accent that made her want to climb him like a firehouse pole.

Ripley laughed despite the ache of desire thrumming through her.

"When I heard you on the radio at Big Lake and watched you handle that plane like a boss, I had to meet you. That's why I drove out to Palmer." He tilted his head with a half-smile and a dimple she'd love to live in.

She leaned back, surprised. "You drove all the way out there to hit on me?"

"No, of course not—well, okay, yeah, sort of—I admired your flying through that hideous weather. I had to meet the woman who made that drop." His blunt honesty skipped her heart.

"Sly dog." Her phone buzzed, and she answered. "Hey, Frank, what's the verdict?"

"Found the problem," Frank's voice was tinny through the speaker. "Faulty temperature sensor was giving false readings, but we're replacing it as a precaution. Also, fixed that vibration you felt in that left engine. Should have you ready to fly by tomorrow morning."

Relief washed through her. "That's great news. Thanks, Frank." As she ended the call, she turned to find Tanner watching her.

"Blazebuster will be ready by morning," she confirmed. "False alarm with the engine."

Tanner nodded, rising from the loveseat. "That's good. One less thing."

"Right?" Ripley rose as well, keenly aware of his fabulous physique and the neck tattoo of a blue dragon with a Pulaski in its claw. She peered at the tattoo, running her finger over it. "Does your dragon have a name?"

He sucked in a breath. "If you keep doing that, you won't be leaving this room. And yes, he has a name. It's Mizuchi... a mythological Japanese dragon that breathes water instead of flames."

"A water-breathing dragon instead of a fire-breathing one?" Now *that* turned her on. She fought for casual. "Perfect for a firefighter." If she stayed any longer, her resolve would crumble. "I'd better go. Early start tomorrow."

"Sleep well," he rumbled at her.

"You too," she replied, stepping into the hallway, already questioning her choice.

Damn, he's mother effing hot. Am I utterly insane?

As the door closed behind her, she all but staggered to the stairwell. She hoped she hadn't hurt his feelings, but she'd spent years safeguarding her heart and wouldn't hand it over to the first charmer who wanted it. What bewildered her was that, in less than a week, Tanner Westlake had slipped past every single defense in her no-way-will-you-break-my-heart arsenal.

What bewildered her even more?

I'm falling for him.

Hard and fast, like a plane plummeting in a downdraft. She had to get a grip—keep reminding herself this was temporary, for the duration of this fire. After that, they would go their separate ways.

As she collapsed onto her bed, she stared at the ceiling, trying to frame this thing with Tanner. While she'd never done the fling thing on a fire before, maybe doing one would help both of them de-stress and let off steam.

As long as they kept it all under wraps.

Chapter 15

Tanner

The digital clock read 5:17 AM, but in Alaska's perpetual summer daylight, sunbeams already filtered through the hotel curtains. He'd slept better than he had in days. He chuckled, thinking Ripley probably had factored into it.

Tanner showered quickly, trying not to dwell on the memory of her beneath his hands. She'd been right to stop things since they were in the middle of a complex firefight. Still, as he pulled on his yellow Nomex shirt and laced up his boots, he couldn't deny the dynamic between them had changed.

The morning briefing at the ICC was concise, with a focused energy running through the team. Containment was now at sixty-eight percent, with expectations to reach eighty by day's end if conditions held. The news should have lifted Tanner's spirits, but the arson angle left him uneasy. People deliberately endangering lives and property wouldn't just walk away—they'd set more fires.

He relieved Cohen from the night shift, then headed into the field, wanting to see the progress firsthand and to talk directly with the crews battling this blaze.

"I'll be on the Aurora Crew's sector," he told Ryan, grabbing his radio and hardhat. "Keep me updated on any developments."

Ryan nodded. "The latest fire weather forecast is improving—winds staying under ten knots, humidity increasing slightly."

"Let's hope it holds," Tanner replied, hefting his day pack. "I want to check on our containment lines and see how mop-up is progressing."

The drive to the fire's edge took him through neighborhoods that had narrowly escaped destruction. Yellow evacuation notices fluttered on mailboxes, a reminder of how close this fire had come. He parked his truck at the established drop point, nodding to the security personnel controlling access to the fire area.

The acrid stench of charred vegetation mixed with the chemical scent of fire retardant hit him as he picked his way through the burned black. The landscape resembled a monochromatic wasteland, trees reduced to skeletal silhouettes against a backdrop of ash and soot. His boots crunched ash and soil as he made his way toward the Aurora Hotshot's position.

He spotted Tara and her crew meticulously inspecting the ground, checking for hot spots and extinguishing lingering embers.

"Morning, Tara," he called, navigating around a fallen spruce.

She wiped sweat from her brow with a sooty glove. "Hey, Tanner. Didn't expect to see you here in the trenches."

"How's it looking?"

She gestured to the surrounding area. "Still finding hot spots in the deep duff layers and around some root systems. Nothing we can't handle."

"Good. Thought I'd poke around here a bit." As he progressed through the burn, he noticed an intensely burned section. Curious about the pattern, he picked through charred debris, the ground still warm beneath his boots—fire could linger in duff and roots for days after flames were extinguished.

A flicker of movement caught his attention. Through the blackened trees, he spotted a small moose calf, spindly legs wobbling as it paced anxiously along a metal fence, the wood posts blackened from the flames. On the other side stood its mother, the massive cow moose snorting and pawing at the ground in agitation.

"Damn," he muttered, immediately recognizing the danger.

The calf had become separated from its mother, with the fence preventing their reunion. A moose cow separated from her calf could charge with deadly force to protect her offspring.

He quickly assessed the situation. The calf was distressed but uninjured, frantically trying to find a way through the fence. The mother's distress was ramping up and her ears lay back as she paced. If the calf remained trapped, it would likely starve, or a bear would get it. If Tanner tried to help, he risked placing himself between a protective mother and her calf—an undesirable position.

Tanner keyed his radio. "Tara, this is Westlake," he said in a low voice. "Encountered a moose calf separated from its mother by a fence. I plan to lift the calf over, but may need help if it doesn't go well."

"Want me to send someone over?" asked Tara.

"Too many people could escalate the situation. I'll let you know if I need it."

Tanner approached cautiously, his movements smooth and deliberate. The calf's eyes grew huge, and it backed away, pressing itself against the fence with frightened bleats. The cow immediately focused on Tanner, her massive head swinging in his direction.

"Easy," he murmured, trying to calm both of them. He knew not to approach the calf.

He scanned the fence line, looking for a section low enough for the calf to cross. About fifteen feet to his right, the fence dipped slightly where it crossed a shallow depression. If he could guide the calf there, the cow could jump over it. Problem was, once she did, she'd be on the same side of the fence that he was.

Keeping one eye on the agitated cow, Tanner herded the calf toward the lower section, where it stopped and bleated. With a guttural bellow that sent adrenaline spiking through Tanner, the cow charged the weakened fence. Nearly seven feet tall at the shoulder and weighing close to a thousand pounds, the moose hit the barrier with shocking force. The fence bowed but held.

Tanner's heart felt like a locomotive on full throttle. The cow backed up, clearly preparing for another charge that could topple the fence. He had seconds to act.

In one swift movement, he lunged forward, grabbing the confused calf around its midsection, its gangly legs kicking in panic as Tanner picked it up.

"Come on, little buddy," he grunted, struggling to hoist the thrashing calf high enough to clear the fence.

With tremendous effort, he boosted the calf over the top, and it tumbled clumsily to the ground with an indignant bleat.

Relief flooded through Tanner—a moment too soon.

The cow, having seen a human handling her baby, charged again with renewed fury. This time, she reared up on her hind legs, powerful front hooves pawing the air. One of those hooves caught Tanner's left arm as he backed off, sending a bolt of white-hot pain through his shoulder. The force of the blow knocked him backward, falling hard onto the ash-covered ground.

In case the moose jumped the fence, Tanner scrambled behind the blackened trunk of a fallen spruce, gasping as pain radiated through his arm. The cow circled back to her calf, nuzzling it briefly before leading it into the unburned forest beyond.

"Thanks for the gratitude," Tanner muttered, gingerly examining his arm. The pain was intense, but he could move his fingers, which meant the bone was intact. It didn't feel broken. Charging moose were never fun.

He used his cell phone, not wanting to broadcast his injury. "Tara, Westlake. Calf is reunited with mother, but I took a hoof to the arm. I'm okay, but I could use some ibuprofen from your first aid kit."

"Copy that," Tara responded. "Should I send someone to help?"

"Unnecessary. Will be there in a while." Pushing to his feet, he got a grip and calmed himself.

He sensed movement in his peripheral vision and turned, expecting another animal. Instead, he glimpsed a human in a black hoodie slipping through the unburned trees about a hundred yards away. Alarm bells rang. This area was closed to the public, with security checkpoints on all access roads.

"Hey! Stop right there!" shouted Tanner, breaking into a run despite the throbbing pain in his arm.

The person glanced back—shadowed face beneath the hood—then bolted deeper into the forest. Tanner pursued, leaping over deadfall and crashing through the underbrush, his lungs burning as he struggled to keep pace. The guy was too fast and disappeared into the dense spruce. Breathing hard, Tanner stopped. Continuing the pursuit alone would be dumb, especially with an arm injury in unfamiliar terrain.

Cell phone in hand, he tapped Jon Silva's number, who immediately picked up.

"Jon, it's Tanner. I just chased a tall guy in a black hoodie through the eastern edge of the burn area. Lost him in the woods, but he shouldn't have been there."

Silva's voice sharpened with interest. "You get a look at his face?"

"Just the hoodie and dark pants. He seemed to know the area—navigated the terrain like he'd been through it before."

"Where exactly are you?"

Tanner rattled off his GPS coordinates from the tracker he carried. He waited while Silva relayed the information to APD and the state troopers.

"What's the latest on the investigation?" Tanner asked, hiking back toward the Aurora Crew's position.

"We have a lead," said Silva. "A guy named Dirk Logan, released from Spring Creek Correctional in Seward three weeks ago. Did five years for arson, for torching cabins in Talkeetna."

"Just in time for fire season," Tanner noted grimly. "You think he's one of our guys?"

"He fits the profile," Silva said. "But the accelerant used in this fire differs from his usual sets, and the scale is beyond anything he's done before."

"Could he have partners? We saw two people when we flew over the other day."

"We're looking into that. Alaska State Troopers still have evidence from his trial, including surveillance footage from one of the Talkeetna fires. We're comparing it to security camera footage from businesses near the point of origin."

Tanner ducked under a low-hanging branch, wincing as the movement jarred his injured arm. "Keep me posted. They might plan something else. I'll sleep easier once these arsonists are behind bars."

After ending the call, Tanner made his way back to Tara and her crew. The hooded figure confirmed his suspicion that the arsonists were still lurking, possibly monitoring the impact of their handiwork as many were prone to do—or worse, planning their next fire set.

By the time he reached his truck, his arm was pulsing with pain. He ignored it and drove to the ICC to meet with law enforcement to tell them about what he'd seen. They assured him they had officers searching that area.

Just as he was heading off in search of ibuprofen, Ryan's voice from the ICC activated Tanner's radio, requesting drops on three spot fires in a remote portion of the Hillside. Tanner stopped and trained his binoculars out the window, scanning the sky for Blazebuster's distinctive silhouette. The air tanker released a graceful red stream and banked away.

"That's my girl," he said out loud to himself.

Ryan surfaced behind him. "Who are you referring to?"

Tanner lowered his binoculars. "Oh, I was just talking to myself."

Just then, Ripley's voice responded to Ryan on the radio. "Heading back to the airport."

Ryan stood next to Tanner, and they gazed out the window at the disappearing plane. "Let me guess which girl you were referring to." He tapped his chin with a thoughtful look. "Do I smell a romance?"

Tanner raised his brows, mustering innocence. "Don't have the slightest idea what you mean."

"Yes, you do." Ryan elbowed him. "We've all done it, you know. How do you think I met Raynie?"

Tanner smirked. "Oh, I don't know—on a fire, maybe? But you weren't her boss."

Ryan laughed. "No, but she was mine. That got a tad messy. Firefighting is hell on relationships, but at least romancing another firefighter lessens the hassles. There's no explaining why you're gone for weeks at a time, and how you almost died on every fire. You can skip straight to the good stuff."

"Good point." Tanner grinned. "On that note, I'm heading out for lunch, stopping by Urgent Care on the way. Had a moose entanglement when I was poking around in the black."

Ryan blinked. "Moose entanglement?"

Tanner explained, ending with a description of the hoof connecting with his arm. He tried lifting it, but it hurt.

"Roll up your sleeve. Let me see."

When Tanner exposed the bruising on his upper and lower arm, Ryan whistled. "Yeah, you better get that checked out. Make sure nothing is broken."

"The con is yours until I get back." Tanner rolled his sleeve back down and paused on his way out the door. "Oh, and I know you'll keep our conversation under wraps. Not a fan of fire gossip."

"It's in the vault," Ryan assured him with a knowing wink.

"At least until this fire is over." Tanner lowered his baseball cap over his face to avoid talking to the ever-present, insistent protestors on the way to his pickup.

He wondered what Ripley was doing right now. After their make-out session last night, he wondered if she'd have dinner with him again tonight. He'd take her to a restaurant this time, so neither would be tempted to cross any professional lines... even though they already had.

The best of intentions...okay, dammit, I am a mother freaking wolf.

Chapter 16

R*ipley*
This morning's drops were flawless, yet beneath it all lurked thoughts of Tanner. As Ripley completed her post-flight checks, last night played on repeat... his hands warm against her skin, the restraint in his eyes when she'd stopped him.

Her phone vibrated, and Tanner's name lit her screen. A nervous flutter took flight in her stomach.

"Beecher," he crooned at her in a velvet tone. "Thought I'd check on Blazebuster's status." A thrill tingled, in addition to the great day she was having so far.

Stop it. You're not some lovesick teenager.

"All fixed and flying." She smiled into the phone. "My mechanic replaced the left engine sensor."

"Want to have dinner tonight?" The question hung in the air between them.

Ripley hesitated, remembering how close they'd come to crossing a line last night. Her body had screamed in protest when she'd stopped his roaming hands. Always that same niggling fear holding her back.

"Dinner sounds good," she said finally. "Maybe in a restaurant this time? Not sure we should be alone together in a hotel room."

She immediately regretted her candid admission and was glad he couldn't see her reddening cheeks. Dammit, she was about to turn forty. Why was she blushing like a moony teenager?

Smooth, Beecher. Real smooth.

He laughed. "I like your blunt honesty. I heard about a place in downtown Anchorage. Great food, good ambiance."

"It's a date. I mean, not a date-date, just—"

"I know what you mean," he cut in with amusement. "Be in the lobby around six. Oh, another thing. I saw someone suspicious in the burn area this morning."

She tightened her grip on the phone. "Where?"

"Eastern perimeter, heading into the unburned section," said Tanner. "Couldn't get a good look at him—just a black hoodie and dark pants. He wasn't fire staff, nor was he allowed to be there."

"One of the arsonists? How many are there, do you think?" she asked.

"Not sure, only that there has to be more than one." He let out a sigh. "Silva says arsonists often revisit the scene of their fire sets—they get a thrill from watching the destruction and the response. And there's more."

Her unease grew as Tanner explained about the pyromaniac recently released from the Spring Creek Correctional Center in Seward. He discussed the evidence suggesting multiple perpetrators.

"Jeez, Tanner, that's not good." She scribbled her signature on a flight data sheet a ground crew member handed to her.

Urgent voices in the background cut him off. "Ripley, winds have kicked up on the northwest flank. Fire's making a run uphill toward the neighborhoods that don't yet have a fuel break. Can you make a full salvo drop on that flank?"

"All over it," she replied. "I'll contact you when I'm airborne."

"Fly safe," he cautioned.

"Always do." She paused. "Oh, and Tanner?"

"Yeah?"

"I'm glad you called." And she meant it.

"Be careful up there." He ended the call.

When she climbed up to her pilot seat, Loman was cycling through the pre-flight checks. "Ryan ordered a full load to a new fire that's sprung up on the northeast flank. He sent the coordinates to our computer."

Loman glanced at the monitor. "Got it." He entered them into the GPS on the instrument panel.

She'd noticed Loman's coolness toward her ever since their awkward hallway encounter the other night. In a way, she was relieved. Maybe he'd stop crushing on her. At least he stayed level while they worked together.

Cleared for takeoff, she fired up the engines and taxied toward the runway. As they lifted off, the sprawling panorama of Anchorage unfolded beneath them, the blackened scar of the fire visible against the green landscape on the lower Hillside. In the distance, a new smoke column rose northeast of the main fire.

Ripley banked the loaded plane toward the Anchorage Hillside, smoke thickening as they approached the fire zone. Visibility was reduced, but she was used to that.

"Air Attack, this is Tanker One-Six-Zero, approaching the drop target," she radioed. "Proceeding according to drop coordinates."

"Copy, One-Six-Zero," responded Ryan. "Bird Dog is in position. Winds are gusting at fifteen knots."

"Affirmative." She scanned the sky for the smaller spotter plane.

Bird Dog appeared in front of her to lead her in. "Tanker One-Six-Zero, this is Bird Dog, ready for more fun. Follow me to the drop zone."

"Copy, Bird Dog." She followed the spotter plane through the thickening smoke, locking onto the blinking lights.

"Drop zone in sight," the Bird Dog pilot announced. "Wind direction holding steady. You're cleared for approach."

"Prepare to release," she told Loman, whose hand gripped the slurry gate control as they waited for Bird Dog to mark the target.

Ripley descended to drop altitude, her hands steady on the controls as she lined up for the run. Through holes in the smoke, she glimpsed the line of insistent flames advancing uphill toward the susceptible homes.

"Three... two... one... Now!" she instructed Loman, who opened the gate release.

She watched her monitor as the red slurry cascaded from Blazebuster's belly, creating a perfect barrier between the flames and the homes. The expected weight change caused the aircraft to lift, giving her the extra boost to climb away from the drop zone.

"Excellent drop, One-Six-Zero," Ryan confirmed on the radio.

Satisfaction flowed through her. This was what she lived for—knowing her actions made a difference on the ground.

"Heading back to base for—"

Loman's shout cut her off. "Watch out!"

Her head snapped up to the windshield in time to see a red and white float plane heading directly toward them, closing fast. Too fast. The aircraft showed no signs of altering course, flying straight at them like a missile.

"What the hell?" She yanked on the controls, attempting to pull Blazebuster into a steep climb to avoid a collision.

The float plane veered at the last second, missing them by mere feet, but the wake turbulence rocked Blazebuster violently. Warning alarms blared as the left engine sputtered, then failed—completely.

"Left engine out!" Ripley shouted, fighting to maintain control as the aircraft listed sharply. Her hands moved reflexively, attempting to restart the engine with her left while clutching the yoke with her right.

The right engine roared, taking on the additional load. She started emergency procedures, her training kicking in. They still maintained altitude. She'd trained for this—she could make it back to the airport on one engine.

Loman shouted, "Single engine protocols, adjust for weight distribution, maintain airspeed!"

"Working it!" Even as she continued attempting to restart the left engine, the right one coughed, sputtered, and went silent.

The sudden absence of engine noise was as shocking as the alarms blaring through the cockpit. Ripley's insides fluttered as Blazebuster rapidly lost altitude. She glanced in horror at the houses below, frantically searching for a way not to crash into them. She banked the aircraft north, higher up the Chugach Mountain slopes, to avoid the homes.

Terror clawed at her. The irony wasn't lost on her—she was following in her father's footsteps, right down to the engine failure.

No. It can't end like this!

"Mayday, mayday, mayday!" she called into the radio. "This is Tanker One-Six-Zero. I've got a deadstick! Both engines failed. We're ditching upslope of the drop zone!"

Loman's face had gone white. "What do we do?"

"Brace for impact and pray." Fright clamped down, but she had to hold steady. "I'll aim for that clearing, but we're coming in fast."

The altimeter spun downward as Ripley struggled to maintain a glide path toward a small opening in the dense spruce. The ground rushed up to meet them with terrifying speed.

A random thought slapped her brain: *I love Tanner, and I'm going to die without telling him.*

"Come on, Blazebuster, I'm not ready to join my dad yet!" She coaxed the aircraft as if it were a living thing. "Just a little further."

They cleared a ridgeline by mere feet, the landing gear scraping treetops. The clearing Ripley had spotted was coming up too fast—but it was their only chance.

"Brace! Brace!" she shouted to Loman.

The first impact was jarring—the landing gear collapsing as they hit the uneven ground. Blazebuster skidded forward, dirt and debris spraying up around them, cracking the windshield as the aircraft tore through the clearing and into the tree line beyond.

The windshield filled with green as they plowed into the spruce forest. Branches tore at the shattered glass, the screech of tearing metal drowning out the impact alarms. Ripley held the yoke in a death grip, trying to maintain control over their trajectory.

Almost there... almost there...

A sudden, massive jolt slammed her sideways inside the cockpit. Her head hit the side window with explosive pain. The last thing she saw was the cockpit interior spinning strangely, and Loman's mouth open in a shout she couldn't hear.

Then darkness claimed her.

Chapter 17

R*ipley*
Consciousness returned in fragments. Pain. Ripley blinked repeatedly, trying to focus. The cockpit was tilted at an unnatural angle, daylight filtering in through the shattered windshield and side window. Her entire body throbbed, but the sharpest pain radiated from her left temple. She reached up to touch it and got a handful of blood. The acrid smell of fuel and smoke filled her nostrils, and disorientation distorted her comprehension of their situation.

Then memory flooded back—the drop, the small plane, the engine failures, the desperate glide toward any clearing they could find.

The crash.

They were down, but they were alive. At least she was.

Ignoring her searing pain and surging panic, she turned her head to look at Loman. He slumped in his seat, eyes closed, a trickle of blood making its way down his forehead.

"Loman," she croaked, her voice raw. "Nubs, can you hear me?"

He didn't respond except for a low moan that escaped his lips. He drooped in his harness, blood trickling from a cut on his forehead, but his chest rose and fell with steady breaths. Relief flooded through her—he was alive.

She took inventory of her own body, carefully testing each limb. Arms, painful but functional. Legs, same. Nothing was broken, though her entire left side ached where the impact had thrown her against the harness. Dizziness and the wet warmth trickling down her temple told her she was bleeding.

She fumbled for her harness release, her movements sluggish. She had to get them both out before the leaking fuel found a spark. Every movement sent spikes of pain through her skull and left arm, but she forced herself to focus.

Check Loman's condition. Evacuate the aircraft. Call for help.

The radio was dead, the instrument panel dark. She reached for her phone, but her pocket was empty. She prayed the satellite phone was still in the emergency kit strapped behind their seats. The ELT—Emergency Locator Transmitter—should broadcast their position automatically.

The smoke worried her the most. Through the shattered windshield, she saw wisps of it threading between the dense spruce, a grim reminder that the fire they'd been fighting was still out there, still advancing. If it reached them before help did... she pushed the thought away. No point dwelling on that horror. She needed to focus on what she could control.

"Loman," she called again, louder this time. "Nubs, we need to get out."

Loman stirred, groaning as consciousness returned. "What... what happened?" he mumbled.

"We're down," Ripley explained, speaking slowly to ensure he understood. "The engines failed after the float plane buzzed us. We crash-landed in the spruce." She brushed an insistent mosquito from her cheek.

His hand went to his forehead, coming away sticky with blood. "Are you okay?"

She freed herself from the seat harness. "Yes. Can you move?"

"Yeah, but my mid-section hurts." Loman fumbled with his own restraints. "My leg hurts like hell. Think it's broken."

"At least we're alive. The ELT should broadcast our position," she said. "I smell fuel, so we need to get out. You know the drill."

"Yeah. I'll need help." He shifted in his seat, wincing at the movement.

"Don't worry." Ripley kicked open her cockpit door, which had jammed during the impact. She noticed her left arm was bleeding as she reached behind the seat for the aircraft's emergency survival pack containing the satellite phone.

She eased herself down to the ground. She had to get Loman out. Climbing over a jumble of partially fallen trees, she tugged Loman's door open and dragged him from his seat, lowering him to the ground. One of his legs didn't look right. He was probably right about it being broken.

She checked for other injuries. "Where does it hurt?"

"Everywhere," he groaned. "Head, ribs... and my leg..."

She was feeling lightheaded from losing blood and knew she had to act fast. "Hold on, I have to stop my bleeding or we'll both be in a world of hurt," she said, clawing the medical kit for gauze and bandages. She yelped in pain when she poured the isopropyl alcohol over the cut high on her forehead and over the cut on her forearm.

She applied a compress with direct pressure to stem the bleeding and held it in place with gauze wrapped around her head and tied in a knot. She did the same with her arm, as best she could with one hand. Loman helped her tie the knot.

She unrolled more gauze and cleansed the cut on Loman's forehead with the alcohol. He hollered just as loud as she had. "Sorry, Nubs, have to ward off infection before stopping the bleeding." She pressed a clean compress to the right side of his head, then wrapped the gauze around his head, cut it with scissors from the kit, and tied it off to hold it in place.

She scissored his pant leg open. "You're right about the break. I need to splint it."

"We look like two Civil War soldiers," joked Loman in a weak voice. "Thanks for helping me, but I'm the one who should be doing all this."

"Why? Because you're a man?" she teased.

"No, because I have military training for shit like this." He smiled at her. "You're still pretty, even with blood dripping down your face."

She knew he wasn't hitting on her. Not at a time like this. He just appreciated her help.

"Thanks, Nubs. Sorry, but there's no chivalry after a plane crash. We help each other." She handed him a water canteen from the pack. "We both need to drink, or we'll get dehydrated."

"Thanks." He gratefully accepted and guzzled. "I smell gas. Pray to God Blazebuster doesn't explode."

"Me, too." Ripley stood to assess the damage. Blazebuster lay broken among the spruce trees, its nose crumpled against the massive tree trunk that had stopped their momentum. One wing had sheared off completely, the other was bent at an impossible angle. Fuel dripped steadily from the ruptured lines.

"Jesus," she muttered, taking in the destruction, knowing the pickle they were in. She set to work finding a straight branch and whittling limbs from it. She eased it next to Loman's injured leg and tied it on with strips of gauze.

They had overshot the clearing, and she had to get them as far away from the plane as she could. "Come on, we have to get away from here." She stood to sling the survival pack over her shoulder, wincing from the pain.

"Find a safe spot, and let's call for extraction," said Loman, waving away mosquitoes.

"Yes." Ripley put Loman's arm around her shoulder to help him through the underbrush, putting distance between themselves and the wreckage. Despite the throbbing pain in her head, Ripley's mind raced. The Cessna 206 float plane had flown directly toward them—no attempt to avoid until the last second. The engine failures immediately after. It wasn't a coincidence.

Someone had tried to kill them.

Her legs were like rubber, and the world tilted alarmingly when she moved too quickly. Once they reached the small clearing about two hundred yards from the crash site, Ripley activated the satellite phone. Her hands shook as she dialed the emergency frequency. She had no idea where her call was going, but she figured it would most likely be routed to the Anchorage Emergency Operations Center.

"This is Ripley Beecher, the pilot captain of Tanker One-Six-Zero. Our aircraft is down, about a mile north of our drop zone. Two souls on board, both survived and ambulatory with minor injuries, except for the broken leg of my first officer. Aircraft is leaking fuel. Request extraction as soon as possible."

Someone somewhere replied, saying help was on the way. There was so much static she could barely make out what they were saying, then she lost the call altogether.

As Ripley lowered the phone, the reality of what had just happened hit her in a wave so powerful she sat abruptly on a fallen log, shaky and nauseous. She pushed herself to stand and staggered away from Loman to vomit. She returned and took out a water canteen from the kit, unscrewed the cap, and sucked down a long drink.

"You okay, Captain?" Loman asked, his own face pale beneath the blood and soot.

She handed him the canteen. "Yeah. Better drink some more. Help is on the way." She slapped a mosquito on her forehead, then instantly regretted it. She pawed through the pack for some bug dope. Finding a small bottle, she slathered her exposed skin and handed it to Loman.

He lay on his back with a forearm over his forehead. "That Cessna float plane... think it was deliberate?" He rubbed bug dope all over his face.

Ripley nodded, regretting the movement as pain lanced her skull. "It came straight for us, then cut away at the last second to catch us in its wake. Too precise to be an accident."

"But why would anyone—" Loman began, then understanding dawned. "The arsonists. You think they're targeting firefighters, too?"

"I don't know. Tanner mentioned seeing suspicious activity this morning." Her thoughts turned to him, and she wondered what he was doing.

He no doubt knew their situation by now and was probably mobilizing the search and rescue operation. A punishing reality struck her: she could have died today. Should have died, given the severity of the crash. The thin line between life and death had never been more fragile.

Along with that realization came another, equally powerful: she didn't want to die with regrets. Didn't want to look back at opportunities lost to fear and caution. Life was too short, too precious to waste on what-ifs and might-have-beens.

She vowed to herself the next time she saw Tanner, things would be different. The fire would still burn, their professional obligations would still be in place, but she wouldn't hide from her feelings anymore. She would try harder at adulting.

Time was an eternity, marked only by the steady drumming of pain in Ripley's head and the occasional murmur from Loman as he drifted in and out of lucidity.

The smoke seemed to thicken.

Or maybe that was just her imagination feeding her fears.

Chapter 18

Tanner

Tanner stood frozen beside Ryan at the Air Attack desk, an icy dread seizing him as seconds stretched into minutes with no response to Ryan's radio calls to Tanker One-Six-Zero. He'd been monitoring the drop from the ICC when the mayday call had cut through the channel, Ripley unnervingly calm as she reported the failure of both engines. Then—nothing.

Just the terrible silence of a dead radio.

He instantly began calculating search grids and survival scenarios. But beneath that, a greater fear—the thought of losing Ripley before he'd had the chance to... to what? Tell her how quickly she'd become important to him? See if they could build a relationship that would last beyond the chaos and intensity of a fire assignment?

She's alive. She has to be alive. He had to keep thinking that, or he'd go nuts.

Ryan tried another approach. "Air Attack to Bird Dog. Do you have a visual on Tanker One-Six-Zero?"

"Negative," came the tense response. "Saw them banking to go north after the drop, heard the mayday, then they disappeared. Smoke's too thick for visual."

Ryan's mouth formed a straight line. "They're down. The question is where, and in what condition. The good news is, even if their radio is out, there's a sat phone onboard. That is, if they're..."

"Don't say it," Tanner cut him off, his mind sprinting through the worst. He visualized twisted metal and flames, with Ripley as a possible casualty, and the possibility tore at his gut.

"Get Mel's helicopter in the air," ordered Tanner, his voice tight. "Juliet is equipped for helitack response. I'll go with him. I still have my helitack certification."

Ryan reached for the radio and hesitated. "Are you sure, Tanner? There's another Turnagain winds forecast for the Anchorage Bowl this afternoon. Could be risky."

"What isn't risky in this fucking business?" Tanner snapped, then immediately regretted his tone. "You know better than anyone. We can't wait. If they survived the crash, they could be injured. And if the fuel ignites..." He couldn't finish. The thought of Ripley trapped in burning wreckage was unthinkable.

He steeled himself. "She's the best pilot I know. If anyone could walk away from this, it's her."

Ryan studied him. "You care about her." It wasn't a question but a statement of fact. "I mean, you really care about her."

Tanner considered denial, then realized it was pointless. "Doesn't change the fact we have an aircrew down and every second matters."

"Gotcha, buddy." Ryan keyed his radio. "Air Attack to Juliet. Mel, we need you airborne ASAP for search and rescue. Tanker One-Six-Zero is down, location unknown. IC will accompany."

"Copy that. Heard the mayday. Any word on the crew?" Mel's voice was strained. "I'm at Merrill Field, refueling. Have Westlake meet me here."

Ryan's cell was blowing up. First, he answered the call from the Anchorage Emergency Center, who relayed the information from Ripley's sat phone call. "Thank you, I'll relay the information to our search and rescue teams."

Relief brightened Ryan's face as he turned to Tanner. "Ripley and Loman survived the crash. She used the sat phone to call the emergency frequency. They went down a mile north of the last drop zone."

"I'm going after them myself," Tanner said gruffly. "Relay their coordinates to Mel and tell him I'm on my way to Merrill Field. Thanks, Ryno." Tanner damn near fainted with relief. He dug into his fire pack for his helitack flight suit and the helmet he carried for just such emergencies.

"I drew a circle around the location." Ryan inserted a map into Tanner's hand. "I also have helitack certification. I'll come with you."

Tanner hesitated. "You sure?"

"Got my gear in the truck. I'll get it."

"Thanks, man," said Tanner, as the two men sprinted out the door.

While Ryan retrieved his gear, Tanner took a quick second to get a sense of the circled location on the map. It was in dense spruce, and Mel would have to hover while Tanner and Ryan lowered to the ground using Juliet's helitack gear.

Tanner broke every speed limit to Merrill Field; only five minutes away, but it seemed to take forever, like he was driving to Mars.

"Hold on, Ripley, we're coming," he muttered after he exited the pickup and grabbed his gear, with Ryan on his heels.

Mel was already in the pilot's seat with rotors spinning. Tanner and Ryan strapped on their helmets, ducked beneath the whirling blades, and climbed inside. Tanner rode up front with Mel, and Ryan sat in the rear compartment. They buckled in, positioning their hot mics to talk through their helmet headsets.

"We have their last known coordinates, but Ripley probably glided further to put distance between her plane and those houses before impact," said Mel before talking to the tower.

"Let's start with the last visual from Bird Dog," suggested Tanner. "The mayday indicated they were going down a mile east of the drop zone."

As Juliet lifted off, the full scope of the fire came into view. Smoke columns twisted and merged in the strengthening winds, creating a turbulent mess of air currents.

Tanner keyed his radio. "ICC, this is Westlake. This Turnagain is kicking up flames. Get the crews on it before she runs again."

"This is gonna be rough," Mel warned as the helicopter bucked in a gust. "These aren't ideal conditions for a search and rescue."

"Hey, if it gets too dangerous—"

"Save it," Mel interrupted. "I'm not turning back until we find them."

They flew in tense silence as they approached the coordinates, each of them scanning below for any sign of the downed tanker. The smoke thickened as they approached the fire's head, reducing visibility to patches between swirling gray clouds.

"How long have you known her?" Tanner asked, partly to distract himself from the fear damn near choking him, and partly because he wanted to know.

Mel adjusted their course to navigate around a smoke column. "Known her most of her life," he replied. "Flew with her dad in the Air Force out of JBER years ago. Tom Beecher was one of the best pilots I ever met—and Ripley's cut from the same cloth."

"You were close with her father?"

"Close enough that when his plane went down fighting a fire in California, I was the one who delivered the news to Ripley and her mother." Mel's voice grew quiet. "Hardest thing I ever did. The look on their faces... I'll never forget it."

Tanner's chest tightened. "She lost her father to aerial firefighting?"

Mel nodded. "That's why she's so meticulous, checks everything twice, and doesn't take unnecessary risks. She wanted to be an aerial firefighter like her dad... like she was trying to make up for his dying."

The pieces of Ripley's guarded persona clicked into place—her professional intensity, her reluctance to get attached, and the rest of the barriers she'd kept solidly in place to protect herself. Now he understood why she resisted involvement.

"I recommended her for the Alaska Fire Service position," Mel continued. "Knew the change would do her good. Flying California fires held too many ghosts."

"Tell me about it," mumbled Tanner.

"Don't let on that I told you about her dad. I'm sure she'll tell you at some point, but normally she doesn't like to talk about it."

"Not a word," said Tanner.

Another gust rocked the helicopter, blowing them sideways. Mel compensated. "Damn winds. In case you didn't know, Turnagain Arm is famous for strong winds and deadly tides. Captain Cook had to 'turn again' when he couldn't find a passage."

"Didn't know that," said Tanner, gripping his seat when the helicopter tilted.

Through a brief clearing in the smoke, Tanner pointed to the red line of slurry that Blazebuster had released. "There's the drop zone. Bird Dog said they headed north from there."

Mel banked Juliet toward the ridgeline, fighting the crosswinds as they searched for any break in the canopy that could indicate a crash site. The turbulence worsened, and the helicopter shuddered against the powerful gusts.

"We're pushing the envelope here," said Mel, his jaw tight with concentration. "If they went down in this, they'll need help fast."

Tanner keyed his mic to the emergency frequency. "Tanker One-Six-Zero, this is Westlake. If you hear this transmission, respond on any channel." He repeated it several times, but the radio remained silent save for the background static.

Tanner pointed through the windshield. "Look!"

A flash of red appeared from below, and as they watched, it arced high above the canopy before bursting into a shower of sparks.

"Emergency flare," said Ryan, pointing. "That's them!"

Mel adjusted their course to circle the location. "Keep your eye on that area."

Tanner's heart leaped. "See a place to set her down?"

"There's no clearing big enough that I can see," he said, compensating for another wind gust.

He dipped Juliet lower, circling where the flare had originated. Through gaps in the trees, Tanner's breath caught, spotting the mangled shape of Blazebuster, its red-and-white fuselage broken and crumpled. One wing had sheared off.

"Hot damn, I'm amazed they survived," breathed Tanner, scanning the ground for movement.

"Pilots always distance themselves from the crash site in case leaking fuel sparks an explosion," said Mel. "I'll circle a wider circumference."

Mel circled while Tanner grew impatient with worry. Finally, in the distance, a flash of bright yellow caught his eye.

"There they are!" Tanner breathed relief as the two figures waved.

"I don't see a safe landing spot," said Mel. "I'll hover while you and Ryan get the rappel lines set up. You rappel down, and Ryan can stay here to pull them inside. Strap one at a time into the harness. When Ryan gives me a thumbs up, I'll winch them up."

"Copy that," replied Tanner, knowing what he had to do.

"Get into position on the skids." Mel brought Juliet to a hover fifty feet above the trees. The winds buffeted the helicopter relentlessly, requiring constant adjustments to steady their hover. "We need to be quick with these winds. I'll hold her steady as I can."

"Understood." Tanner crawled to the rear compartment where the rappel gear was attached, and he and Ryan set to work hooking everything up. Tanner secured the harness around his chest and legs, then Ryan attached Tanner's harness to the rescue line in the helicopter's winch system.

It was tricky for Mel to hover low enough, yet high enough to stay above the tall trees.

Tanner moved to the rear door, sliding it open against the rushing air. The downdraft from the rotors whipped through the cabin, and the noise was deafening despite his helmet. Fifty feet below, Ripley stood a suitable distance away from the rotor wash, looking up, shielding her eyes. Loman sat on the ground beside her.

"Ready?" Mel streamed in through Tanner's headset.

Tanner eyed the length of the line. "Can you bring her down fifteen feet?"

"Affirmative, but no more than that." Mel lowered the helicopter, which was no easy feat with the wind gusts.

"Ryan will let you know when to lower me." Tanner stepped out onto the skids and braced himself, ready to ride the ropes. He leaned back almost to an upside-down position as the rocking helicopter hovered. A powerful gust swung them, and Mel revved the rotors to counter the offset.

Ryan braced himself in the open door, waiting for Tanner's okay.

"Go!" yelled Tanner. *Almost there, Ripley. Hold on.*

Mel hit the release, and Tanner began lowering. Despite Mel's best efforts, Juliet swung wildly, causing Tanner to sway like a puppet on a string. He prayed he wouldn't lose the burger he had for lunch.

The descent was controlled but jarring, the lines playing out as he descended through the turbulent air. He spun slightly, his body buffeted by the gusting winds. The ground rushed up, and he flexed his knees, ready for impact.

His boots touched down, and he unclipped from the main harness, keeping his helmet on to maintain communication with Mel. He reached Ripley and noted Loman had a branch strapped to his lower leg. Both had gauze around their heads and were covered in soot and dirt. Ripley had a bandage on her forearm, but otherwise they looked okay.

When he turned to face Ripley, she shrieked and hurled herself into his arms. "Oh my God, Tanner!" she shouted above the rotor noise. "Thank God, you found us!" Trembling, she buried her face in his shoulder. It was chilly on this slope with the Turnagain winds, but he suspected trauma was the larger reason for her shaking.

"What are your injuries? Can you both move?" he shouted.

Ripley nodded, hollering, "I'm okay. Loman has a broken leg, so take him first."

"No, you're going first. Loman will be trickier. Ryan's in the chopper. He'll pull you inside," he shouted, noting Ripley's dilated eyes. He had to take her to a hospital before she slipped into shock. He was amazed she was even functioning.

He quickly strapped her into the harness and signaled Ryan. The lines tightened as Mel lifted her to the chopper. Tanner watched, not relaxing until she reached the skids. Ryan helped her climb onto one, then hoisted her inside the helicopter. Soon after, the harness fell again.

Tanner strapped Loman in, instructing him to use his good leg to get on the skid. He gave Ryan a thumbs up and held his breath while Ripley and Ryan tugged Loman into the helicopter. Then she lowered the harness to him. He grabbed the survival pack from the ground, strapped himself in, and signaled thumbs up.

As he reached the helicopter skids, a wind gust nearly blew the chopper out of the hover. Mel fought to hold Juliet steady in the violent air currents while Tanner struggled to grab a skid and hoist himself up so Ripley and Ryan could pull him inside.

Ripley slid the door shut and sank onto the floor next to Loman, who was slipping in and out of consciousness.

"All souls onboard!" Tanner shouted to Mel, who immediately lifted away.

"Everyone okay back there?" Mel called over the intercom.

"Affirmative." Tanner removed a helmet from a compartment and handed it to Ripley so they could talk on the headsets.

Tanner spoke into his hot mic. "Mel, they need medical attention, so head to the helispot at Providence Hospital. I'll let them know." He reached for his cell and notified the emergency room they would be landing.

"Copy," said Mel, still fighting the wind gusts.

As Juliet banked toward Providence on the east side of town, Tanner stayed on the floor of the rear compartment next to Ripley while Ryan took the co-pilot seat. He also wanted to keep an eye on Loman, who seemed in pain.

"I gave Nubs a couple of painkillers from my medical kit," said Ripley.

"How are you feeling?" Tanner checked beneath her bandage, noticing a sizeable laceration on the side of her head. She'd stemmed the bleeding, but he didn't like the looks of it. He checked the gash on her arm, which wasn't too bad, then took her hand in his.

"Lightheaded, but okay... now that you're here."

Tanner checked Loman's break in his lower leg. "Compound fracture," he muttered, unscrewing his canteen and holding it to Loman's lips, but he was too out of it to sip.

Tanner put his arm around her, and she rested her head on his shoulder. "You're okay now. I've got you."

"A float plane buzzed us. Came straight at us. A Cessna 206, I think. Happened fast."

"We'll find out who did it, don't worry," assured Tanner. "Right now, you're safe. Just focus on getting patched up."

"That was some flying on Mel's part," she said softly. "Didn't think anyone would attempt a rescue in these conditions."

"Did you think I would leave you there?" teased Mel from the pilot seat.

They touched down at Providence's helipad, and a medical team rushed toward them with gurneys. Only then did Tanner allow himself to fully process what had just happened—what could have happened.

As Mel powered down Juliet's rotors and the medical team loaded Ripley and Loman onto the gurneys, Tanner provided summaries of their conditions, then watched as they were wheeled from the heliport.

Mel appeared next to him. "Go with her. I'll handle the debrief with Ryan."

Tanner hesitated, torn between his duties and his want to ensure Ripley was truly okay.

"You can't do anything at the ICC that Ryan can't handle," Mel pointed out. "Ripley would rather see your ugly mug than mine."

"Tell Ryan to hold down the fort until I get there. And thank him for me." Tanner clapped Mel on the shoulder in a silent thanks before jogging after the medical team. He caught up just as they were wheeling Ripley and Loman through the emergency room doors.

"I'm staying with her," he told the nurse who walked alongside Ripley's gurney.

"Are you family?" she asked the standard question.

He met Ripley's gaze over the nurse's shoulder, and she spoke up.

"Yes, he's family and needs to stay with me." She reached for his hand, and he took it without hesitation.

Her claim made him mushy inside. Proud. Needed.

A doctor approached as Ripley and Loman were delivered to different curtained rooms. He saw Ripley first, asking her questions about the crash, the day and year, and who was the president. She answered all correctly, which relieved Tanner.

For now, the fire would have to wait. His responsibilities as IC would have to wait. Because in this moment, with the image of Ripley's crumpled plane searing into his memory, he could no longer deny what his heart had been telling him since the day they met.

He'd fallen in love with Ripley Beecher. And he'd nearly lost her before finding the courage to admit it.

Chapter 19

R*ipley*

She opened her eyes from a deep sleep, like she was surfacing from deep water. The antiseptic smell hit her first, then the steady beep of monitors, followed by a warmth on her hand. Her lids fluttered open to see Tanner slumped in a plastic chair beside her hospital bed, his large hand cradling hers as he dozed. Soot and grime streaked his face, reminding her of a battle-weary archangel sent to earth to fight alongside the mortals.

Memories of the crash flooded back—the terror of both engines failing, the desperate glide toward the clearing, the moment of impact. Struggling for survival. Lying on spongy ground. Dozing off... waking to the whump of helicopter rotors.

She'd forced herself to stand, ignoring the dizziness to signal their position... panicking about finding the flare gun, shooting it, and watching the flare arc high above the trees. She and Loman had struggled out of their flight suits to take off their yellow fire shirts to wave for greater visibility.

She'd cried with joy when the helicopter hovered overhead, and she saw who had lowered from it. She recalled flinging herself into Tanner's arms... her knight in shining Nomex.

He came for us. He actually came for us himself.

The realization hit her with startling clarity. Somewhere between his calm, sexy voice that first day during the Big Lake fire, and working with him these past several weeks, she'd fallen hard. And she might have died without telling him.

The flight to Providence Hospital had passed in a blur of pain and fatigue, except for Tanner's closeness, giving her strength with his calm reassurance. And the way he'd held onto her during the helicopter ride, then slipping into incident command mode, barking orders at the medical team... no one had ever protected her like that.

When they'd landed, everything was a rush of medical personnel, gurneys, and urgent questions, with Tanner providing details of the crash and their injuries. As they'd wheeled her away, she couldn't take her eyes from him. Oddly, nothing else was important now: her rules about workplace romance, protecting her reputation, not getting attached—these were nothing but dumb-assed lies she'd told herself for so long she believed them.

She still couldn't believe Tanner had come to get her and Loman. When had anyone cared enough to risk their own safety for her? When had anyone gazed at her the way Tanner did—like she was precious and irreplaceable?

She thought of all this as she watched him sleep, his face sooty with stubble on his jaw, and exhaustion etched in the lines around his eyes. His fire shirt was blackened with ash and dirt, his reddish-brown hair mussed, and there was ash under his fingernails. He looked like he'd been through hell.

Oh, wait a minute—he had—and so had she.

She squeezed his hand, and he opened his eyes. "Hey, how are you feeling?"

"Like I crash-landed a plane in a forest," she said in a hoarse voice. "But alive. Thanks to you."

His grip on her hand tightened. "Thanks to Mel and your incredible flying. It was a team effort. Your doctor is a small plane pilot and complimented you on a textbook emergency landing procedure when I told him what happened."

"How's Loman?"

"Stable. Broken leg, some bruised ribs, and a concussion. They're keeping him a few days for observation, but otherwise, he'll be fine." Tanner's thumb resumed with those gentle circles on the back of her hand.

"Did the doctor say I have a concussion?"

"No," he replied. "You have a laceration that required stitches, but no concussion."

"Thank goodness," she said, relieved. "If I had one, I would be grounded for two solid months. Loman won't be able to fly for at least that long. How long was I sleeping?" She peered at the twilight out the window.

"A couple hours."

"You've been here all this time?"

He answered with a nod and a weary smile.

"Thanks so much for staying here with me," she choked off, thick with emotion.

A nurse appeared inside the curtain. "You've been discharged. Here are pain meds if you need them." She held up a prescription bottle.

"Thanks," said Ripley, taking them and shaking two into her hand.

Tanner handed her a glass of water, and when the nurse left, he leaned toward her. "You scared the hell out of me today, Beecher."

"I scared the hell out of me today, too," she groaned, swallowing the tablets and water.

"Let's get you ready to go." He helped her out of bed and handed her an oversized Missoula Smokejumper T-shirt. "I wore this under my fire shirt. It's a little cleaner than your war-torn Nomex, even though it's pitted out."

She laughed. "Thanks, Westlake. Beggars can't be choosers." She held up her blackened, tattered fire shirt. "I'm hard on government issue, huh?" She still had on her green Nomex pants.

He helped her out of the hospital gown and slipped his T-shirt over her head. She breathed in his familiar scent, finding comfort in it. He handed her hospital slippers instead of her dirty boots.

"Would you mind driving me to the hotel?" she asked. "I want to sleep in a proper bed."

"Happy to. Mel and Ryan dropped my truck off." He took her elbow to support her as she wobbled slightly. After she signed out, he tucked her inside his pickup and drove out of the hospital parking lot.

The drive to the Greatland Suites passed in comfortable silence as she watched the familiar landmarks of Anchorage slide by. It was surreal to be back in civilization after the terror of the crash, to see people going about their normal lives, oblivious to what was going on behind the scenes to protect their city. She didn't turn on the radio—didn't want reminders.

"Shouldn't you be at the ICC?" she asked, resting her head back. "What's the fire doing?"

"Cohen is handling things for the night shift. Thanks to your slurry drop, the Aurora Hotshots completed the dozer line on the northeast flank, slowing the flames' advance toward one of the Hillside subdivisions. However, there's a delay with the permitting of operating dozers next to the wetlands boundary."

"Got to love the bureaucracy." She paused. "I feel terrible about Blazebuster. I'm sentimental about that plane. We've been through a lot together. StormAir won't be pleased, either."

"The NTSB is investigating the crash. Mel got the tail number of the Cessna from the Merrill Field tower records. They'll want to interview you, but that can wait until you're up to it."

"Did Ryan say when Blazebuster will be retrieved?" Her heart ached at the thought of her aircraft, broken and abandoned on the Anchorage Hillside. She'd lost more than a plane—she'd lost a trusted companion who'd carried her safely through her aerial firefights.

"Ryan talked to StormAir. They're arranging with JBER to retrieve Blazebuster with a Chinook once the weather settles down," Tanner assured her. "Dave Doss has placed you on mandatory administrative leave until he clears you to fly again."

"Standard procedure after an incident like this," she mumbled.

Flying was the furthest thing from her mind right now. For once, something else mattered more than getting back in the cockpit.

"I lost my cell phone in the crash," she groaned. "I'm sure there's a myriad of people trying to reach me right now."

"I have Ryan and our fire information officer handling it. When they can't get you, they call the ICC. No worries, everyone has your back."

"Thanks for all that. Jeez, Tanner, you've done so much for me..." She was at a loss for how to show him how much she appreciated what he'd done for her and Loman.

At the hotel, Tanner helped her to her room, his hand on the small of her back as they rode the elevator and walked down the quiet hallway. His touch was reassuring.

"You need rest," he said as she unlocked her door. "I'll bring you some food later."

"I need a shower, too, but these meds just hit me," she said, her eyelids drooping. "There's no way I can navigate a shower right now." All she wanted was a bed.

"Then take one when you wake up." He lowered the shade on the window to block the insistent daylight.

"I'll sleep on top of the covers until I get a shower later." She eased herself onto the bed, every muscle screaming in protest. Remembering what she'd vowed, how could she find the right words? "Tanner."

"What is it? Would you like me to get you anything?"

"How can I possibly thank you? For coming to get us, and for staying with me in the ER..." she closed her eyes as her pain numbed.

"How could I *not* come? When I heard your mayday, when we couldn't raise you on the radio, I went ballistic with worry." He sat on the edge of the bed. "No way was I willing to lose you."

Ripley didn't want him to go. The thought of being alone right now, with nothing but her petrifying thoughts and the echo of metal scraping against trees, sped up her breathing.

"Lie with me, okay? Just until I fall asleep. I don't want to be alone." She needed Tanner to stay close right now; he was the oasis in her storm.

"All right." He took off his boots and crawled onto the bed to lie beside her. The only sounds were their quiet breathing and the hum of the hotel's air conditioning.

She had to tell him before she fell asleep. She had to. This was a big step for her, but a necessary one.

I made a vow...

She talked slowly, the drowsiness taking over. "While my plane was... going down... all I could think of was... what I didn't tell you," she slurred.

Tanner brushed her hair back. "What didn't you tell me?"

"How much you...how much I..." Her pain meds kicked in and she couldn't finish.

"Go to sleep. You've earned it." He kissed her forehead as she succumbed to inertia, loving the sound of his voice.

WHEN RIPLEY PRIED HER eyes open, she had no idea where she was. She lay still to get her bearings and shake off the heavy slumber. Twilight had settled in. The days were shorter now after the solstice. Parking lot lights blinked on through the curtain gap.

She was a thousand times better, despite her muscle soreness and tender side. The cut on her arm stung a little, along with the one on her head. She fingered the three stitches on her hairline and slowly sat up, staring at the pile of filthy fire clothes on the floor.

Stepping into the shower, she let the water massage her scalp. She shampooed her hair repeatedly to get rid of the grittiness. Gray water swirled at her feet when she rinsed herself.

Afterward, she put on the smokejumper T-shirt Tanner had given her after she aired it out. It was a perfect nightshirt and hung just below her hind end.

The blow dryer's warmth soothed her as she dried her hair, and it felt like heaven when she applied lotion to her parched skin. A pang of hunger reminded her Tanner had suggested ordering takeout. Just as she picked up the receiver of her room phone, a knock on the door stopped her call.

She peeked through the peephole to see Tanner lift two large brown shopping bags. She swung open the door and inhaled his freshly showered scent. The sight of him in jeans and a henley shirt instead of his usual Nomex had her in a double-take.

"You look rested. How are you feeling?" He breezed past her to set the bags on the table.

"New and improved. I needed that sleep."

"Picked up some Thai food." He lifted a tall cardboard cup out of the bag and handed it to her. "Got you a Thai iced tea."

"Mm, thanks," she purred, sipping the sweet drink that was bliss on her parched throat. "The doctor cleared me for normal activity, as long as I take it easy."

"Define normal activity," he said with a slight grin, his eyes roaming over her. "Not that I like my T-shirt on you," he drawled in that low rumble of his.

Heat bloomed low in her belly at his suggestive tone, along with remembering she wasn't wearing underwear. She glanced down to make sure the T-shirt covered her lady parts.

"Normal activity depends on what you have in mind."

The way his eyes darkened charged the air between them now that they were alone, with nothing to interrupt them. Unless Cohen needed him at the ICC. She knew they'd crossed an invisible threshold today with the way the events had unfolded; a solid bond bound her to him after rescuing her from the crash.

"Thought we could have a quiet evening after the day we had."

"Great minds. I was just about to call you." She dug into a bag and lifted a container of green curry with chicken and rice. "Thanks for this. I'm famished." She removed the lid and dove in with her chopsticks, seating herself on the loveseat.

"I've had time to think after waking with a clearer head," she said slowly. "Most of our conversations are always about the job. I mean, of course they are, because we work together." She glanced up, her chopsticks paused in midair. "I don't even know what your favorite color is. What kind of music do you like? What do you drive back home? We know little about each other aside from the job."

"All good points." He took a bite of pad Thai and chewed. "Where do you want to start?"

"Well, for starters, we haven't talked about where we go from here, if this is a temporary fling, or what. If it isn't temporary, then how will it work when we live thousands of miles apart, chasing fires to hell and back?"

His chin dipped in agreement as he maneuvered the chopsticks around a piece of chicken. "First off, this isn't a fling, and I think you know that by now. Today was a wake-up call... nearly losing you hit home hard for me."

She set her cardboard container on the table and sipped her iced tea in somewhat of a daze. "Wow, Tanner. Okay, how about we start here: tell me about Montana. What do you do when you're not fighting fire?"

Tanner settled beside her on the small loveseat, close enough that her bare thigh touched his jeans. "I have a log home south of Missoula, nothing fancy. Floor-to-ceiling windows that look out at the Bitterroot Mountains, and a wraparound deck where I drink my coffee in the mornings." He paused. "It gets lonely sometimes, especially during the off-season."

"I can relate to that," she said, sipping her tea. "My place in Fairbanks is sometimes too quiet and empty. Especially after moving up here from California, where I had more friends." She glanced at him. "I don't even know how old you are."

"Forty-two. So, what do you do when you're not flying?" he asked. "And by the way, my favorite color is green. I like alternative and indie rock, and I drive a green Mustang."

She laughed. "Now we're getting somewhere. Okay, so I read a lot. Mostly thrillers and mysteries. Anything without fire. I inherited a small garden with my rental that I'm terrible at maintaining. Back in California, I volunteered at an aviation museum when I had time." She hesitated. "I don't have many friends here yet, outside of work. Haven't been in Alaska long enough. Also, it's easier to keep people at a distance."

His hand found hers, fingers intertwining. "You did that at first with me. What changed?"

"You." Her answer came without hesitation. "You changed everything."

They locked gazes, the weight of unspoken things hanging between them. Tanner finished his meal and set aside the container. "You keep asking me what happens next. Do you want to know?"

"Well, yeah." She held her breath, unsure what to expect.

He shrugged. "I don't know, Ripley. I don't know what happens next." He leveled his gaze. "I want you to know this isn't some random fire romance for me. I don't have flings with women when working fires, like some guys do. What I feel for you won't stop when we demobilize."

Her breath caught in her lungs, and she gulped. "You really mean that? But the logistics are—"

"Screw the logistics." He heaved out a sigh. "I don't care if we live in different states and only see each other between fires. I'd rather have a complicated relationship with you than a shallow one with someone else." He was exploding her defenses, like a hot knife through butter.

"But what if we grow apart, or things don't work out?" she tossed back.

"You're a fearless pilot. Why are you worried about this?" He eased into a close-mouthed smile. "Come on, Beecher, look at the big picture."

"I'm trying."

"Well, try harder. What if it *does* work? What if we're stronger together than apart?" His hands cupped her cheeks. "I almost lost you today. When I saw that wreckage, I knew I'd rather risk everything with you than wonder the rest of my life what could have been."

"I feel the same way about you... but I'm scared. You don't understand..."

"I understand more than you think I do. You've lost those you loved, and it hurts like hell. You're afraid it'll happen again. Ripley, you won't lose me... I'm not going anywhere. What does your heart tell you?"

"Everything you say makes my heart remember its own purpose. Like it knows it has come home," she said softly. This was a person who understood her. He knew what lived in her soul, dissolving the ramparts around her tightly guarded heart.

She leaned forward and pressed her lips to his, and his hand caressed her cheek as her distance resolve evaporated. His gentleness gave way to urgency as she fisted her hands in his shirt. Suppressed desire poured out of her like slurry on a runaway blaze.

"Tanner, make love to me," she murmured, crumbling the last of her former resolve. "I could have died today. Please... make love to me."

"Your injuries, you need to take care—" His eyes flick up to meet hers.

"I need a lot of things," she cut in. "Right now, I need you the most."

His eyes searched hers. "I don't want to hurt you."

"You won't. I want this... I want you." She'd gone out on a limb because telling him this took a helluva lot more guts than when she'd learned to fly. "I just crashed a two-million-dollar airplane, and the only thing I cared about was never again being able to do this." She leaned in and kissed him with all the fervor and determination that made her fearless in the cockpit.

"Feels good to hear you say that." Tanner tugged her to her feet, then reached for the bottom of her T-shirt and lifted it over her head. He mumbled under his breath when he discovered she wore nothing underneath. His eyes took their time taking her in, and had darkened the moment he saw her naked.

She grasped the bottom of his shirt, and he brushed her hand away to do it himself. "Don't overexert yourself." He lifted it off and dropped it.

She chuckled. "Undressing you is hardly a workout." She moved her hands to unsnap and unzip his jeans, and again, he brushed her hands away.

"It sure is after a plane crash," he insisted.

"Come on, I want to do my share," she protested, not minding one bit that he finished the job and shoved everything down. She was long past caring about their work relationship, now that she was certain they both wanted this.

She took her time grazing his bare chest and stomach with her eyes, delighted with what she saw. Her palms explored his warm skin, and she leaned into him to kiss where she figured his heart was. His hands glided from her bare stomach to her breasts, where he hesitated. She held her breath, anticipating his touch, then let it out when he bent to kiss each of them.

When his lips found the bruises on her side, he pressed soft kisses to each one. She winced when he glazed over the tender spot on her side where her seat belt had dug into her.

He straightened to look at her. "Am I hurting you?"

She shook her head, blinking back the water pooling in her eyes. "It's just that... no one's ever been this gentle with me."

"You deserve to be cherished." He brought his lips to hers. "You deserve someone who appreciates how precious you are." His hand skimmed down to her center, his lips sliding down her neck. When he found her ear, her very soul quivered when he kissed it. She'd never been worshiped like this, and it was intoxicating.

She explored the broad plane of his back, the solid strength of his shoulders as he slipped his tongue into her mouth, massaging it, exploring. His kiss was erotic, driving her insane as he massaged her. He knew how to kiss... and kiss... and kiss. He slid down her body and got on his knees, kissing and licking her down low.

"Oh... you're killin' me, Westlake," she moaned, nearly levitating off the floor. Her lady parts fired up like plane engines before liftoff.

"That's my objective." Leave it to an incident commander to say that.

Tanner took her hand and led her to the bed, helping her to lie on her back. He lowered himself beside her and bent to take her nipple into his mouth, driving her wild. Every touch amped up her pulsating ache for him. No turning back now—not that she wanted to. She was putty in his hands, happy to hand him the controls for this flight. For once, she wasn't the one in charge.

She had to have him. *Now*.

As if reading her mind, his hand groped the nightstand for his wallet and pulled out a condom. He rolled it on and moved over her, melding his body with hers. Her need for him grew to a fever pitch as the pressure between her legs ached to be gratified. She pressed against him, loving his chest pressing into hers.

"Cripes, Tanner, get inside... now!" she urged, her voice breathy but insistent. He'd become a parachute for her soft landing... a life raft for her weary body and soul.

When he settled between her thighs, his weight supported on his forearms to spare her bruised body... she arched against him, her gaze fastening to his. He entered her slowly, and she loved the tenderness in his eyes as she took him inside of her.

They were claiming each other, marking territory, saying without words they belonged to one another... and God help anyone who got in the way.

A low moan moved through him, and it reverberated through her. There was so much they still didn't know about each other... how could she have spent nearly half of her lifetime without knowing him? They could have been together all this time.

"Don't you dare stop, Westlake," she threatened, wrapping her legs around his hips to draw him deeper. She moved hard into him, the way she flew her plane. Her side hurt and she didn't care. This was too important. *He* was too important.

"Why. Would. I. Do that?" he panted, picking up the pace, yet still careful to be gentle.

They moved together in their own unique rhythm, loving the respite from the demands of their world. Ripley spiraled higher, every nerve ending alight with sensation. When she released, she called out his name, her hands clutching his shoulders as white hot pleasure rocked her.

His own followed with his face buried in the curve of her neck, his solid frame shuddering as he breathed out in a long, slow exhale, "Beeee-cher." The way he said it made her want to chuckle, so instead she grinned; happy to be in this moment, happy to be close to him.

Afterward, they lay tangled, neither wanting to separate. When he finally rolled off, she rested her head on the front of his shoulder, the thump of his heart vibrating her ear. In the evening twilight, she studied his glistening body, marred by scars from years of firefighting. Battle scars, like her own. Her fingers glided along a silvery four-inch scar that ran between his ribs.

"How'd you get this beauty?"

"Tree branch. And not a friendly one." He caught her hand and brought it to his lips. "During my second year as a smokejumper, my parachute caught a gust and blew me into a stand of lodgepole pine. Damn near impaled me."

She slid down his body to kiss his scar, imagining a younger, reckless Tanner, eager and wild, just like she used to be. She found a smaller scar on his leg. "And this?"

"Fell off a log and caught a rock."

She laughed. "We're a perfect pair. Battle-scarred and stubborn as hell. And we still come back for more."

"That we do." He folded an arm and rested his head on it. There were large black and blue bruises on his upper arm.

"Jeez, Tanner, what happened to your arm?"

"Oh," he chuckled. "Got into a fight with a moose."

"You're not serious." Her mouth hung open. "When?"

"The other day when I was poking around looking for clues to who started these fires. A mama moose and her calf somehow got separated by a fence and I tried to help."

She bent her head to kiss his bruises.

"That feels better."

"You know what? We blew past the friendship part," she pointed out, propping her head up with an elbow on the bed.

"No, we didn't. This is the beginning of a beautiful friendship... only with benefits." Tanner gave her a lopsided grin.

"I like the benefits part." She fiddled with his chest hair.

"Time for you to rest after what you've been through. I promise you we'll find out who brought down your plane. Mel and Ryan are working on it."

"Thanks, I appreciate that." Her mind raced ahead to tomorrow and the uncertainty that awaited them. "What happens now?"

"We'll figure it out." His arms tightened around her. "One day at a time, one fire at a time."

"I'm not good with relationships," she confessed. "I'm used to flying solo. That's why I'm so bossy."

"You aren't flying solo anymore." He motioned to her, then to himself. "This is formation flying—I'm your wingman, and you're my wing woman."

"The funny thing about damn near dying is that it puts things into perspective. Makes you realize what really matters," she said.

"Copy that, Captain." His smile was sunshine streaming through the smoke. He kissed her so fervently she wanted him to make love to her again.

He got up to rid himself of his condom, then returned with a glass of water and a hand towel. Seeing his naked form standing over her made her squirm with an even greater desire she couldn't quell, even if she wanted to.

"Thought you'd like to know Loman will be discharged in a few days, then he's flying up to Fairbanks to recover. Ryan wanted me to pass that along," he informed her.

"Glad he's okay. I'll miss him, actually." She yawned, eyeing him. "Want to have a sleepover or go back to your room?"

He glanced down at himself, then grinned. "Since I'm buck-assed naked, I'll stay."

"Then get that luscious tush back in here." She flung back the sheet and comforter.

"Twist my arm." He set his phone alarm. "I'm jealous you get to sleep in tomorrow. By the way, that's a direct order from your incident commander."

"I love hosting sleepovers. I should do it more often." She wrapped herself around him and kissed him goodnight.

"Okay, but no pillow fights or tickle fests," he teased.

"Oh, come on, be a good sport!" she shot back, tossing a pillow at him.

Right away, he fell asleep while she marveled at how her world had flipped all in one day. Somewhere between the terror of the crash and the sanctuary of Tanner's arms, she'd opened her heart for the first time in God knows how long. A month ago, she'd been content with her solitary existence, convinced that caring deeply was a luxury she couldn't afford. Now, she couldn't imagine tomorrow without him. For a woman who'd spent her life flying solo, formation flying no longer seemed formidable.

She wondered about the future of their relationship. It was like uncharted airspace—different bases, different lives, unique challenges that would test them once this fire ended. She closed her eyes, but before she sank into dreamland, she made a crucial decision that would have terrified her a week ago—she was ready to fight for whatever this was they had together—and for him.

And Ripley had never lost a fight in her life.

Chapter 20

Tanner

He woke to the soft buzz of his phone vibrating against the nightstand. The sunny morning filtered through the curtains, casting a golden glow across the room. At first, he didn't know where he was, but when he swiveled his head, Ripley slept peacefully beside him.

He reached for his phone, not wanting to disturb her. Silva's name flashed on the screen.

"Westlake," he answered quietly, easing out of bed and padding to the bathroom where he could talk without waking Ripley.

"Hey, Tanner. Can you get to the staging area by 0700 for our click-bait operation?"

He glanced at his phone, bleary-eyed. He'd forgotten that Silva had been planning a way to catch the arsonists. "Yeah. Got an update?"

"Trail cameras picked up activity in the burn zone around midnight. Could be the guy you saw in the black hoodie. They're getting bolder, like they're taunting us." He paused. "Want in on the action?"

"Yeah," said Tanner, without hesitation. "What do you want me to do?"

"Tell you when you get here," replied Silva. "Be at the roadblock on Elmore Road at 0700."

"Copy that." He ended the call and took a moment to gather his thoughts.

After yesterday with Ripley's crash, the rescue, and the night they'd spent together—he'd hoped for a minute or two of peace before diving back into the arson investigation. Unfortunately, arsonists waited for no one.

When he emerged from the bathroom, Ripley was awake, and propped up on one elbow, watching him with those sky-blue eyes. If the rest of her expression was any indication, she seemed to like what she saw.

"Good morning, starshine." Tanner sat on the edge of the bed. "Silva called. Trail cameras picked up our hoodie friend last night. Law enforcement is moving forward with a surveillance operation. I offered my help and support."

"Of course you did." She smiled. "I'm coming with you." Ripley pushed back the covers.

"Whoa, wait a minute. You were in a plane crash yesterday. Normal activity, remember?"

Her chin lifted in that stubborn way he both admired and found exasperating. "I'm better today. I'll go nuts in this hotel room while you're gallivanting around chasing arsonists. Who, I might add, tried to kill me. I have a dog in this fight."

"You're still on administrative leave."

"For flying, yes. Not for anything else," she countered. "Don't stress, I'll be incognito. I'll dress in civilian clothes and disguise myself with a baseball hat and sunglasses, like Clint Eastwood does."

"He tends to stand out in a crowd, so that doesn't work for him," retorted Tanner. "Ripley, if Dave Doss, NTSB, or anyone else finds out..."

She cut him off. "They won't unless you tell them. Besides, I won't be in the air."

They stared at each other in a showdown of wills. Tanner was smart enough to recognize a losing battle when he saw one. Unless he tied her to a chair, she'd be in the ICC, anyway. Plus, there was logic to her argument: whoever had caused her to crash might try another attempt on her life. She'd be safer with him than alone in her hotel room.

"All right," he conceded. "But stay close. If things go south, you do what I say without argument. Deal?"

"You're my boss, right, Commander?" She flashed him a coy smile with a come-hither look. "So, yeah, it's a deal."

Unable to resist, he took her in his arms and planted a kiss on her that practically undid them both. He'd better get them away from the bed and out of this room before he lost complete and total control, along with his job.

SILVA'S STAGING AREA was a small clearing at the burn zone's edge, hidden by spruce trees that had survived the fire. Alaska State Troopers and APD officers were already present when Tanner arrived with Ripley. She wore jeans and a BLM jacket with a matching cap, looking more like an agency official than an aerial firefighter.

Silva met them as they climbed out of the truck, his brows rising slightly at seeing Ripley. "Good morning, Captain Beecher. Didn't expect to see you out and about so soon."

Tanner pulled him aside. "She's technically on admin leave, but she wanted to take part. Since someone tried to kill her, she's not willing to sit this one out. Just act like she's a BLM fire investigator assisting me, okay?"

A corner of Silva's mouth lifted. "Now she's the boss, and you're her subordinate? Sounds kinky, like role play." He lowered his Ray-Bans to wink at Tanner. "If you say so, you sly dog."

"Tell anyone, and I'll have to kill you," deadpanned Tanner.

Silva motioned for Ripley to join them and handed her a burner phone. "Looks like you're assisting the IC today, Investigator Beecher. Exchange cell numbers. Not everything will be on the radio, if you get my drift." He lowered his shades once more in a you-better-go-along-with-this look.

"Takes more than a plane crash to keep me down," she sniffed. "I'm on it."

"Alrighty, then." Silva turned to Tanner. "We have surveillance set up around the area where our friends have been frequenting. Motion sensors and hidden trail cameras with real-time feeds have clued us in. APD has officers stationed at likely exit points."

"What's the draw?" Tanner asked, examining the map Silva spread on the hood of his vehicle.

"Unattended equipment cache. Fuel, drip torches, the stuff that would be irresistible to anyone looking to start more fires." Silva pointed to a marked location on the map. "We've made it look like it was forgotten and left behind during yesterday's evacuation from a subdivision. We're figuring out where to observe."

Ripley pointed to a spot on the map, half a mile from the bait. "What about here? This rock ridge would give a perfect vantage point to surveil the entire operation. Trust me, I've flown over this more times than I can count. If I were scoping things out, that's where I'd set up."

Both men's brows lifted. She had a good point. The ridge offered an excellent view while providing cover.

Silva nodded. "I'll send a team to that area. Thanks, Ripley."

As he moved off to talk to law enforcement, Tanner eyed her suspiciously. "Where the heck did you learn to think like an arsonist?"

"I worked on a handline crew in Northern California, fighting fire in the summers between semesters at Humboldt State. One summer, we had a string of premeditated fires set by the same person. After the third set, a couple of us studied the cases to understand the pattern. We went into thinking-like-an-arsonist mode and helped catch the guy."

"For a minute there, I thought you'd say you were a pyromaniac, so you became a firefighter to legally set backburn fires."

She recoiled as if he'd said she was a serial killer, then feigned a flabbergasted look. "How did you know?"

"I'm onto you, Beecher," he teased, then sobered. "Time to get serious. Let's exchange cell numbers. Call me."

She tapped her IC icon, and he turned away to answer. "You were fantastic last night, Captain Beecher," he breathed in a sexy drawl.

She nervously glanced around. "Trying to out us, Westlake? Knock it the hell off!" She gave him an eyeroll as he turned around, ending their call. "Okay, what's our role in this?"

Tanner pointed to the ridge she'd suggested. "Silva wants us to monitor from up there while law enforcement moves into position. If the arsonists take the bait, we help coordinate the response."

"Sounds good," she responded.

They hiked the short distance up to the ridge and hid behind a rock pile. Tanner silenced his radio. He'd see the light blink if someone tried contacting him. Now it was a waiting game. Time wore on with no sign of anyone. Tanner sensed Ripley's growing restlessness beside him and figured her injuries were bothering her.

"Doing okay?" he asked as she huddled next to him.

Her hand went unconsciously to her forehead. "Just a slight headache. No big deal."

Tanner's radio blinked, and he turned off the mute. "This is APD. We have movement. Someone's approaching the cache."

Tanner tensed as a figure emerged from between the trees, moving with purpose toward the scattered equipment. "I don't think that's our hoodie guy. Different build, different clothes."

This man wasn't the person Tanner had chased through the forest. He was shorter, stockier, and dressed in camouflage pants and a dark green jacket. The guy lifted the drip torch, examined it briefly, then dropped it and retreated.

Tanner sucked his teeth. "He's scouting around."

He grabbed his radio. "He seems suspicious. There may be others nearby."

The radio erupted as officers chased the guy who'd broken into a run.

Silva appeared behind Tanner and Ripley, barking orders into his radio, directing others to cut off the runner's escape route.

Tanner spotted movement, and his blood ran cold. "There's another guy moving fast!" It was the guy he'd chased before, flitting between trees at the opposite end of the surveillance area—far from where the attention was focused.

"He's creating a diversion. Ripley, come with me!" Tanner sprinted to his vehicle and had the engine running before Ripley had closed her door.

"What are you doing?" she asked as they bounced over the uneven terrain.

"Cutting them off before they reach the tree line," replied Tanner, scanning the landscape. "If they get into the trees again, it'll be hard to catch them."

They exited the truck on a dirt road at the edge of a burned area. "I'm calling your cell, so we stay connected."

"Okay." She pulled out her burner phone and tapped to connect with Tanner.

"I'll go north around that stand of snags," said Tanner. "You head down this drainage and keep visual contact. If you see them, tell me on the phone. Turn on your speaker." They both tapped their phones.

"Be careful." Her eyes met his with an intensity that conveyed more than it had a few short days ago.

His instinct was to pull her close. Instead, he said, "Remember, observation only. Do not engage if you spot them."

They separated, moving stealthily through the blackened landscape. The charred ground crunched beneath Tanner's boots as he navigated through the skeletal remains of what had once been a vibrant forest. Smoke still hung in the air, though the fire had moved on from this area.

Ripley's voice came through the speaker. "There's movement two hundred yards ahead of me. It's the dark hoodie guy, moving toward some standing dead trees."

Tanner calculated quickly. "I can cut him off. Stay back and let me know where he goes."

"He's carrying something. Looks like a daypack."

Tanner picked up his pace, angling through the burned landscape to catch up to them. Adrenaline pounded as he stayed low to avoid being spotted.

Ripley again. "Tanner, he's stopped. Kneeling down doing something. Can't tell from here, but he's fiddling with something on the ground."

Tanner was close enough now to make out the figure in the distance, hunched on the ground. He needed to move before the man finished whatever he was doing. The terrain between them was open, offering no cover.

Ripley shouted, "Tanner, he spotted me and took off!"

He abandoned stealth and broke into an all-out sprint. Ahead, he could see the black-hooded figure running through the burned trees with Ripley a hundred yards behind.

"Ripley, fall back!" he shouted into his phone. Either she didn't hear, or she ignored him.

The chase led them deeper into the burn zone, and the man was fast. He clearly knew the terrain, weaving around obstacles with ease.

Tanner pushed harder, gaining ground on the hoodie guy and Ripley. Each breath burned his lungs as he closed the gap.

A thunderous crack split the air, and he instinctively ducked as a massive snag—a fire-weakened, dead tree—collapsed, sending up a cloud of ash and debris that had him coughing as he ran.

"Ripley!" he shouted into his phone, his stomach plummeting after losing sight of her.

"I'm okay but just spotted the other guy and they're both getting away!" she hollered.

Tanner scrambled around the fallen tree, relieved when Ripley came into view. She was covered in ash but unharmed, pointing to a dense stand of unburned trees where their quarry had disappeared. By the time they reached the edge of the unburned forest, the men had been swallowed by the impenetrable green wall of spruce.

"Damn it," Tanner muttered, bending over with his hands on his knees, panting. "We almost had them."

Ripley did the same, her breathing equally labored. She winced, her soreness evident.

"I want you to return to the truck, Ripley. You're pushing too hard."

"I saw their faces!" she spat out. "For a split second before they took off," she panted.

Tanner straightened. "Did you recognize them?"

"Enough to know that neither looked like the Seward prisoner Silva showed us. These guys are younger. Early thirties, maybe. One had a scar on his left cheek."

"That's more than we had before. Let's go back. Disconnect the phones." He gave Silva a quick call to update him.

As they made their way back through the burn zone, Tanner noticed Ripley lagging slightly, her movements becoming more cautious. He slowed his pace to match hers, worried that her injuries were causing more trouble than she let on.

"Headache getting worse?"

"Nothing I can't handle," she said quickly, still huffing.

"Ripley—"

"I'm fine," she cut in. "I helped you make progress, right?"

He couldn't argue with that. "Yes, but you're recovering from a crash. There's no shame in admitting you need to take it easy."

Her gaze fixed on the path ahead. "It's not about shame. It's about being sidelined when I could be helping. When people are in danger."

Tanner recognized the drive that pushed her—the same protective instinct that pushed him through to exhaustion. He couldn't help but empathize.

"I understand," he said. "Please don't push yourself so hard that you end up back in the hospital. I don't want to rescue you from another dangerous situation."

"Hey, I rescue people too, you know," she gently reminded. "Tiring of playing the hero?"

"I'll carry you out of as many burning forests as necessary," he retorted. "However, I'd prefer it not to become a daily occurrence."

Her smile softened. "Duly noted."

They returned to the staging area on Elmore Road. Silva approached. "We lost the first guy. But not before he dropped this." He held up an evidence bag containing some kind of electronic device.

"What is it?" Tanner asked, inspecting it through the plastic.

"Remote detonator. And not one your average pyromaniac picks up at the hardware store." Silva's expression was grim. "This is looking less like random arson and more like a coordinated operation."

"Coordinated by whom?" Ripley asked. "And to what end?"

Silva shook his head. "That's the golden question. What did you find on your end?"

Tanner explained their pursuit of both men, while Ripley described the brief glimpse she'd caught of one man's face.

"A scar on the left cheek," Silva repeated, making notes. "That might help narrow things down. And you're certain they were setting something?"

"Positive," Ripley confirmed. "Though I couldn't see exactly what."

"I have news you both need to hear." Silva led them away from the main activity. "We've identified the plane that caused Ripley's crash. It was registered to a company based in the Cayman Islands and was recently purchased by a subsidiary of Northstar Minerals."

Tanner frowned. "A mining company?"

Silva nodded. "They've been pushing for a way to mine critical rare minerals in the areas that have burned this summer."

"Critical rare minerals? In East Anchorage?" Ripley was incredulous. "Are you suggesting a mining company is behind these fires? Not only is that ludicrous, but it's also insane!"

"I'm not suggesting anything yet," Silva cautioned. "Just connecting dots. Environmental regulations and local opposition have blocked the company from developing. Fires conveniently destroy protected habitats, making development arguments easier. And then there's this."

He pulled out his phone, showing them a news article. The headline read: *Insurance Company Denies Claims for Fire-Damaged Properties Citing Acts of God.*

"If these fires were proven to be arson rather than natural causes, those insurance claims would have to be paid," Silva pointed out. "Which would make a lot of properties suddenly affordable to a company with deep pockets."

Tanner's mind raced with the implications. "So, you think someone at Northstar is coordinating these fires to both remove environmental protections and drive down property values?"

"It's a theory," Silva acknowledged. "One we're investigating carefully. But it would explain the sophistication of the operation, the resources behind it, and the targeted nature of the fires."

Ripley went pale. "They tried to kill us to keep this quiet."

"Or to slow the firefighting efforts. Either way, this just became a much bigger investigation." Silva's radio erupted.

"Silva, this is APD. We've found an incendiary device. It's a—" The transmission cut off in a rush of static, followed by a boom that vibrated the ground like an earth tremor.

"Get everyone back!" Silva shouted, running toward his vehicle. "We have a detonation!"

In the distance, a black column of smoke rose above the Anchorage Hillside.

Chapter 21

ipley

R Tanner and Ripley returned to the ICC after the Aurora Hotshots quickly contained the explosion-driven fire. The incident drove home the seriousness of the situation. They weren't dealing with drunk college kids playing with matches or someone with a grudge against Anchorage. They were dealing with organized, resourceful bastards, who were getting bolder by the second.

Ripley was still officially grounded from flying, but she'd otherwise made herself useful. The fire still raged through beetle-killed trees, but luckily, every effort to prevent it from spreading up the Hillside had so far been successful. She'd watched as another air tanker made the drops she should be making, intensifying her longing to be airborne.

Today, she was a tactical observer in a state truck, relaying real-time fire behavior information back to the ICC to help Tanner coordinate the overall response.

The burner phone Silva had given her vibrated. "How's it looking, gorgeous?"

"Hope no one heard you say that." Secretly, she loved the rush of their hidden involvement. As a constant rule follower, it made her feel like she was getting away with something.

"Chillax, I'm in my truck," he reassured her. "I can say anything I want in the privacy of my truck."

"The initial dozer line is holding, and the Aurora Crew is almost done extending it to upper O'Malley Road."

"What's the fire doing?" he asked.

"There's increased activity near the power substation on the lower Hillside. The fire's pushing that way with the afternoon winds."

"That substation powers half of Anchorage, including hospitals and other essential services," he replied. "I'd hate to drop retardant near it."

"What about a backburn? Create a buffer zone around the substation by burning out the fuels before the main fire gets there." She mentally mapped the area, having flown over it several times. "The substation access road would make a good anchor to build a fuel break around it."

"Good idea. How long do you think it'll take?"

"Not long with the Aurora Hotshots and other hotshot crews. I'm happy to help out, too," she added.

"Okay, I'll let Tara know and dispatch the hotshots. Can you drive to the substation to scope out the on-site conditions? I need someone who is skilled at sizing things up," he said provocatively.

"Sizing things up?" she echoed. This should *not* be turning her on in the middle of a workday, but she liked that he valued her expertise, so she let that innuendo slide. "I'm on my way. I'll report back in thirty."

"Bye, gorgeous," he breathed, making her neck hairs stand on end.

"Keep it real, Westlake," she chided, ending the call. What she really thought was how well she and Tanner worked together, especially after the trauma of her crash and the harrowing search for her attacker; their collaboration felt seamless and natural.

The drive to the substation took her along winding roads, skirting the fire's eastern edge. The complex was a sprawling maze of transformers and switches surrounded by a chain-link fence. Two utility trucks sat outside, workers in hard hats, deep in conversation.

Ripley flashed her BLM ID. "Ripley Beecher. Has anyone contacted you about keeping the fire off the substation?"

"Jim Hendricks, Chugach Electric," the older man replied. "Tanner Westlake said you were coming with crews to backburn. What's the plan?"

"We'll establish a control line at twenty-five hundred feet and backburn toward the fire," she said, remembering similar operations in California. "The steep slope and gusty winds require extra distance."

"That'll work. I'll show you around."

The situation was better than expected—the access road created a natural firebreak on one side, a creek offered protection on the other, and fuel loads were relatively light.

She called Tanner with the good news. "A backburn here is doable. Wind direction is favorable for the next six to eight hours. If we hurry, we can secure this site before the head of the fire reaches it."

"Aurora Crew should be there any minute," responded Tanner. "I'll send an engine and a water tender truck for backup."

"I'll mark the control line." She retrieved the flagging tape from her pack. "Talk to you later. She ended the call, glad that he kept things on the straight and narrow. One thing she appreciated about Tanner; when he focused on the job, he didn't screw around—just like she did when airborne.

By the time Tara arrived with her crew, Ripley had a plan mapped out, and Tara listened attentively as she explained the fuels reduction strategy.

"Solid plan," said Tara. "We'll have this done before dinner."

What followed was a masterclass in wildland firefighting efficiency as the Aurora Hotshots executed backburning operations, with Ripley working alongside them. Her experience on handline crews proved invaluable as they ignited controlled burns to consume fuel ahead of the main fire. The work was deeply satisfying after being grounded from flying.

Tanner showed up six hours later to assess their progress, and Ripley greeted him with a drip torch in hand.

"I leave you alone for a few hours, and you're already playing with fire." The corner of his mouth quirked up in a half-smile.

Ripley wiped her forehead with her sleeve. "Some skills you never forget. The backburn went perfectly, gobbling fuels with minimal smoke. One substation has been saved... without retardant, I might add." She swept her arm in a grand gesture, proud of their hard work.

"Tara's impressed with how you planned this," remarked Tanner, as everyone was winding down and loading equipment into the trucks.

Ripley shrugged modestly. "The Aurora Hotshots did all the hard work."

"Don't sell yourself short." He studied her with an intensity that turned her on out here in the wild. "You're as good on the ground as you are in the air."

Tara moved up, wiping her forehead. "East Anchorage will keep their power. Good job, Beecher." She looked at Tanner. "This woman knows her stuff."

"That's why I asked her to help," he responded with a nonchalance Ripley found endearing.

After the Aurora Hotshots packed up and left, Tanner and Ripley watched the distant glow of the main fire reflected against the smoke-filled sky.

"Score one for us," he said, letting out a long sigh. "Now to wrangle the rest of this thing."

Ripley bumped his shoulder. "Small victories prevent colossal disasters."

He bumped her back. "We make a good team."

She leaned all the way into him. "On and off the job." Understanding passed between them that needed no words.

She could get used to this.

Chapter 22

R*ipley*
Back at the ICC, the mood was cautiously optimistic at the progress being made on containment. The eastern flank, which had threatened heavily populated areas on the Anchorage Hillside, was mostly under control.

"Containment is at seventy percent," announced Tanner. "If the weather holds, we should reach eighty percent hopefully by tomorrow night."

A cheer went up from the battle-worn firefighters and support staff. After days of this continuous burn, the tide was finally turning.

When Tanner finished for the day and turned the command center over to Cohen for the night, he caught Ripley's attention from across the room and pointed to his cell phone. A silent message passed between them.

When her phone pinged a notification, she read his text.

I know a place for dinner. Nice and private.

Do tell! she texted back.

Meet me in the hotel parking lot. I'll be the one in the state fire truck.

Ripley laughed out loud, pretending not to notice Tanner leaving the command center. She gave him a five-minute lead, then moseyed out to the state truck he'd gotten for her to use. She drove across town and pulled into the hotel parking lot. She parked next to him, then casually glanced around and hopped into his truck, pulling her baseball cap down over her sunglasses. She slunk down in her seat.

Tanner threw his head back and laughed. "Excuse me, ma'am, but are you with the CIA?"

"This is a covert operation," she deadpanned, trying to keep a straight face. "We shouldn't be seen together off duty."

"In that case, I'm taking you to a covert location." He pulled out and headed down Northern Lights toward the airport. To her relief, he passed the airport turnoff and drove out to a parking lot that overlooked Cook Inlet. He backed into a space, switched off the ignition, then reached behind him to retrieve a portable soft-cooler bag.

They climbed out, and Tanner lowered the tailgate of the truck, shook out a red and white checkered tablecloth, and rested the square insulated bag on it. He unzipped it and lifted out two large styrofoam food containers and a bottle of red wine, which he handed to her. The food aroma made her mouth water.

She peeked into the bag for a corkscrew opener and set to work, twisting it into the bottle. He set out plastic stemware as if they were dining in a fine restaurant.

"How did you manage this?" Ripley laughed, genuinely impressed, as he laid out the impromptu picnic on the truck's tailgate. "Where'd you get the tablecloth?"

"I'm full of surprises," he said smugly, obviously enjoying her delight with his choice of venue.

A passenger jet descended from across the inlet, seemingly to land on them. Ripley surveyed the belly of the Alaska Airlines plane as it roared over them to land on the international airport runway.

"The hotel clerk recommended this." Tanner waited for the noise to subside before pouring wine into a plastic glass. "Thought you'd feel at home out here, and no fire people are likely to show up." He held the glass out to her by the stem.

"Look at you, acting like a local. An end-of-the-runway picnic." She grinned.

"Figured you'd like the ambiance." He eyed another incoming plane, this time an Air Canada flight.

"A man after my own heart." She appreciated him going out of his way for her.

They leaned side by side against the tailgate, gazing at the soft alpenglow on Sleeping Lady Mountain on the far side of Cook Inlet. Their conversation flowed easily between plane landings. Tanner told stories of his early days as a rookie smokejumper, of the mistakes he'd made and the lessons he'd learned. Ripley shared memories of her dad, how he'd taught her to fly when her feet could barely reach the floor.

"He'd be proud of you," said Tanner when she finished a story about her first solo flight. "The way you handle aircraft, and the decisions you make under pressure."

A lump formed in her throat. "Truth be told, I became a tanker pilot to feel closer to him. And to understand why he loved flying air tankers so much that he was willing to risk everything."

"And do you? Understand it now?"

"There's nothing like it—knowing that what you do makes a difference, that people's homes and lives are safer because of how you fly, where you drop." She smiled ruefully. "Even when it ends in a crash landing."

Tanner shook his head. "I'm still amazed you and Loman walked away from that crash."

"Dad must have dispatched a guardian angel to help us that day." She'd thought about it a lot, and that was her figurative conclusion.

"I'm thankful that he did." Tanner pressed his lips to hers, and she turned into him, sliding her arms around him, loving the taste of the cabernet on his tongue.

Another plane flew over, and she wondered if anyone saw them kissing. She didn't care who saw them now; not after what they'd been through together. Alaska's evening twilight settled around them, and they eventually wrapped up their kiss. The inlet waters leveled into a slack tide, while a barge parted the seawater on a return trip back to Seattle.

"I meant what I said about figuring things out when this fire assignment ends." His sexy drawl squished her insides the same as when she first heard him on the radio.

"I meant what I said, too."

"But?" he prompted, reading her hesitation.

"I'm grounded for a few more days pending the NTSB investigation. You're commanding a complex firefighting operation while arsonists consider us the enemy. Mixing our personal lives in the middle of this has been a..."

"A clusterfuck," Tanner finished for her.

"Exactly. I've worked my ass off to get where I am. All it takes is one accusation that I'm sleeping with the IC for favorable treatment, and my career is toast. You know how this works."

"So, what are you saying?"

"Just that we need to be careful in public. Sneaking around like this feels like we're tempting fate."

"We can do our jobs and still sneak around," he pointed out, bemused. "Speaking of which, I could use your continued expertise with fire behavior analysis and strategic planning."

Her brows shot up. "High praise, coming from a smokejumper."

"Not just any smokejumper. A Zulie," he corrected with a serious expression.

"Ooh, a *Zulie!*" she echoed emphatically, feigning amazement. "Sorry, didn't realize I was in the presence of greatness."

He looked down his nose at her, his mouth twitching. "I'll forgive you this time."

An ocean breeze lifted his hair as another plane roared overhead. Her heart skipped at his closeness—he was the type of rugged hotness she'd always avoided—the type that was usually consumed by ego. Yet Tanner was different; beneath that eye-candy exterior he carried quiet strength and a genuine compassion that had dissolved her resistance and utterly disarmed her.

"Maybe we could go to your room to discuss fire behavior analysis and strategic planning," she suggested innocently.

"Maybe we could." A grin spread across his face. "What about professional distance?"

"We're just two colleagues discussing business after hours," she justified.

"Don't have to tell me twice."

They packed up and drove back to the hotel, each entering separately. Tanner took the elevator, and she tapped up the stairs to the second floor. They met at his door and burst out laughing at their silliness.

He paused with the key card in his hand. "Would you like to come in to discuss fire behavior, Captain Beecher?" he asked in a business tone.

"I'd be delighted, Commander Westlake."

"Keep it professional," he teased in a low voice, as he inched closer. The heat that flared in his eyes sent sparks through her.

"Always." Her pulse kicked up as he invaded her space. "Open the damn door already!" She snatched his key card and waved it over the lock. She opened the door, and he followed her in.

When it slammed shut behind them, he backed her up and pinned her hands against the wall, licking her ear and breathing hot air on her neck until she moaned.

"Now, what did you say about fire behavior?" he breathed against her lips, nipping her lower one with his teeth.

She blanked. "Fire. Burns. Hot," she squeaked out, and he crushed her mouth with his, dancing his tongue so sensuously she never wanted him to stop.

He lifted off. "How analytical. In the interest of sticking to business, you should return to your room after." He kissed her neck, and her head fell back to give him access.

She gasped. "After what?"

"After this." His hands released hers to slide under her yellow shirt. To speed things up, she pushed him away to lift her shirt over her head, then reached behind to unclasp her bra.

Without missing a beat, he ditched the bra. "All this sneaking around turns me on."

"Me, too," she panted.

"If anyone says anything..." He lifted off his shirt. "I'll tell them they're mistaken." He undid his pants and ditched those, too. "I'll say," he crooned, "I'm not involved with Beecher. Why would I want to sleep..." He got rid of her pants. "With a tanker pilot?" He looked her over like she was a twenty-course meal he was about to devour.

To say she was drunk with desire was an understatement. "Because a tanker pilot can fly you higher than you've ever been." She reached down to touch him, surprised she didn't have to reach far at all.

They stumbled to his bed, and he whipped off the comforter before falling together onto the sheets. Ripley delighted in how he made lovemaking fun and sexy at the same time. His lips traced a torturous path from her neck down to her center, setting her ablaze until she begged for mercy. When his mouth was on her, she forgot everything: her name, his name, where they were, and why she'd resisted him. All she knew was she didn't want him to stop.

When he slid back up her body to settle himself inside of her, she tried slowing things down to savor every second of this erotic sensation. But passion won out, moving both of them with increasing urgency, panting each other's names. Her sparks exploded into flame, and his flare gun shot up into the evening sky.

Afterward, they were spent. When their breathing slowed, she snuggled into his side and swung her leg over him to keep him close.

He rubbed her back. "Your mind is going ninety. I can feel it."

"Work stuff." She poked him. "For real this time. Getting back in the air. And when Blazebuster will be retrieved."

"The Chinook is scheduled to lift it out tomorrow and load it onto a truck to go to StormAir in Canada."

"I wonder if there's any chance to salvage it."

"We'll see." He pulled her tight against him. "If not, we have other tankers on standby."

"The thought of flying another plane feels like a betrayal." She rose to put on her yellow fire shirt.

"What are you doing?" he said in surprise.

"Going back to my room."

"Like that?" he snickered.

She glanced down at herself and laughed. "Wondered why my shirt was so big. I put yours on by mistake!"

"I'd pay money to see you show up to work in my fire shirt." He patted the spot next to him. "Now take it off and get back in here. We need to discuss fire behavior."

She did what he said. After all, he was her boss.

Chapter 23

anner

The next morning in the command center, Tanner studied the weather forecast on his digital tablet. His jaw tightened at the implications. After days of hard-won progress on the Elmore fire, Mother Nature was about to throw them a not-so-desirable curveball. He tapped the National Weather Service number in Anchorage and put the meteorologist on speaker.

"How confident are we in this forecast?" he asked.

"Pretty confident. We're looking at a dry front moving through tomorrow, with sustained winds of thirty-five knots, gusting to forty-five. Behind that, a thunderstorm system with lightning potential," replied the meteorologist.

"Great, a one-two punch. Rain?" he asked hopefully.

"Unfortunately, not until the bitter end of this weather event, if at all."

"What a lovely combination," muttered Tanner, rubbing a hand across his face.

"Also, the winds will change direction from southwest to northwest," added the weather person.

Tanner flashed Ryan a grim look. "If that happens, then the eastern flank will become the head of the fire—blowing it toward the city. The Hillside will be the least of our problems."

The room fell silent as the implications sank in. At eighty percent containment, they had been on the verge of turning the corner on this fire. Now, with this setback, the possibility of losing it loomed large.

"How much time do we have?" Tanner asked the meteorologist.

"Twenty-four hours before the front arrives with the high wind event," she replied. "Thunderstorm to follow."

"Okay, thanks for the info." He ended the call, his mind ticking through contingencies, weighing options and priorities. He turned to Ryan. "We'll need to strengthen our eastern containment lines. Double the width of the dozer lines where the terrain permits. Burn out all remaining fuels between our lines and the active fire edge."

Ryan nodded. "Air Attack operations will be challenging at forty knots. As you know, gusts stronger than that will make dropping water or slurry next to impossible. The agency only permits experienced pilots to fly in these conditions." He glanced over at Mel, who nodded in agreement.

"We need to prepare the public," Tanner continued. "If the weather materializes as predicted, we may need to do additional evacuations, especially along the lower Hillside neighborhoods."

The meeting broke up, with division leaders hurrying to execute the new priorities. Tanner stepped into the back conference room to the desk he'd set up for himself. The swirling patterns of the approaching front on his tablet seemed malevolent, as if the fire had summoned an ally to undo their containment progress.

"Not good news, I take it," commented Ripley from behind him.

Tanner turned to see her leaning against the doorframe, freshly showered, with still-damp hair falling past her shoulders. Made her look downright sexy. He wondered if any of the mostly male fire staff noticed.

"Well, it's not good." He gestured at his desktop monitor. "We have a wind shift on the way that could push the fire into the city."

Ripley smoothed her hair into a ponytail as she squinted at the forecast. "The eastern flank is still vulnerable, even with the backburns we did."

"The Aurora Crew and other hotshots have been mopping up the black. But all it takes is burning debris tossed ahead of the fire to mess things up. Remember the Palisades?" Tanner sighed.

She closed her eyes, shaking her head. "We can't afford that. What's the plan?"

"Reinforce the eastern lines. I'm putting our hotshots in those areas."

"What about aerial resources?" asked Ripley. "We'll have a narrow window for drops before conditions make it too dangerous to fly."

"Ryan has a Canadian tanker pilot on standby, Ted Bishop. Know him?"

She shook her head. "I've heard the name, but don't know him."

"We'll have him hit the eastern flank hard before the front arrives." He glanced at her, sensing her frustration at not being allowed to fly. "I could use your expertise on target selection. You know the effectiveness of aerial drops better than anyone here."

She brightened. "I'll identify the highest priority drop zones, based on fire behavior predictions."

"Perfect. I know you'd rather be flying, but this will give us a fighting chance." He fought the urge to touch her since others were in the room. "I'm meeting with Silva in a few minutes. Why don't you sit in?"

"I'll be there." Ripley scrutinized the topographic maps and the BLM Master Title Plats, showing land ownership of East Anchorage, stretched along the long conference table.

Jon Silva breezed in with Detective Martinez from the Anchorage Police Department. "We've got something to show you."

Tanner motioned at Ripley, then led the three of them into a smaller office across the hall.

Silva pulled his digital tablet from a briefcase and retrieved an image. "We obtained airport surveillance footage from the day of Ripley's crash. This is from a security camera at Merrill Field, showing the Cessna that buzzed your aircraft."

The grainy image showed a man walking toward the small plane, his face partially obscured by a baseball cap, but his profile was visible.

"Do we have an ID?" Tanner asked.

"Not yet," Martinez replied. "But we have this." She swiped to another image, showing the same man's hand as he reached for the aircraft door. On his wrist was a distinctive tattoo—a stylized flame design.

"And here's where it gets interesting," Silva continued, bringing up another image. This one was from a social media post—a group photograph of employees at a corporate event. In the back row was a man with a similar profile; his sleeves were rolled up, revealing an identical tattoo on his wrist.

"The caption identifies this as the annual leadership retreat for Northstar Minerals, Inc.," Martinez explained. "We're working to identify this guy, but it supports our theory about corporate involvement."

Tanner studied the images, processing the implications. "So, we're looking at a planned operation, possibly bankrolled by a mining company that stands to benefit from these fires."

"It's still circumstantial," Silva cautioned. "But it's the strongest lead we have so far."

After Silva and Martinez departed, Tanner and Ripley remained in the small office, exchanging disbelieving stares.

"What are you thinking?" asked Ripley, fiddling with a pencil.

"I'm thinking if a corporation is behind these fires, they won't stop just because we're getting close," Tanner replied grimly. "In fact, they might kick things up a notch, especially with this incoming weather system. Perfect cover for more ignitions while we scramble just to hang onto our containment."

"Yeah, this really sucks," she said.

His fist slammed the table. "Can't tell you how much this pisses me off! Endangering our firefighters is bullshit! They already came after you and Loman."

This was the first time she'd seen him angry, and he could see by the astonished look on her face it had taken her by surprise. But hell, he was human, like everyone else.

"Hey, Westlake. Look at me." Her fingers made a V, and she pointed them at her eyes. "Get a grip."

He flicked his eyes at her and blew out air, checking himself. "Okay."

She gave him a half-smile. "We all lose our cool in this business, then we dig in again. Okay, let's strategize." She rose and moved into the conference room, pointing to a map. "If I were an arsonist for hire, I'd target these areas on the other side of our dozer lines." She pointed to locations near unburned neighborhoods. "Maximum impact, especially with the forecasted winds."

"You're right." He was impressed by her tactical thinking. "I'll request APD and the state troopers to position patrols in those areas to monitor for any suspicious activity."

"Tell them to monitor all access points—roads, trails, and the like," she added. "The arsonists seem familiar with the terrain, so they must be using routes that aren't obvious."

Tanner requested the law enforcement resources, then briefed Cohen and Ryan, asking them to fill everyone in on their protection strategy. When he emerged from the conference room, the ICC hummed with activity, everyone preparing for the approaching weather system.

Ripley followed him out. "I'll sit in on Ryan's Air Attack meeting. Dinner later?"

Tanner stared ahead, like he was ignoring her. "My room, 1700 hours?"

"Copy that."

Tanner watched her stroll over to the Air Attack group, noting how seamlessly she'd integrated into his overhead team and how well they worked together.

The afternoon whizzed by in a blur as Tanner coordinated with local and state agencies, crew bosses, and division supervisors. The atmosphere was tense but determined—all fire staff understood the challenge they faced; many of them had battled similar situations in California, Colorado, and other places where wildfires had threatened to engulf entire cities.

By late afternoon, dark clouds gathered on the horizon, the harbinger of tomorrow's approaching front. Tanner stood outside the ICC, eyeing them with a mixture of assessment and personal dread. Weather was the one variable they couldn't control, the one factor that could negate all their strategic planning and physical labor in a matter of hours.

Ryan joined him, eyeing the incoming weather. "Weather is looking ugly."

Tanner heaved out a sigh. "Not liking the looks of it."

"The crews have made good progress widening the containment lines," Ryan reported.

"Good. What about the aerial drops Ripley recommended?"

"Bishop made two of them on the eastern flank." Ryan gave him a sidelong glance. "Ripley knows her stuff. It's great to have her perspective, even if she can't fly."

"One of the best I've worked with. Her experience in the air and on the ground gives her unique perspectives in a firefight." Although Tanner delivered his matter-of-fact statement as a supervisor, he sensed Ryan saw right through it, judging from his impish grin.

To Ryan's credit, he didn't comment. "I still have things to finish up here. Get some rest while you can. Tomorrow will be a long one."

"Aren't they all?" Tanner knew he'd toss and turn all night, under the weight of responsibility bearing down on him from the forbidding weather system threatening to inflict new challenges on their firefight.

As the evening sun cast long shadows across the parking lot, Tanner conceded that he'd done all he could for the time being. Plans were in place, and crews were positioned. He left the ICC in Cohen's capable hands for the nighttime hours.

He was halfway to his truck when his phone buzzed with a text from Ripley.

Still on for dinner?

His response was immediate: *Absolutely. Be there in thirty.*

Tanner's spirits lifted as he drove to the hotel, where he showered and washed away the tension of the day. As he dressed in clean jeans and a fresh shirt, he took more care than usual with his appearance, a realization that made him look critically at his own reflection.

How long had it been since he cared about his appearance? At forty-two, he wasn't getting younger, and his job had consumed him these past few years. He gave himself a hard look.

It's time I do something about my life. And I know just the person I want to do it with.

Chapter 24

R*ipley*
    Ripley moved the brown paper bag to her other hand and knocked on Tanner's door. She'd let her hair down after her shower and thrown on jeans and her favorite blue tank top—the one that always made her feel confident. When the door opened, the way his gaze swept over her confirmed she'd made the right choice.

"I come bearing dinner," she announced with a smile. "That Italian place near the ICC I've been wanting to try. I don't feel like going out tonight."

"Me, neither." Tanner stepped aside to let her in, tracking her with his appreciative gaze.

She set the bag on the small table by the window. "Pretty sure half the ICC suspects something's going on between us. Ryan keeps giving me these knowing looks and smiling."

"He's more perceptive than most. I've known him a long time." Tanner helped unpack the containers of pasta and salad. "He's also discreet. He was Tara's training instructor when she first transferred to the Alaska Fire Service. He rescued her from a fire shelter after a hellacious burnover in Alaska's Interior. She and her crewmate barely survived."

Ripley's fork froze halfway to her mouth. "That was Tara? I heard about that after it went viral through the entire wildland fire community." She had a newfound respect for the auburn-haired Aurora Hotshots supervisor. "No wonder she's so tough—she literally went through hell and lived to tell the tale."

Ripley moved to the window, looking at the distant glow of the fire as it lay down for the night. "It's going to be bad tomorrow, isn't it?" It was more fact than question.

"We're as prepared as we can be, I guess," he said wearily, moving to stand next to her. "Hope nothing bad happens."

She turned to face him. "We need to play devil's advocate. If the NorthStar company is truly behind these fire sets, tomorrow's weather will create the perfect storm of opportunity for them."

He gave her a look of dread. "What do you think they'll do?"

"If it were me, I'd start multiple new ignitions, timed to coincide with the wind shift. They know our resources are already stretched thin. If they start several new fires simultaneously, we'd have to triage and make impossible choices about what to protect."

He nodded slowly, and she could tell his wheels were spinning. "Wait until we're stretched to the max, then strike where it hurts to create an impossible situation for the firefight."

He tugged his eyebrow, a habit she was beginning to recognize as a sign of stress. The weight of his command must be wearing on him. "Just once, I'd like to fight a fire that isn't complicated by greed and malice."

Ripley's hand found his, intertwining their fingers. "You're the best person for this job. You've got this. Try not to worry."

"Thanks for putting up with my whining," he drawled in that sexy voice that reminded her of actor Sam Elliot. "And for letting me share my truth and admit my screw-ups without judgment. That means a lot."

"That's what friends are for." She prized his trust in her with the partnership they'd formed in a short amount of time.

In the spirit of partnership, Ripley wanted to help him relax. Guiding him to a chair, she delighted in his shocked expression when she removed all of her clothes. After ordering him to lower his pants, she found he was ready for her and lowered herself onto him with a soft moan. She focused on his pleasure rather than her own, and it was a refreshing change from thinking only of herself.

"Oh, Tanner!" she soon cried out, with a mind-bending peak of release. As her private explosion catapulted her into euphoria, Tanner stiffened and shuddered.

"You feel so good," he groaned out, and she knew she'd accomplished her mission.

"Good, now you're relaxed." Together they stilled, his heart thumping against hers. She couldn't remember the last time, if ever, she'd had this intense of an orgasm—this deep of an intimate experience—with anyone.

"Thank you, I needed that."

As she held him in a tight embrace, she practically heard the gears turning in his head. "You're thinking too loud," she murmured, nuzzling his ear.

"I'm thinking we had our dessert before dinner."

"You're right." She laughed, climbing off of him and retreating to the bathroom to clean herself up.

He followed. "I can't stop going over tomorrow's contingencies. Hard to turn it off completely."

They returned to the table to eat the pasta and salad she'd brought.

She noted the tension lines around his eyes. "Talk it through if that helps. Two minds are better than one."

"I keep thinking about that Cessna that buzzed your tanker." Tanner bit into his garlic bread and swallowed. "I worry about them doing it again with our other pilots. I had Ryan talk to the Merrill Field and Anchorage flight control towers about restricting the air space within the fire's perimeter."

"I've thought about that, too. Merrill Field already had a restriction in place when I flew you up for the recon flight the day I arrived, so the Cessna must have ignored the restriction. Arson is often about power and control, so when money is on the table, it's an exponential threat."

"Which makes them even more dangerous," Tanner concluded. "If Northstar is behind this, they have resources and planning capacity. Tomorrow's weather will be a good thing for them and a bad thing for us."

Ripley's head lifted, her forkful of penne frozen in midair. "We've overlooked the obvious. We need to expand surveillance to other likely targets. Not just the fire perimeter, but high-value infrastructure that would create maximum disruption if lost."

He stiffened. "Like what?"

"Well, we already have the one substation protected." She ticked them off methodically. "But what about other electrical substations and communications towers, like cell towers? The natural gas distribution hub? Places where a fire or other drastic measures might cause cascading failures across multiple systems."

Tanner rose from his chair. "Brilliant! Why didn't I think of that?"

"Because you're too overloaded. Don't beat yourself up."

He glanced at the clock. "I'm sending a group text to Silva, Cohen, and Ryan to set up a meeting with the municipal agencies and law enforcement." He snatched his phone and tapped it like a chimp on speed.

"There goes everyone's sleep for the night," she joked, although nothing was funny about this.

Tanner's phone blew up. Silva was the first. "Hey, Jon, we've been thinking on too narrow of a scope. We need to put surveillance on the list that I texted." He listened while Silva talked. "Right. More law enforcement. Okay, see you first thing in the morning."

He'd scarcely ended that call when his phone vibrated with Cohen. Tanner explained the same thing, asking him to call Ryan. When he finished, he placed his phone face down on the table.

"Ripley, you're a genius. Thanks for pointing that out." He finished inhaling his food. "I'm ready for some shut-eye."

"Me, too." They crawled into his bed, and she snuggled into him. "You've been running on fumes since this fire started."

She wasn't wrong. The weight he carried—command decisions, public pressure, the arson investigation, protecting the city of Anchorage—would max out even the toughest of people. Sharing the burden seemed to ease his mind, and she was happy to do it.

"I owe you," he said, kissing her forehead.

"You owe me nothing. Not after rescuing me from my plane crash. I'm happy to help however I can. Now go to sleep and dream about your water dragon, Mizuchi." She kissed the tattoo on his neck.

His breathing gradually evened out as he drifted off. Whatever challenges awaited them at dawn, they would face together. She wished more than anything that Blazebuster wasn't lying broken in the woods, so she could get back in the air.

Tomorrow might bring hell on earth, but tonight, she was exactly where she wanted to be.

Chapter 25

T*anner*

Dawn broke gray and threatening as Tanner pulled into the ICC parking lot. The weather front rolled toward them like a dark wall, ready to unleash its fury. He stepped from his truck just as Ryan climbed out of his vehicle.

"Barometric pressure's dropping fast," noted Ryan. "We might see the wind shift sooner than we expected."

Tanner's mouth was a straight line. "Tell everyone the morning briefing starts in five minutes."

"Got it." Ryan ducked back inside, and Tanner followed. Cohen quickly briefed him about last night's crew actions while a tense energy filled the room. The overall mood reflected the gravity of their situation.

Tanner addressed the assembled agency heads, law enforcement, and the ICC team. "The incoming wind event will drive flames toward Anchorage. Structure protection, public safety, and firefighter safety remain top priorities. I want all available resources at the ready." He reviewed contingency plans, including Ready-Set-Go evacuation procedures.

When the briefing concluded, Silva approached with a file folder. "Got the preliminary lab results on the lighter police officers found near the point of origin. The craftsmanship is distinctive—handmade by an artisan in Seward who specializes in custom pieces for corporate gifts."

Tanner's interest sharpened. "Any Northstar connection?"

"Not yet. If there is, it's a roundabout one, but we're looking into it. The lighter was one of a batch commissioned five years ago as executive gifts for a company called Frontier Exploration."

"Never heard of them."

"That's because they don't exist anymore," Silva explained. "They were acquired three years ago by—"

"Let me guess. Northstar Minerals Development," Tanner finished.

Silva nodded. "Yep. Thanks for the heads-up last night on the critical systems protection." He handed Tanner a map with marked positions. "Here are the critical sites around Anchorage that law enforcement and the municipality will be monitoring."

Tanner scanned the map, noting the locations he and Ripley had discussed. "Add the natural gas distribution hub near Campbell Airstrip. And maybe the cell tower above Flattop Mountain. Knocking those out would create significant disruption."

"I've requested additional staff from APD and the State Troopers, but with evacuation support and traffic control, they'll be stretched," said Silva.

"Keep me updated with the investigation," said Tanner. "If we can catch these people before they set more fires, that'll be one less headache."

"Will do. Keep your radio handy." Silva dashed off.

Tanner found Ripley in the operations section, reviewing satellite imagery with Ryan. They looked up when he approached. "We've identified three spots of concern based on overnight infrared. Adding them to the drop priorities," said Ripley.

"Good work," replied Tanner, his eyes meeting Ripley's briefly.

A dispatcher appeared. "Tanner, you have a call on our ICC landline. The mayor wants an update on evacuation preparations."

"I'll take it at my desk," he said, heading in that direction. "Ryan, Ripley, keep me posted on aerial activity."

"You got it," replied Ryan.

Shortly before noon, Tanner received a weather update. "Gusts are at fifty knots instead of forty-five at the leading edge of the front. Moving faster than predicted." He keyed his radio. "All crews and strike team leaders, this is the IC. Stronger winds are arriving sooner than we planned."

The room fell silent as the consequences sank in. They had prepared as best they could, reinforcing lines and positioning crews, but nature was about to test their efforts.

Ripley snapped her fingers and pointed to her cell phone, just as Tanner's phone pinged with her text: *A pilot friend at Lake Hood just texted that a Cessna 206 just took off. Same tail number as the one that buzzed me!*

He snapped his gaze to hers. Her stricken expression mirrored his own dread at the implications. Why would a pilot risk flying in extreme conditions—unless he'd been ordered to for some purpose? A purpose he didn't like.

Tanner strode outside, not wanting anyone to hear his conversation. He called Silva, who picked up right away. "One of our bad guys is airborne. The same float plane that caused Ripley's crash. Took off from Lake Hood within the last fifteen minutes."

"In this weather?" Silva sounded incredulous. "That's suicide."

"Or it's someone who thinks the risk is worth wreaking havoc." Tanner scanned the turbulent sky. "They could set multiple ignitions from the air, timed with the wind shift for maximum impact."

"I'll alert the Alaska State Troopers and APD to scramble their helicopter if conditions allow."

"Do it fast," Tanner urged. "We may be out of time."

As if to punctuate his words, birch trees next to the middle school bent suddenly, branches whipping in a gust that came out of nowhere. The wind shift had arrived.

Tanner's radio erupted with calls from fire crews requesting resources as the fire responded to the new wind direction. He maintained a steady focus, issuing clear directives and allocating resources, all the while worrying about the airborne Cessna. He hoped for the best and expected the worst.

As the fire grew more aggressive under the lash of strengthening winds, Tanner knew they were entering the decisive phase of this battle. The next few hours would determine whether they'd lose everything they'd fought for.

Apprehension seeped into his gut... the real fight was just beginning.

Chapter 26

R *ipley*
Seeing the weather roll in firsthand out the window of the ICC made Ripley's neck prickle. "Where did Tanner disappear to?" she asked Ryan, scanning the busy command center.

"On a call with the Fire Marshal," he replied. "Discussing worst-case scenarios if winds push the fire toward Anchorage."

Tanner emerged from a small office, his face tight with concern. "Winds are already gusting at forty, with some weather stations reporting fifty."

Ripley calculated how the gusts would affect the fire's behavior. "We could see flame lengths over a hundred feet. Rate of spread could triple."

"That's what we're afraid of," agreed Tanner. "We're prepared to start evacuations for neighborhoods in Muldoon. The State Troopers are notifying homeowners to be on a 'Set' status."

Ryan stepped over. "Bad news. Bishop, our tanker pilot, had a car accident on the Glenn Highway. Ambulance is on the way, but he's out of commission for the time being."

"How bad?" inquired Tanner.

"Not life-threatening. A broken arm and other injuries. His Subaru is totaled, and he can't pilot a tanker."

"What about the planned drops on the eastern flank?" asked Tanner, his eyes meeting Ripley's. They both knew how critical those drops were with the approaching weather.

"The new air tanker is fueled and loaded at Ted Stevens International, but we have no pilot. Other pilots are working the Interior fires," Ryan informed him.

Ripley's heart sped. The DASH 8-400AT was a newer model, but the only modification was StormAir's proprietary tank system. She'd been cross certified to fly the modified tanker, having trained on it just last year.

She stepped forward. "I can fly it."

Tanner and Ryan turned to her, surprise evident on their faces.

"You're on mandatory administrative leave until Dave Doss clears you to fly again," reminded Tanner. "Standard procedure, you know that."

"I'm medically cleared, though," she countered. "The only reason I'm still grounded is the NTSB investigation."

"Which is still ongoing," Tanner fired back.

She turned to her air attack supervisor. "Ryan, I'm one of only six pilots in Alaska currently certified on the DASH 8-400AT with its pressurized retardant delivery system. If those drops don't happen before this storm ramps up, we're looking at a catastrophic spread not only to the Anchorage Hillside, but to the east side of the city!"

"I was just notified a tanker pilot arrived last night from the lower forty-eight, so we might have it covered. Dave Doss must have requested him. I'll talk to him and see if he'll allow you to fly." Ryan stepped away to make the call.

"He has to let me fly," she muttered. This wasn't about her—it was about protecting homes and lives with the skills she uniquely possessed.

Tanner crossed his arms. "Are you sure about this?"

"Yes! I'm sure," she snapped. "Sorry, but I told you I have medical clearance. My head is clear, and my reflexes are good. I can do this."

"I know you can," he mumbled. "That's what worries me."

Ryan returned, looking grim. "Doss says it's a no-go, too soon after your crash. He dispatched the new arrival to fly the new Q400AT tanker, so he should be at Anchorage International airport now. We're planning a drop in the next forty minutes to beat the weather."

"Who's the pilot?" asked Ripley.

"Colt Strickland," replied Ryan.

Ripley froze in her tracks. "Colt Strickland from California?" Her voice rose an octave, causing Tanner to stare at her.

Ryan's brows rose. "I take it you know him?"

She backpedaled. "I've heard of him." Of course she knew him. She dated him back when they trained together to fly tankers at the California aerial training center.

Boy, do I know him.

"Strickland is looking for a first officer," said Ryan.

"Oh, really?" she blurted with a cheerful smile. "I might know someone. I'll contact Strickland. I'll take care of it, Ryan." She flashed an even wider smile.

"Who's Colt Strickland?" Tanner asked.

Before Ripley could open her mouth, his phone sounded, and he stepped away to take the call. She stood in a daze, her mind going a hundred miles an hour.

Holy crap! Colt Strickland will be dropping on the Elmore fire?

They'd dated sporadically but were never truly close. It had been a friends-with-benefits relationship, free of emotional drama, which suited them fine back then. When training ended, Strickland wanted to continue their arrangement, but Ripley broke it off, tired of how hollow it felt.

Thunder rumbled in the distance. Through the window, Ripley observed treetops bending in the strong winds.

She had an idea. A bit on the deceptive side, but an idea, nonetheless.

"Ryan, I'm going to the restroom," she announced casually. "Back in a minute."

He glanced up from a monitor while a staffer furiously typed on a keyboard. "Sounds good."

No one thought anything of it as Ripley strolled calmly toward the hall, then out the door. Once out of sight, she raced to her borrowed pickup.

The thunder grew louder, and the wind whipped her hair across her face as she climbed in and started the engine. Her heart thumped as she sped to the Anchorage airport. The rational part of her screamed that what she was about to do was against protocol, but the part of her that had become a firefighter in the first place—the part ruled by selfless dedication and protective instincts—propelled her forward. She remembered her dad saying she was too "alpha" because she had to be in on the action.

She flashed her Alaska Fire Service ID to the airport security guard, who waved her through without question. The new air tanker stood gleaming on the tarmac, the ground crew bustling around it with final preparations.

"Where's Strickland?" she called out.

"In the hangar," said a mechanic, wiping his hands with a greasy cloth.

She must be crazy, but this was one way to get airborne without piloting. Technically, she wasn't violating her pilot grounding, she reasoned, as she strolled inside the hangar.

Strickland stood talking to Frank, the mechanic, as he signed the incident flight sheet.

She swaggered up to him. "Look what the fire dragged in."

His surprised look made her laugh. "Beecher! How the heck are you? I heard you'd transferred up here after the L.A. fires."

"I understand you need a first officer. I'm available to do it." She snatched her flight suit from the rack and stepped into it.

"I heard you crashed a tanker," he said, none too lightly. "That means you're grounded."

"It wasn't pilot error. A small plane deliberately buzzed us as we were making a drop," she quipped. "It caused me to lose power."

"But aren't you still grounded?"

"From piloting, yes. But not as a passenger."

"I can use someone for the gate controls." He gave her a suggestive look. "You're not doing this expecting something in return, are you?"

She scowled. "I expect nothing in return. I'm not that person anymore, Strickland. Anyway, I'm seeing someone and I just need to get back in the air."

He shrugged. "Okay, fair enough."

"Uh... just one thing. Don't mention my name on the radio. Certain people don't have to know I'm on this flight. I'm going crazy on the ground and need to be in the air. You know how it is." She lifted a helmet from her cubby.

"I don't blame you for that. I won't tell if you won't." He winked in that same provocative way he always had before their encounters... the kind she preferred to forget.

"Aircraft is prepped and ready," the lead mechanic called out. "Full load of retardant, fuel tanks topped off. Better make it quick. They're talking about grounding all aircraft due to extreme winds."

As they strode to the plane and climbed into the cockpit, Strickland grinned. "We'll catch up later. Good to have you as my wingman."

"Wing woman," she corrected, putting on her helmet and buckling in. "Weird to be on this side of the plane, though. Let's restrict our comms to the intercom instead of the aviation frequency."

"Paranoid?" Strickland fired up the engines and lifted the air tanker smoothly, climbing through the increasingly turbulent sky. The storm system loomed ahead like a dark castle wall as they flew toward the Chugach mountains.

As they approached the fire zone, he whistled. "Flame lengths must be a hundred feet."

"It gets turbulent next to the mountains," she warned. "I've made several drops, and it's never smooth." She pointed at the monitor. "See that red dotted line? It's the wetlands boundary. Don't drop inside of it."

"Roger that." Strickland tightened his grip on the yoke.

The plane bounced and buffeted in the wind like a cork in rough water. The tanker dropped, as if falling through an invisible hole in the sky. Ripley's stomach jumped to her throat when the aircraft plummeted several feet in a matter of seconds before catching air with a bone-jarring impact that rattled every rivet.

Strickland switched to the aviation frequency. "Air Attack, this is Tanker Four-Seven-Four. Proceeding to the drop zone."

"Copy that, Four-Seven-Four," said Ryan. "Bird Dog is en route to your position. Be advised, we're seeing extreme fire behavior. Multiple spot fires ahead of the main front."

"Understood. What's my target?" asked Strickland.

"Two targets. Split your load: hit the evacuation routes from the Lower Hillside, then where flames are encroaching into neighborhoods in Muldoon. Sending the coordinates now."

The latitude and longitude coordinates appeared on the monitor. The aircraft bucked like a bronco, forcing Strickland to fight the controls.

The spotter plane appeared ahead, its smaller form bobbing even more violently in the wind currents. "Tanker Four-Seven-Four, this is Bird Dog. Leading you to the drop zone. Buckle in tight—conditions are deteriorating."

"Copy that, Bird Dog. On your six."

Ripley wished she were at the controls, but she'd flown with Strickland before and had confidence in his piloting skills. She made sure to stay off the air ops frequency so Tanner wouldn't lose his shit at her being up here.

As they approached the fire's edge, Ripley noted that Ryan's assessment of extreme fire behavior was an understatement. The fire crowned through the spruce, leaping from tree to tree with frightening speed. Smoke columns twisted and bent in the fickle winds, creating a turbulent mess that threatened both aircraft.

"Anchorage Tower to all aircraft," came an unfamiliar voice on the aviation frequency. "Be advised, we are issuing a severe turbulence warning for the Anchorage area. Wind shear reported at multiple altitudes."

Bird Dog banked sharply, leading them to the critical area where the fire burned toward evacuation routes on the Hillside.

"Drop zone approaching," Bird Dog called. "Wind gusting at forty knots."

Ripley calculated how the wind would affect their drop. "With these powerful gusts, we'll need to release earlier than normal to ensure our first load hits the target zone," she said to Strickland on the private intercom.

He nodded, focusing on the spotter plane's blinking lights in the smoke.

Ripley closed her hand around the gate release as Strickland fought the controls to line up with the target area. The aircraft shuddered violently as it crossed the thermal updrafts of the fire.

"Looking good, Four-Seven-Four," the Bird Dog pilot encouraged. "Marking the spot now."

As the spotter plane let out the smoke trail, Strickland called out, "Ready in four, three, two, one... Release!"

Ripley opened the first gate, feeling the lessening of the aircraft as gallons of slurry streamed from its belly. On the monitor, they both tracked the red stream as a wind gust threatened to blow them off target.

"Direct hit!" Bird Dog confirmed. "Excellent drop, Four-Seven-Four."

Ripley bit her lip to keep from saying, "Copy that, thanks, Bird Dog!" It was weird to be in the co-pilot seat, for sure.

The spotter plane replied, "I'll lead you through the next drop near Muldoon."

"Copy that," replied Strickland.

Ripley couldn't tell the smoke from the dark clouds. The air was less violent as they flew north.

"Here we go, Four-Seven-Four," said Bird Dog, letting out smoke.

The tanker bucked and strained, but after that last rodeo, the second drop was a piece of cake.

"Three, two, one...Release!" directed Strickland, and Ripley cut loose the second load of slurry next to the Muldoon neighborhoods.

"Good job," said Bird Dog. She heard the smile in the pilot's voice, wishing the compliment was for her.

Strickland banked toward the airport and landed the tanker. When Ripley climbed down from the cockpit, she gulped upon seeing Tanner leaning on his truck with folded arms, none too happy.

"Fancy meeting you here," she said cheerfully. "Guess I'm busted. Am I in trouble?"

"What do *you* think?" His expression matched the thunderclouds above. "What the hell were you doing?"

"Strickland didn't have a first officer, so I filled in." She held up her hands in surrender. "These hands didn't touch the controls, I swear. Well, except for the slurry gates."

"We could both get into big trouble for this." He gave her an exasperated look. "This stays between us, understand? Good thing you stayed off the radio."

"No one has to know." She shrugged.

"Don't do it again. Ripley, you just—"

"I just what?" she snapped. "Just what, Tanner? Broke protocol? I couldn't sit in the damn command center knowing people's homes might burn when I could help prevent it." Her words tumbled out in a swift torrent.

"Save it." He placed his hands on his hips. "I knew something was up when Ryan told you another tanker pilot was sent in to fly this fire. I suppose you know him?"

Right then, Strickland appeared next to her and put a hand on her shoulder. "Thanks for helping today, Captain." He shot her his *Top Gun* smile and lifted his gaze to Tanner's "Incident Commander" baseball cap. He extended his hand. "Ah, so you're the IC. Colt Strickland, also on contract with StormAir."

Tanner dipped a nod, and she noted him sizing up the handsome, dark-haired pilot. "Pleased to meet you. Impressive job on the drops." Tanner forced a smile, his jealousy obvious to her.

"Thanks." Strickland returned the smile, then strode toward the hangar.

"No one is to know you were airborne, not even as a passenger." Tanner ran his fingers through his hair. "Had I been in your situation, I may have done the same thing. But if Doss finds out..."

"Technically, I'm not grounded from being a passenger." She moved close, cupping his cheek. "I'm impressed you figured out where I was."

"You are indeed a wild woman, Beecher," he said, shaking his head. "Don't get yourself fired. Speaking of fire, if you two hadn't laid down that slurry when you did, the evacuation routes would have been cut off."

"Wait, what are you talking about? I wasn't on that flight, I didn't drop slurry. It wasn't *my* hand on that gate release." She batted her baby blues at him. "You must be mistaking me for someone else."

"Yeah, right," he said, going along with her little ruse. "I forgot. It was only Strickland on that flight. Think he'll say anything?"

"Unlikely." Ripley smiled. "I know for a fact he won't."

He narrowed his eyes. "How's that?"

"Because I used to date him."

Tanner looked like he'd been slapped with retardant. "When? Back in California? Is that why you volunteered to fly with him?"

She snorted. "Hardly. It ended years ago after tanker training. Besides, it wasn't really a relationship. It was a..." She twirled her forefinger.

"Co-workers with benefits," he finished with a half-smile.

She relaxed when his dimple appeared, the one she liked to lose herself in.

"Sorry about that long bathroom break," quipped Ripley as they ambled to their vehicles. "See you back at the ranch." She gave him a peck on the cheek.

He pointed at her with a stern look. "Don't do that again."

She blew him a lighthearted kiss, then hopped inside her truck, invigorated from having been in the air again.

She loved that he'd driven to the airport to see her. Though he hadn't liked what she did, he seemed to understand helping Strickland was better than twiddling her thumbs when she could be useful in the air. Her reckless decision could have landed Tanner in deep trouble, something she hadn't considered.

He was right—Doss better not find out, or there would be hell to pay.

Chapter 27

Tanner

The storm that had rolled through overnight left an eerie calm in its wake. By morning, the rain had dampened portions of the fire, creating a patchwork of extinguished areas interspersed with stubbornly burning hot spots. Scattered across the Anchorage Hillside, fresh smoke columns rose like funeral pyres—new fires that hadn't been there when the storm began.

Tanner stood at a monitor in the command center watching drone videos of overflights when his radio interrupted him. "IC, this is Tara with the Aurora Hotshots. We have several new ignitions that started overnight. Also, humidity's dropping, and winds are picking up again."

"Copy that," he said, with a sinking feeling in his gut.

"A hot, dry high-pressure system is moving in for the next seventy-two hours, along with more wind."

"Can't we get a break from the winds?" groused Tanner. "Thanks Tara. Hold what you can but prioritize crew safety."

Cohen offered him a fresh cup of coffee. "Had a rough night. The storm gave us a reprieve in some areas while complicating our situation in others. The containment percentage has plummeted from eighty to sixty percent."

Tanner gratefully accepted the coffee. "Thanks. Go get some shut-eye, Cohen. I'll take it from here."

"I'll stay for the fire briefing, then head back to the hotel," replied Cohen, yawning.

Tanner stepped to the map table where Ryan was marking the newest ignitions. "How's it looking?"

Ryan straightened, gesturing to reconnaissance photos on monitors. "Twelve new ignition points across the Hillside and East Anchorage neighborhoods. As if they were strategically positioned."

Tanner's blood ran cold. "The Cessna. Just as I suspected."

"By some miracle, we extinguished most of them," said Cohen. "The Alaska State Troopers found the Cessna abandoned at a private airstrip up in the lower Mat-Su Valley. No sign of the pilot, but they found delayed incendiary devices that could be deployed from the air."

"Cripes," muttered Ryan. "They used the storm as cover."

"The devices were timed to ignite while winds were still strong enough to move the fires rapidly," said Cohen. "Whoever planned this knew exactly what they were doing. The Aurora Hotshots have been working nonstop to contain most of the blazes."

Tanner stepped to the podium for the morning fire briefing. Ripley took a seat in front. Her presence seemed like the sun just came out... then vanished behind a cloud when Strickland sat next to her. It stuck in Tanner's craw to see them smiling and laughing together.

Get over it, Westlake. You have a job to do.

"I won't sugarcoat this," began Tanner. "We're facing several new ignitions from last night, reduced resources due to competing fires, and weather that favors fire growth for the next three days."

He paused to let the new reality sink in. "We're outnumbered and outflanked. The fire is threatening both critical infrastructure and neighborhoods. We have limited resources, which means there could be some tough choices. We're consolidating efforts, focusing on human lives and essential infrastructure."

As he outlined the new strategy, the reporters in the room erupted with questions. "We've heard these fires were caused by arson. Can you address that?"

Tanner eyed the State Fire Marshal and the law enforcement agency heads. "Would you like to take this, gentlemen?"

The Fire Marshal stepped to the podium and relayed what was known so far. He left out the part about last night's new starts, possibly set deliberately. He concluded by saying that everything was still under investigation.

More reporters bombarded Tanner with questions, and he summoned his media person to field them, which she did expertly.

When the briefing concluded, Tanner stepped back to the conference room, followed by Ripley, studying a map of new fire starts.

"What do you think?" asked Tanner.

Her finger pointed to three separate fires in proximity. "If these three converge into one blaze, winds will blow flames toward the four subdivisions in Alpine Meadows on the lower Hillside, then the flames will move into Anchorage."

"I've dispatched Tara and her hotshots to reinforce that section."

"Won't be enough," Ripley said bluntly. "You need to hit it from both directions—ground and air—with everything you've got, or you'll lose the whole thing. Get Mel to make water drops with Juliet. And..." He sensed it pained her to say the next thing. "Get Strickland to make drops with Blazebuster Two."

Tanner grinned. "I like how you name the tankers, like they're good friends."

"They are." She lowered her voice. "I wish you could have been in Four-Seven-Four, Tanner. She took a beating and performed beautifully. I'd give my left arm to fly her."

She was right about the three fires merging into one. He'd thought of it, too. He was loving this woman. Not only because she was hot, although that didn't hurt, but she was so good with direct attack strategy.

Ryan returned. "Alpine Meadows is reporting flame lengths over seventy feet, with flying debris spotting a quarter of a mile ahead."

Tanner snapped his fingers. "Get everyone back in the briefing room. *Now*."

Within minutes, key leadership had reassembled.

"Change of plans," announced Tanner. "We're putting most of our resources on one critical area—the convergence zone threatening Alpine Meadows." He outlined the strategy, committing to an all-or-nothing initial attack. "We're facing a threat that demands extraordinary response."

"I've learned something important this week." His gaze caught Ripley's. "When we trust one another and put everything on the line to do our jobs—each of us is capable of extraordinary things. This fire has tested us and forced us to adapt. We're the people who don't back down from a fight. Let's show the city of Anchorage who we are. No structures will burn. Not on our watch." Tanner took a breath. "All right, let's go, people! Make it count!"

Clapping and cheering erupted as everyone rushed to do their jobs.

Ripley moved up to him. "Cool speech, Commander. Let me know what you need me to do and consider it done." Her words were music to his ears.

"Get your fire gear and let's go."

Tanner and Ripley drove out to establish a command post near Alpine Meadows. Crews arrived in waves, engines lined access roads, and helicopters were in the air, dropping water. Strickland dropped the slurry, and Tanner noticed Ripley's gaze never left the air tanker.

Ryan had instructed Mel and the other helicopter operators to draft water from Sand Lake as the closest freshwater source to the Hillside. Slinging water over Anchorage wasn't desirable, but they had little choice. Couldn't drop saltwater, or the boreal forest would turn into a wasteland.

Slowly, the tide turned as the firefight intensified. The aggressive aerial attack broke the crown fire pattern, holding the flames behind their fire line. Backburns had robbed the fire of fuel. For once, the weather cooperated.

Tanner and Ripley noticed the large smoke columns had dissipated.

"We've done it," said Tanner. "We're actually holding the line."

"About time," said Ripley. "Good job, Commander."

As they got into Tanner's truck, Silva's voice came over the radio. "Westlake, can you return to the command center? Big developments on the investigation."

Tanner was glad he didn't mention arson on the radio. He didn't want a panic on his hands. He reached over and took Ripley's hand. "What you did today, predicting the convergence, was spot on. You're as good on the ground as you are in the air, Miss Fire Behavior."

"That might be the nicest thing you've ever said to me, Westlake." Her wide smile told him she appreciated his compliment.

"Truly. I don't dispense praise often." He wanted to pull over and plant a kiss on those luscious lips.

"Can't wait to see what Silva has for us," she said.

He liked the word "us." It was a partner term, and he hoped they'd continue their partnership until every spark of this deadly blaze was dead out. While he wasn't sure what the future held, one thing was for sure...

Some flames were worth every risk.

Chapter 28

R*ipley*
When she and Tanner entered the command center, Silva pounced on them with his news, swiping his digital tablet.

"We have solid IDs on both suspects. Facial recognition from security cameras matched FBI databases. Primary suspect is Marcus Reynolds, a former forestry technician turned eco-terrorist. His partner is James Keller, ex-military, with demolitions training."

Silva held up his tablet, displaying the photos—the same faces Ripley had glimpsed during previous encounters. Reynolds had the distinctive facial scar she remembered, while Keller's military tattoo was evident.

"They're serial arsonists, suspects in a series of destructive fires along the West Coast over the past three years," Silva continued. "Portland, Seattle, Vancouver. Their MO is consistent—target the urban-wildland interface to maximize property damage and resource strain."

"What about the Northstar Minerals Development connection?" asked Ripley.

"That's where it gets interesting," Silva replied. "No direct connection to Northstar. The corporate angle was deliberate to throw us off. Reynolds used to work for environmental agencies that opposed development. When legal channels failed, he used fire to destroy areas corporations wanted to build on."

"Twisted logic," commented Ripley. "Burn it to save it? Yeah, that makes sense."

"We believe they're planning something else." Silva pulled up a map showing an area on the unburned green side of the current containment lines. "Trail cameras picked up movement here this morning. We need to move fast to verify the suspect's location."

"But only with backup from law enforcement," Tanner said firmly.

"Tanner, I'm a U.S. Forest Service LEI special agent, Law Enforcement and Investigations, with arrest authority. I've handled serious criminal stuff." He lifted his jacket, revealing his service weapon.

"Whoa," chuckled Tanner. "In that case, I'll go with you. Ryan can fill in for me while I'm gone."

"I'll go too!" added Ripley enthusiastically. "I've spotted these guys before. Plus, I can help identify their fire patterns."

"Ripley, you should stay here," said Tanner.

She knew he said it from a place of concern, but it still ruffled her feathers. "And do what? I've seen both these guys! I'll know if they're the same ones in the photos."

Silva nodded. "She's right. Three pairs of eyes are better than one. But we observe only—let APD make the arrests when they arrive. No one plays hero." He pointed at both of them.

RIPLEY CROUCHED BETWEEN Tanner and Silva on an overlook, squinting through hazy smoke at the two men methodically placing accelerant trails below. It didn't take rocket science to recognize the devastating pattern they were creating.

"They're setting up multiple ignition points," she whispered, with barely controlled anger. "This will overwhelm our containment lines."

The distant roar of the fire's head infused the air with tension, while airborne ash drifted around them like gray snow.

"I notified APD. They'll be here soon," said Silva, holding his camera.

"Not soon enough. They're about to ignite their sets," Tanner said grimly, watching Reynolds pull an ignition device from his pack. "We need to stop them."

He must have spoken louder than he'd intended, because Keller's head jerked up, spotting their position. "We have company!" he shouted to his cohort.

Both men bolted—Reynolds toward the access road, and Keller in the opposite direction.

"I'm going after Reynolds," Silva called, already in motion. "Don't let Keller get away. Hold him until the cops get here!"

Smoke swirled around Tanner and Ripley as they scrambled after Keller through the choking haze, coughing as they inhaled the thick air. Keller crashed through the underbrush, his figure appearing and disappearing like a ghost in the drifting smoke.

Ripley circled left, thundering down the mountain, while Tanner veered right so they could corner him. Residual smoke stung her eyes as she fought to maintain visual contact with their target. She reached a clearing and positioned herself behind a large spruce. Through the gray haze, she could barely make out Keller's form until he was almost upon her.

She stepped out to block his path. "Stop! You won't get away with this!"

Keller lunged forward, tackling her. They hit the ground hard, rolling through duff and drifting ash. Ripley fought to control him as they rolled in the dirt. He was a lot stronger than she was, and he pinned her to the ground.

"I know that voice from radio transmissions. You're the tanker pilot," he snarled. "You should have died in that crash."

Fear and fury exploded from her. "And you're a murderous lunatic!"

When his grip loosened, she kicked him off. Keller scrambled to his feet, a hunting knife appearing in his hand.

"Ripley!" Tanner's shout echoed through the trees as he crashed into the clearing, panting heavily and coughing. When he spotted Keller, his face hardened into rage.

Keller spun toward the new threat, giving Ripley precious seconds to roll away. Tanner lunged without hesitation, tackling Keller around the waist before the knife could find its target. The two men went down hard, grappling for control of the weapon, their struggle punctuated by fits of coughing. Tanner was larger, but Keller had military training.

The knife slashed wildly as they fought.

"Sometimes you must destroy to protect," Keller gasped, trying to bring the blade down.

Tanner caught his wrist, muscles straining. "You're motherfucking insane!" he hissed through gritted teeth. Sweat mixed with soot streaked his face and neck as he fought to keep the knife away from his throat.

Ripley's heart thundered seeing the man she loved fight for his life. Desperate for a weapon, she grabbed a fallen branch. When Keller's back was to her, she swung hard, connecting with his skull. He crumpled, the knife spinning away.

"Federal agent! Stand down!" Silva emerged from the trees with his service weapon drawn.

Reynolds appeared behind him with a pistol in his hand, his face twisted in pain and rage.

"Behind you!" Ripley screamed.

Silva spun around just as Reynolds fired. The shot went wide, and Silva returned fire, his bullet catching Reynolds in the shoulder. The arsonist stumbled back but kept his gun raised.

In the meantime, Tanner dove for Keller's dropped knife as the desperate man tried to retrieve it. They grappled again in a fierce fight, and Keller got the knife, while Reynolds aimed his pistol at Tanner's head, yelling nonsense about burning fires.

Driven by fierce protectiveness, Ripley threw herself forward, tackling Reynolds from the side. His shot went into the treetops as they hit the ground and pain shot through her shoulder when she landed on a branch.

"APD! Everyone stand down!" Police officers emerged from the smoke, swarming the clearing with weapons drawn. In seconds, Keller and Reynolds were in cuffs. Reynolds howled about his bleeding shoulder while Keller complained his head had been split open.

Silva helped Ripley to her feet while Tanner checked the shallow cut on her collarbone where Keller's knife had grazed her.

"Just a scratch," she assured him, her voice shaking.

"Way too close," said Tanner, his breathing ragged. "You should've stayed behind. What was I thinking, letting you do this? This was not the normal activity your doctor talked about after your crash!" he hollered at her.

"I had to do this!" she hollered back, meeting his anger. Her headache had returned, and her hand flew to her temple. She supposed she shouldn't have pushed herself as hard as she did.

An officer took their statements, then processed the scene and left the area. Tanner and Ripley headed toward their truck and beelined for their water bottles, while Silva stayed behind to assist the officers.

Silva showed up fifteen minutes later. "Both are in custody and confessed to having enough incendiary devices to light up half of Anchorage. Reynolds also confessed to hiring the Cessna pilot to buzz you."

"He confessed all that without an attorney?" asked Tanner.

"Sang like a canary when Detective Martinez showed up and told him everything they had on him so far. I have paperwork to do, so see you both later." Silva climbed into his pickup and drove off down the road, dust kicking up behind him.

"See why I had to do this, Westlake?" muttered Ripley. "Did he hurt you?"

Tanner rolled his shoulder. "He did a number on my moose arm, but that's about it. I held him off before he got any licks in."

"Thank goodness. Where'd you learn to fight like that?"

He eyed her. "I'm a street fighter from way back."

Her brows lifted. "You never cease to amaze me, Westlake."

Tanner had his arm tightly around her, and she was glad for it, as she was lightheaded and praying she wouldn't faint.

"Promise me. No more unnecessary risks." Tanner reached inside the truck and handed her another water bottle. "Drink this whole thing. You're dehydrated."

She took it and guzzled it greedily, then handed the bottle back to him.

"No. All of it," he instructed firmly, shoving it back at her. She noticed a bruise on his cheekbone.

"Stop telling me what to do, Westlake," she snapped, her head pounding.

"I'm your boss, remember? Now drink." His tone was rough, but she couldn't fault him after the fight he'd just had. Still, after her own tussle, she didn't appreciate being talked to that way.

Glaring at him, she sipped more, then shoved the plastic bottle at him and climbed into the truck. Seeing Tanner fighting for his life had scared her to death, which was the real reason for her anger. That, and coming face to face with the despicable people who'd caused her to crash.

"You fighting that loser scared the crap out of me," she blurted. "Sorry, I took it out on you," she mumbled.

"Me, too," he grumbled back, sliding into the driver's seat. "Didn't mean to yell at you. Seeing that knife at your throat had me seeing red."

They rode in silence for a while, each of them processing what had just happened.

"The arsonists might be caught, but our work is far from over," said Tanner. "I'd better get back to the ICC, and you need to go rest. Doss put you on admin leave for a reason... and it wasn't to chase bad guys through the woods."

"I know." Despite the pounding in her head and the soreness, the real blaze—the one burning between her and Tanner—had grown into a positive life force, one with staying power.

A blaze she hoped would never be extinguished, like it almost had today.

Chapter 29

Tanner

When Mel called Tanner to see if Ripley could join him for a recon flight, Tanner discussed it with Ryan, and neither saw any reason she couldn't fly as a passenger. She was grounded from flying planes but not from riding in helicopters. He dropped her off at Merrill Field, then headed to the ICC.

Once there, his cell phone buzzed. "We're back to sixty percent. Fire jumped the eastern flank again."

Tanner raised his binoculars. The orange wall of flame that seemed manageable yesterday was being driven by more gusting winds. Once again, crown fires sparked through dense spruce with flames leaping from treetop to treetop.

Ryan rushed up, his radio in his hand. "Flames are running uphill toward Hillside Haven Assisted Living." Yesterday's success capturing the arsonists had seemed like a turning point; now, Mother Nature reminded Tanner who was really in charge.

"IC, this is Juliet," radioed Ripley over rotor noise. "I'm looking at the fire that jumped the eastern fuel break. Spot fires half a mile beyond containment."

"Copy that. What's your assessment?" he asked.

She paused. "There's a natural fuel break about half a mile from the assisted living facility. Dispatch a hotshot crew to backburn between the facility and the main front."

"Good idea." He radioed Ryan to send up another hotshot crew.

Tara's voice cut through the radio chatter. "Hillside Haven is having evacuation problems. Forty-six residents, many with mobility issues. They only have two wheelchair-equipped vans. They're scrambling for additional resources."

"How long until the fire reaches their location?"

"At current rate of spread? An hour and a half."

"Thanks. IC clear." Tanner's heart skipped a beat. "Ryan, redirect every available Type 1 and Type 2 crew to Hillside Haven immediately." He grabbed his fire pack and dove into his truck, speeding up to the assisted living facility as fast as he dared.

THE CHAOS AT HILLSIDE Haven confirmed Tanner's worst fears. Staff members wheeled residents onto the circular drive while others gathered medications, oxygen tanks, and medical equipment. Two small vans were filled with elderly residents peering anxiously through the windows.

The facility director—a harried woman in scrubs—spotted him. "Thank God you're here. We need more vehicles. We have twenty additional residents waiting to evacuate, ten requiring wheelchairs, and three on oxygen."

Inside the building, Tanner saw the remaining six residents gathered in the main lobby area—elderly men and women clutching small bags, some of whom seemed disoriented by the chaos.

"We have vehicles on the way," he assured them.

Two crew-cab pickups arrived with Tara and Kenzie at the wheel. Tanner quickly coordinated, loading as many residents as possible into both trucks.

"Tanner!" Tara waved him over urgently. "The fire has reached the access road. If we don't get these last vehicles out now, the road may become impassable."

Above them, Mel circled Juliet, doing reconnaissance with Ripley on the radio.

Tanner had an idea, and he jogged over to where Tupa and Rego from the Aurora Hotshot crew were sawing trees.

"Help me get the last six residents out to the front lawn," he instructed. "We're going to airlift them out." Tanner keyed his radio. "Westlake to Juliet. Ask Mel if he can retrieve the last six residents. Fire is cutting off our road access. There's a level spot in front of the building for him to land."

"We're on our way," Ripley responded.

Tanner and the two men ran inside the building and helped the residents out to the area in front of the living facility. Relief flooded through him once everyone had gathered on the front patio. Soon, the distinctive whump of rotors filled the air as Juliet descended into the large clearing in front of the facility.

"Haven't seen this much excitement since the '64 earthquake," one older man called out as Tanner helped him duck under the spinning blades. Despite the urgency, Tanner smiled at the man's resilient spirit.

Ripley jumped out to help load the residents. When the last resident was inside and secured, she turned to Tanner.

"What about you? We can squeeze you in!" she hollered over the rotor noise.

"No, I'm driving out right now." He pointed to his truck and waved her to board the helicopter. He almost said he loved her, but they hadn't yet crossed that threshold.

A gust of super-heated wind swept through the parking lot, carrying glowing embers that hissed against the asphalt. The crackle of flames consuming trees grew louder.

While Mel had lifted off with the six evacuees, Tanner's relief was short-lived. Both crew-cab trucks with residents had returned, skidding to a stop. Tara and Kenzie jumped out.

"A burning spruce fell across the road!" Tara called out as they ran toward him. "It's blocking our only escape."

Trepidation squeezed Tanner's chest as he keyed his radio. "Westlake to Juliet. Road's blocked—can you check for alternate routes?"

"Turning around now," Ripley responded. After a pause, she relayed, "No other roads or trails visible."

"Damn, we'll have to shelter in place," replied Tanner, staring at Tara. "We'd better get busy moving the residents to safety."

"Copy that," said Ripley. "Be careful down there." He sensed the worry in her voice.

"Kenzie, please inform the crew we'll need to chop up the tree and get it off the road as soon as it's safe to do so," said Tara. "It's the only way out."

"We'll have to wait until flames pass through," intoned Kenzie, sprinting off to spread the word.

Tanner had to think fast; two truckloads of vulnerable residents plus himself and the Aurora Crew were directly in the path of the advancing wildfire. He sprang into emergency mode. "Tara, have Kenzie keep the residents calm while the rest of us prepare defensible space. We can't let the building burn."

"Consider it done." Tara dashed off while Tanner assessed their position.

The main building sat on three partially cleared acres, built with concrete and steel—relatively fire-resistant. A large parking area and the front clearing provided sixty feet of defensible space, but dense vegetation on one side posed the greatest threat. He had to make a critical decision.

"Westlake to ICC," he radioed. "Need water drops and slurry on the Hillside Haven facility. Establishing a safety zone inside of the building for trapped residents. We need drops fast. A salvo load on the building would be an immense help."

"Copy," Cohen responded. "Ryan sent helicopters to sling water loads. We'll have Strickland drop the slurry."

"Thanks!" Tara returned to help Tanner move the residents back into the building. First he announced, "Ladies and gentlemen, firefighters are on their way to help. We're creating a safety zone around the property. The building is fairly fire resistant, and we'll keep the air conditioning running unless we lose power."

Tanner shouted to Kenzie, "Gather medical supplies from inside and identify those with respiratory conditions. Tell the people not to worry when the slurry covers the building."

While Tara, Kenzie and the others moved the residents back inside the building, a helicopter landed, depositing the Pioneer Peak Hotshots with tools and equipment. Tara organized them quickly—she put Tupa in charge to have the crew remove trees and shrubs, clearing ground cover down to mineral soil all around the building. The place buzzed with chainsaws and rotor noise.

Tanner picked up a chainsaw and cut spruce on the building's vulnerable side, felling trees away from the structure. As helicopters began water drops to saturate the remaining vegetation, his plan was set in motion: the Aurora Crew and the Pioneer Peak Hotshots would maintain the fuel break and suppress spot fires within their perimeter.

"Juliet, where's the fire?" he radioed as the helicopter reappeared overhead in between the smoke.

"The head will reach you in twenty minutes," Ripley responded. "She's throwing burning debris like a hell bitch."

"Thanks, Juliet," radioed Tanner.

"Spot fires!" Tara called out.

The next minutes blurred into chaos. The fire announced itself with ember showers riding gusting winds, followed by an advancing wall of flame consuming everything around them. The noise was terrifying—a roar punctuated by sharp cracks of trees exploding as sap boiled.

Tanner had no choice but to prepare for the worst. Ripley's voice had become a lifeline, providing a play-by-play of the fire's approach, which was critical for everyone trapped on the side of this mountain.

Damn! Where the hell is that slurry?

Chapter 30

R*ipley*
"Wind shift coming in hot from the east," warned Mel, steadying Juliet as another gust buffeted the helicopter. "Fifty-knot gusts at this altitude."

After dropping the residents off at the Providence medical center, Mel flew Juliet back to circle Hillside Haven. Ripley gripped the edge of her seat as she fixated on the apocalyptic scene below. The entire slope had transformed into a war zone—flames crowning through the forest canopy, smoke columns twisting into sinister thunderheads, and in the center of it all, the Hillside Haven facility where Tanner and the Aurora Hotshots fought desperately to create a defensible space for the trapped evacuees.

"Can you get us lower?" she asked, needing a better view of the rapidly deteriorating situation.

Mel descended through the turbulent air, shuddering the Bell helicopter. "Lower than this, and we'll get caught in the downdrafts."

Ripley's heartbeat roared at the disaster unfolding below. The fire had split into two fronts, circling around both sides of the assisted living facility. From her aerial perspective, she saw what Tanner and the others couldn't from the ground—they were about to be surrounded.

Alarmed, she spoke into the radio, fear speeding up her spine. "Tanner, you have two major fire fronts moving uphill on both sides of the facility."

Static filled the radio before his voice cut through, steady as ever despite the grim news. "Copy that. Working like dogs down here. Where's our slurry?"

"I'll check." She radioed Ryan. "Where's Strickland? He was supposed to drop slurry at Hillside Haven."

Ryan came back. "He isn't flying. The Anchorage control tower has grounded all takeoffs from the international airport because of the high winds."

Her heart jumped. *No!*

"Copy that, thanks." Ripley studied the fire's movement, calculating the rate of spread. She keyed her radio. "Juliet to IC. Flames will reach Hillside Haven in twenty minutes, maybe less with these wind conditions."

Tanner's hesitation in responding hung in the charged air between them: he was facing a burnover situation, the most dangerous scenario any firefighter could encounter. Their only option was to shelter in place and hope the defensible space would be enough for them to survive the blaze as it burned through.

Ripley's mind raced, seeking alternatives. She keyed her radio again. "Tanner, can you get everyone inside the building, including all firefighters?"

"The residents are already inside. Crews are cutting defensible space. Why?" he asked.

"Just do it, Tanner. Get everyone inside." The thought of Tanner and the rest facing a burnover with the elderly residents made her chest hurt.

"Mel," she blurted, turning to the veteran helicopter pilot. "Take me to Anchorage International as fast as you can fly."

Mel gave her a sharp look. "All aircraft are grounded, Ripley. I've been instructed to return to Merrill Field."

Ripley stared down at the facility, where tiny figures in yellow Nomex moved with urgent purpose, preparing for the burnover. One of those figures was Tanner—the man who had rappelled from a helicopter in impossible winds to rescue her and her first officer—she owed him.

Big time.

"This is an extreme situation. Too much is at stake and we're out of time."

"You aren't thinking what I think you're thinking, are you?" Mel flashed her a side-eye, like she'd lost her mind.

She left no room for argument. "There's a new DASH 8-400AT at the airport, prepped and loaded. You need to get me there now!"

"You can't fly in this. Even if you weren't grounded, no sane pilot would attempt a drop in these conditions."

"Then I guess I'm not sane." She leveled her gaze. "I refuse to sit up here and watch the burnover when I can do something. They could die without intervention. I'm that intervention."

Mel bucked the winds and sped to the airport. "For the record, this is certifiably insane. But if anyone can pull it off, it's Tom Beecher's daughter."

The mention of her father—his skills, his legacy, his ultimate sacrifice—gave Ripley the courage she needed to pull this off. She'd spent years trying to escape his shadow, to forge her own path. Now she drew strength from his sacrifice.

"Thanks, Mel," she said, her mind racing.

Mel pushed the helicopter to its maximum speed, despite the winds. "Just come back alive. That's all I ask."

The tanker base at Anchorage International was operating with a skeleton crew when they landed. Ripley sprinted from the helicopter to the operations office.

The duty officer glanced up in surprise as she burst in. "Hello, Captain Beecher."

"I need the DASH 8-400AT prepped for immediate takeoff," she barked. "With a full load of slurry."

The officer frowned. "All air tanker operations are suspended because of extreme winds."

"This is an emergency authorization," she lied. "We have firefighters and elderly residents trapped up at Hillside Haven. Without air support, they're facing a burnover situation."

He hesitated, then nodded toward the hangar. "The tanker is already loaded from this morning's canceled mission. But I need proper authorization before—"

"It's coming through now. Watch your monitor," Ripley lied smoothly, rushing toward the door. "We don't have time to waste."

She half-expected him to stop her. Instead, he picked up a phone, presumably to verify her story with the air attack supervisor. By the time he learned she didn't have the authority to fly, she'd be airborne.

The newer air tanker sat on the tarmac like a slumbering beast. Unlike Blazebuster, this aircraft didn't carry the emotional attachment of years spent flying together. It was a newer model with a few more bells and whistles—a bird whose capabilities and limitations were as familiar to her as her old friend.

"Hey you guys! I left something in the cockpit," she shouted to the ground crew, hair whipping around her face. She had no time for truth-telling.

Ripley climbed into the cockpit and began her startup sequence. This tanker had updated avionics and the enhanced StormAir retardant delivery system that required specialized certification she happened to have. Despite the differences, the controls were essentially the same, a reassurance she counted on.

What's a little wind and turbulence—nothing I haven't been through before. Not my first rodeo.

As she settled into the pilot's seat, the co-pilot's door flew open. Mel climbed into the seat beside her, his expression a mix of utter resignation and what-the-hell-am-I-doing.

"Mel! Why are you here?" she demanded.

"Helping you save the day." He strapped himself in. "Making sure I have another story to tell the grandkids if I ever get around to having any."

Ripley flipped switches at warp speed while she talked. "You realize we could both lose our jobs. But, thank you."

"Don't thank me yet," he replied. "Not until we survive this maverick stunt you're pulling."

As the engines spooled up, the plane's radio sprang to life.

"Anchorage Tower to Tanker Four-Seven-Four," said a stern female voice. "You are *not* authorized for takeoff. All aircraft are grounded until further notice."

Ripley forced herself to take a deep breath. This was it—the moment where she'd either succeed or fail before leaving the ground. She thought of Tanner and keyed her mic.

"Anchorage Tower, this is Four-Seven-Four with a required emergency response to the Hillside Haven evacuation zone," she rapid-fired. "Authorization from Incident Command for life-saving drop." She tossed in the last for extra measure.

A pause, during which Ripley held her breath.

"Tanker Four-Seven-Four, hold for verification."

Mel shot her a look. "They're calling the ICC. We've got maybe ten seconds before they shut us down."

She gave him a wicked smile, and without hesitation, she advanced the throttles. The powerful turboprops responded. "Sorry, Anchorage Tower. No time to wait," she muttered as they began rolling.

"Four-Seven-Four, you are not cleared for takeoff! Repeat, you are not cleared!"

The frantic calls from the tower faded as they sped down the runway. Ripley focused entirely on the aircraft, feeling it vibrate as she built speed. As she pushed the throttles forward, a familiar surge of adrenaline coursed through her upon liftoff. The tanker responded beautifully as it broke gravity, the powerful turboprops humming with restrained energy.

"They'll pull your license for this," commented Mel as they banked toward the Hillside.

"Not my problem right now." Experience told her the turbulence would worsen as they neared the mountains. She fought through the increasingly choppy air, each wind gust seizing the aircraft and tossing it around like a toy plane.

The four-minute flight to Hillside Haven was challenging with intensifying winds that created such violent turbulence, they tested the robust flight controls. She gripped the yoke, fighting to keep the nose level as another gust slammed the port side, rolling the aircraft fifteen degrees before Ripley could counter. At this rate, the slurry would be a strawberry milkshake by the time she cut it loose.

"Damn it," she muttered through gritted teeth as the tanker bucked and swayed. The turbulence was so severe that her vision bounced, and she strained to read the gauges.

Mel stayed quiet as the storm tossed them like a sock in a washing machine. If Ripley's stomach zigzagged with each powerful gust, surely Mel's did, too. "This must be what it feels like to be a hurricane tracker," she said lightly, trying to coax a smile from Mel.

He bobbed his head up and down, hanging on for dear life. Mel may be the master of his domain with rotor aircraft, but fixed wings weren't in his wheelhouse. She could tell by his ashen face.

Another violent updraft caught the underbelly of the aircraft, lifting it abruptly, then a downdraft slammed the plane, nearly rotating them sideways. Ripley's harness cut into her shoulders as G-forces threw her against the straps.

"Who-wee! This is like flying through a tornado!" hollered Mel, as the engines whined to find stable air.

By the time they approached the Anchorage hillside, the fire had surrounded Hillside Haven, creating a nightmarish island of flames. Ripley circled to assess her target, since she didn't have Bird Dog to lead her in. It was too smoky to see what was going on with the firefighters on the ground. She was out of time to make two drops—she'd have to pull this off with one 2,600-gallon salvo dump.

No room for fuckups.

"Not good," Mel breathed beside her. "They're completely cut off."

Ripley didn't respond, her focus entirely on assessing the approach. The standard drop pattern was impossible in these conditions; the winds would carry the slurry away from the target zone, rendering it useless. She needed a different approach to deliver the payload precisely where it was needed.

"I'll attack it low from the southwest, where the winds are creating a downslope effect. Use that to stabilize for the drop, then execute a steep climb out to the northeast."

Mel stared at her. "That's insane. You'd have to come in under a hundred feet AGL in these conditions. One downdraft, and we'll crash on that mountain."

Ripley met his gaze briefly. "I need you to radio Tanner. Tell him to make sure everyone is gathered inside the center of the building, including the firefighters. And Mel?" She hesitated. "Tell him if this doesn't work, that I was sorry I couldn't keep my promise."

He gave her an alarmed look, but he followed her orders. He keyed the radio. "Tanker Four-Seven-Four to IC. Tanner, do you copy?"

Static, then Tanner responded. "Mel? What are you doing on a tanker frequency?"

"I'm on a tanker inbound to your position with a salvo load," explained Mel, as Ripley lined up the aircraft for the approach.

Right away, a cell phone sounded. Mel dug into his pocket to answer and spoke into it. "Sorry, Tanner, Beecher can't talk. She's a little busy at the moment."

"He wants me to put him on speaker," he told Ripley, bouncing and nearly dropping the phone.

When she dipped a nod, Mel held it out. "She can hear you," he hollered.

"What the actual fuck, Ripley?" shouted Tanner. "All aircraft are grounded! Return to base immediately!"

"You aren't the boss of me up here," she hollered back.

"Want to make a bet? I mean it, Beecher, go back!" If she didn't know any better, she'd say he was justifiably pissed. Whether it was fear or anger, hearing Tanner only strengthened her resolve.

"Too late, she's on approach, dude," said Mel into his phone.

"Mel, grip the release and get ready!" She gritted her teeth, battling the weather like she was Michael the Archangel.

"I'm dropping a salvo drop at low altitude so the winds won't blow it off target," she shouted. "Westlake, make sure everyone is inside the building like Mel told you. We only have one shot at this."

"But the risk is too—"

"Too late for discussion!" Ripley cut in. "Get all firefighters inside. Now, Westlake! Do it! Let me know when every person is inside that building." She was glad they were on a different frequency for tankers, since she was barking orders to the IC.

"Don't kill yourself or I'll kill you again!" sputtered Tanner. He ended the call.

She shot Mel a humorous look as the cockpit bounced. "Think he's pissed?"

The tanker bucked violently in the fickle air as Ripley listened to the radio traffic, with Tanner ordering both hotshot crews to shelter inside the building. Almost immediately Tanner was back on the radio, his voice tight. "Everyone's in. Fly safe, Beecher. I mean it!"

Ripley fought the controls to line her aircraft up for the approach path. Normally, she dropped slurry at a minimum altitude of two hundred feet above ground level. She planned to drop at less than half that, skimming the treetops to deliver the slurry precisely where it was needed. Any higher and the winds would blow it off the mark. She had no choice in this fifty-five-knot blow.

"Coming up on final approach. Mel, get ready to open the gates when I tell you!" She gritted her teeth, tightening her hold on the yoke.

Mel gripped the release system controls. "Got it."

She descended through five hundred feet, the aircraft bucking and shuddering as violent gusts assaulted it from multiple directions. Hillside Haven grew larger as they flew terrifyingly close to the ground. The fire front surrounded the facility, consuming all in its path.

At three hundred feet, a vicious downdraft caught the aircraft, driving them toward the ground with sickening speed. Ripley fought the controls, muscles straining as she corrected their descent rate. The tanker responded sluggishly when the roiling air challenged it.

"Two hundred feet," Mel called out, monitoring their altitude. "One-fifty... Ripley, we're too low!"

She lowered the aircraft to one hundred feet AGL, nearly kissing the ground. They were now within the thermal boundary of the fire, where strong air currents buffeted the tanker.

The onboard computer intoned, TERRAIN! TERRAIN! PULL UP! PULL UP!

"Get ready, Mel!" she hollered over the damn computer. "Three! Two! One! Release!"

Mel opened the gates and let the slurry fly, surveying the monitor. By some sweet miracle, Ripley had wrestled the plane to stay on course as a cascade of retardant slapped the desired mark to minimize drift from the relentless winds.

"Pull up, dammit!" Mel shouted as treetops materialized in their windshield, turbulence pushing them dangerously close to the canopy.

Ripley hauled back on the controls, demanding everything this new tanker had to give. For a heart-stopping second, the aircraft hung in the air as the winds fought its forward trajectory. The nose suddenly pitched up, and they climbed at a steep angle, engines straining as they clawed for altitude. She prayed they wouldn't stall.

"We're clear!" Mel confirmed as they ascended above five hundred feet. "Damn, Ripley, that was close. I've never seen flying like that."

"I just committed career suicide." The turbulence continued to kick her ass, her hands white-knuckled on the controls as she gained altitude. Only then did she allow herself to exhale.

"Ask Tanner if it worked," she said anxiously as they flew across Anchorage to the tanker base.

"Four-Seven-Four to IC," radioed Mel. "What's your status?"

Tanner replied. "You gave us the window we needed. Flames have been knocked down enough to drive out of here. AFD Wildfire Division crew and the Aurora Hotshots are running chainsaws to cut the tree and get it off the road. Land that aircraft safely, Captain Beecher. That's an order."

"Copy that." Ripley tingled at him going all incident commander on her. It turned her on, now that she was incredibly relieved everyone was okay. She couldn't wait to hug the hell out of Tanner... and do other various and sundry things when they each got back to the hotel.

The Anchorage runway rose to meet Ripley as she touched down, the *thunk* of wheels hitting asphalt. When she parked the plane by the hangar, the wind lifted the wings as if the plane wanted to be airborne again.

"Four-Seven-Four wants to go back up," she joked.

Mel chuckled, removing his helmet. "Got to hand it to you, Beecher. That was some flying. Your dad would be proud. Not only the flying—though that was some crazy-assed aerial firefighting—but the fine woman you've become."

Ripley blinked against the unexpected sting of tears. "Thanks, Mel. That means everything."

"And on that note, it's been an honor working with you. I have to go put Juliet to bed." Mel winked, then exited the aircraft, the wind whipping his hair as he crossed the tarmac to his helicopter.

Ripley was in no hurry to greet her fate. She'd hijacked a tanker; she knew what came next—disciplinary hearings and the end of her career as an aerial firefighter.

But Tanner and the others were alive!

She slowly unbuckled and sat back, admiring the shiny new instrument panel as she did her post-flight shutdown procedures. She gave it a pat when she finished.

"It's been an honor flying with you, Blazebuster Two," she said to the plane.

The ground crew jogged over with a thumbs-up, and she returned it, grinning. One guy pointed at her, then patted his heart, and she burst out laughing. Felt good to laugh after this harrowing flight.

Tanner spoke on the main fire frequency. "Four-Seven-Four, Westlake here. Thank you, Captain Beecher. I know what you sacrificed to help us." His saying this on the open fire channel hitched her breath. She wondered if he was on the main frequency to justify what she'd done.

She reached for her cell phone, then stopped herself. She was tired of sneaking around and hiding her relationship with Tanner. It didn't matter to her anymore.

"I don't care who knows we're involved," she muttered. "I've lost my job, anyway."

She keyed the radio. "I kept my promise to be careful."

"Next time I tell you to be careful, maybe I'll be a bit more specific," he shot back, sounding rather pissed.

She matched his tone. "Next time you're trapped in a wildfire, maybe don't expect me to twiddle my thumbs and watch."

There was a pause, then his sexy drawl slid across the airwaves. "When I saw that tanker coming in so low it was practically up my ass, I knew there was only one person crazy enough to drop a salvo load in a mother-freaking cyclone. No one else could be that insane. And that's when I knew."

"Knew what?" she radioed back with her eyes closed, waiting for the virtual Pulaski to fall and chop off her head.

The chatter that normally filled the radio had fallen silent. Ripley bet every firefighter, pilot, and support staff in the city of Anchorage was listening to this juicy exchange between the IC and his tanker pilot, who'd just done the impossible.

"That it was the crazy-assed tanker pilot I'd fallen in love with."

Ripley froze, too dumbfounded to respond. *He'd said that, knowing everyone heard it!*

Now everyone knew Tanner Westlake was in love with Captain Ripley Beecher. Damn the repercussions of him being her boss. She was in big trouble for the unauthorized flight, but she didn't care. Tanner was alive, and he'd publicly professed his love, which rocked her to the core.

It would have been nice if he'd told her privately first. But that was the world of wildland fire; the right time for things like this rarely presented themselves. And despite efforts to stay on an even keel with co-workers, people still got attracted, still fell in love, and there wasn't a damn thing they could do about it. He'd sent her heart into freefall.

She switched off the plane radio and practically ejected from her seat in her rush to go be with him. To hug him. And kiss him. And make love with him.

Then do it all over again.

RIPLEY'S HAND TREMBLED as she raised it to knock on Tanner's hotel room door. Adrenaline from her successful flight had already coursed through her veins, but it was nothing compared to the emotional storm now raging inside her.

All the way from the airport, Tanner's words had played on repeat: "*...that crazy-assed tanker pilot I've fallen in love with.*"

The door opened before she could knock, and there he was—hair disheveled, soot streaking his face, yellow shirt torn at the shoulder. Despite his weariness, his gray eyes blazed with an intensity that caught her breath.

"Ripley." He breathed her name like a prayer.

"Told you I'd keep my promise." Her voice shook, and she trembled, needing to feel him.

"You fantastic, reckless, impossible woman." He yanked her into the room and against his chest in one fluid motion, the door slamming behind them.

His arms wrapped around her so tightly she could barely breathe. She buried her face in his neck, the scent of him mixed with smoke, sweat, and the realization she could've lost him forever.

"When I saw you coming in so low, I was convinced you'd crash, trying to save us."

"I couldn't lose you," she choked out, drawing back to cradle his face. "I had to fly low, or the winds would have sucked away my drop."

She saw her own desperate need reflected in his gray eyes as his demanding mouth crushed hers, tasting of smoke and grateful appreciation. She kissed him fiercely, her fingers tangling in his hair. She tugged him closer, wanting all of him inside of her as soon as possible.

He broke away and grabbed her wrist. "Come on, we both need a shower. Get this fire stink off of us."

Reluctantly, she let go as he hauled her into the bathroom. He peeled off her flight suit and the Nomex underneath, then removed his own fire clothes. She hadn't the energy to do much of anything and loved that he took care of it. Both stood naked, streaked with soot and sweat, looking as though they'd not only been to hell and back but had orbited it several times over.

Tanner turned on the shower, guided her in, then stepped in behind her, closing the glass door. The space was meant for one person, so they stood close to each other, and took turns letting the spray pummel their backs, like a massage.

Squirting body wash into his hand, he rubbed her skin front and back, taking special care with her lady parts. Dizzy with arousal, his sensuous touch made Ripley ache in places she didn't know existed.

When he finished, he shampooed her hair, taking care not to disturb the cut healing on her hairline. To show him how much she appreciated having him wash her hair with a gentle massage, she took him in her hands and lowered herself to pleasure him. She grazed kisses along the insides of his thighs, and she thought he would come undone. When she took him in her mouth, he braced himself with a hand on the wall, moaning louder. She delighted in making him feel good.

He lifted her to him and kissed her, water droplets running down their faces. Guiding her to the shower ledge, he pulled her down to straddle him. Ever so slowly, she lowered herself onto him and closed her eyes as she slowly slid up and down, while his tongue stroked hers. His hands grabbed her rear end to tug her harder against him. The water spraying her back made this even more erotic, if that was even possible.

When each of them crested, she collapsed into him, and they stayed locked together, the warm water slicking their bodies.

"God, Ripley, you mean so much to me. I love you," he whispered against her lips.

Tears she'd been forcing back finally spilled. Ripley tried to return his sentiment, but the words stuck in her throat. Nothing would come out. Fear kept the words locked inside.

Instead, her body spoke for her. Pressing kisses to his throat, she whispered his name as an "I love you." She wanted him to stay inside her, loving the intimacy, but they were water-logged. After rinsing off and stepping from the shower, they quickly dried and beelined for his bed to make love again.

Afterward, they lay tangled in the sheets while she curled against his warm skin, outlining his neck tattoo with her finger. "Mizuchi watched over you today, along with an entire flock of guardian angels."

"Mizuchi is your spirit animal, too." He gave her a rueful smile. "But I don't think he can prevent you from losing your pilot license."

"I'll get it back someday. You're alive, and I'm alive. That's all that matters."

"You're my she-ro, Ripley Beecher," he said in a goofy voice, giving her a tender kiss.

She tried again to say the words, wanted to say them, but still, she was afraid.

Dammit, why can't I get past this? I do love him!

Instead, she reveled in the feel of him and his body warmth, with the comforting reassurance that both of them having survived the odds.

For now, that had to be enough.

Chapter 31

Tanner

The next morning, Cohen approached Tanner with good news. "The Aurora Hotshots and other hotshot crews are working mop-up. That'll keep them busy for a few days."

Tanner nodded, updating the status board. "What's our situation?"

"We're at 90% containment. The spot fires from yesterday's wind event have been contained." Cohen's exhausted face broke into a smile. "We're gaining on this thing."

"Let's not jinx it," Tanner cautioned. After everything they'd been through with the arsonists, the evacuations, the harrowing rescue at the assisted living facility—they deserved a split-second of cautious optimism.

His phone buzzed with a text from Silva.

Keller and Reynolds have been transported to a federal detention center!

A weight lifted as Tanner read the message. With the arsonists in custody and the fire yielding to their efforts, they were on the downward slope now.

Cohen handed Tanner and Ryan an updated situation report. "Heard that Dave Doss flew down because of what Ripley did yesterday."

"Yeah." Ryan nodded toward a small side office with the door still closed. "They've been in there for over an hour."

"Did you tell Doss about the people she saved, including you?" Cohen asked Tanner.

"Yeah, but he was still pretty steamed, despite her death-defying rescue mission." Tanner knew there'd be consequences, but he personally couldn't condemn her actions.

"That woman doesn't back down from anything, does she?" Ryan gave Tanner a knowing smile. "I can see why you're in love with her."

Tanner's face heated. "Got a bit carried away on the radio."

"Your secret's out now." Ryan laughed. "Everyone at the ICC heard it on the main frequency. They cheered when you spilled the beans. Some ladies stood up and hollered, 'I knew it, I knew it!'"

The door opened from the small office, and Ripley emerged. She headed to the ladies' room while Doss approached Tanner. "Westlake, I'd like a word."

They stepped into the small conference room. "Beecher is suspended from flight duties for the rest of this incident," Doss informed him. "After that, there'll be a disciplinary hearing in Fairbanks."

Tanner had expected nothing less. "And her status here?"

"After the stunt she pulled yesterday, I wouldn't blame you if you sent her packing. But if you want to keep her for other duties, I'll leave that up to you."

"Beecher knows fire behavior and incident management like she knows flying," said Tanner. "I'd like her to stay until we finish here."

"All right, your call. But keep her on a tight leash." Doss strode out of the room.

Tanner was relieved to have dodged that bullet. He wasn't ready for Ripley to demobilize.

Ripley ducked in, closing the door behind her. "Tight leash, huh? Good luck with that," she quipped, obviously having overheard their conversation.

"How bad was it?" he asked, surprised at her unemotional composure.

"Standard lecture about obeying protocols, reasons for admin leave, reckless endangerment, yadda yadda." Ripley shrugged. "He didn't fire me, so that was a shocker."

"When I picked Doss up from the airport this morning, he was pretty heated," said Tanner. "When he heard what you did yesterday, he said his first impulse was to call the state troopers to 'have your ass hauled to jail.'"

Ripley guffawed. "He wanted to have me arrested?"

"He was only blowing smoke. I talked him down," said Tanner. "Reminded him that, regardless of the protocol breach, your action saved lives."

"That's why he didn't fire me?" She gazed at him like he'd just leaped a tall building in a single bound. "I owe you another one."

Tanner gave her a dismissive wave. "No, you don't. I'm the one who owes you."

"Right. May I remind you that you rescued my sorry ass from the tanker crash?"

"Let's not play who-owes-who volleyball." His grin widened. "Come with me, I want to show you something." He motioned her to follow.

Ten minutes later, they drove through the blackened forest on the road that led to the Stuckagain Heights trailhead.

Ripley stared out the window at the burned devastation. "Finally, we're up to 90% containment. That's a major milestone."

"Yep, now that the weather is behaving itself." Tanner swerved around a blackened log. "With the forecast holding stable and no more arson to worry about, we might actually see the end of this fire."

He parked in front of the overlook with a sweeping view of the landscape. "I wanted to show you this so you could see for yourself what you helped to save."

They stepped out of the truck and walked to the edge of the overlook. The contrast was stark: blackened skeletons of spruce and birch across hundreds of acres to their left, and the unburned green trees to their right, interspersed with wide swaths of red slurry.

They gazed at the scorched blight on the magnificent Anchorage Hillside, much of it a sullied, denuded landscape. Twisted, fire-killed spruce remained upright like dark, skeletal sentinels, their brittle remains a ghastly witness to the devastation. Others had succumbed to the ash-covered confusion on the forest floor. The sun burned red in the blanket of smoke still hovering over the city.

They observed it in silence until Ripley spoke. "Never underestimate the power of fire. Like stormy air, it's impossible to tame."

"That's for sure," he said, gazing into the distance. "This is what happens when fuels aren't reduced in a forest, but no one wants to budget for it. Hopefully, the local and state agencies will do it, so this doesn't happen again."

"Let's hope so." Ripley motioned toward a passenger plane lifting over Anchorage, no doubt heading to the lower forty-eight. "From the air, we mostly see smoke and flames because our focus is on making sure the slurry hits our targets. Then we fly back to base to refuel and do it again. We rarely see the results up close."

"Well, now you do." He handed her binoculars so she could see Hillside Haven and the patches of green decorated with red from her slurry drop. "I wanted you to see what you saved after breaking every aviation rule in the book and risking your life."

She faced him, her golden ponytail waving in the breeze. "I'd do it again in a heartbeat."

"You're something, you know that?" He tugged her to him and gave her a tender kiss.

When he lifted, she chuckled. "Couldn't believe you said what you did on the main radio frequency. But you know what? I don't care. Not anymore... not after almost losing you."

He laughed. "Good. Because the proverbial cat is out of the bag, and there's no going back. I was so blown away by what you did, I let my guard down," he drawled with an impish grin.

She smirked. "Oh, ya think? Now God and everybody knows."

He gave her a careless shrug. "I'm not embarrassed. I meant every word." He squeezed her shoulder. "When is your disciplinary hearing?"

"Doss said I'd be contacted after containment is declared," she replied.

He gave her a direct look. "Whatever happens, you need to know the entire wildland community is behind you. Everyone's talking about what you did. You have my undying support. I'm with you all the way."

"And then what? Where do we go from here?" she said, exasperation evident in her expression. "When this project fire ends, you'll return to Montana, and I'll go to Fairbanks, separated by another country. How will this work?"

They'd been avoiding this harsh reality that complicated their growing feelings for each other. Tanner had asked himself how their relationship would work countless times, always circling back to the same conclusion.

"Not sure yet," he admitted. "But I know that in twenty years of firefighting, I've never looked forward to working each day on a fire as I have with this one. All because I got to see you every day. I'm not willing to walk away just because it's complicated. I like what we have."

"What is it we have, exactly?"

"I'll lay it out for you," he said. "You're a kindred spirit, and I feel like we get each other. You give off an energy that... ready for a cliché? You make me want to be a better firefighter."

Amusement crossed her face. "Is that all? What about being a better man?"

"Well, yeah. That, too. Let's take this one day at a time until we demobilize and give it some thought between now and then. We'll figure it out together."

"Together. I like the sound of that," she purred, arousing him. "We've turned a corner on this fire, hopefully. Unless something weird happens."

"Knock on wood." Tanner closed the distance, his lips finding hers.

She drew back. "I avoided all involvement until you came along with your sexy voice, badass looks, and that hot dragon tattoo. Then every resolve I had went up in smoke. Thanks for that, by the way."

He laughed. "Sexy voice and badass looks? Jeez, Beecher, you make me blush. After my divorce, I'd talked myself into believing my job made relationships impossible. It was too much to ask someone to accept the long absences and unpredictability of my job."

"And now?" she prompted.

"Finding someone who understands my work and my lifestyle has changed everything." The radio in his holster clicked with static, a reminder their fire world still turned.

"IC, this is Ryan. Silva wants to brief us on the arson investigation."

"Copy that," Tanner responded. "Heading there now." As he and Ripley walked back to the truck, they shared a serene silence. They'd admitted what they meant to each other. She still hadn't said she loved him, but he figured she just needed some time. He didn't want to pressure her into anything she wasn't ready for.

"Regardless of what happens at the hearing," he said, switching on the ignition. "We'll face it together. That's a promise."

She patted his thigh. "I'm holding you to that, Commander Westlake."

Tanner's newfound sense of peace had everything to do with the woman beside him. A turning point had indeed been reached, not just with the fire, but with their relationship. He'd met the love of his life. Now he couldn't wait to get his life figured out.

Chapter 32

Ripley

The ICC briefing room was packed when they arrived, with the usual agency heads, the mayor's staff, and fire staff. Tanner strode to the front to have a conversation with Silva and Detective Martinez from the Anchorage Police Department.

Ripley slipped into a seat in the back row, self-conscious of her ambiguous status. She felt like she was in aviation limbo—not quite suspended but not fully reinstated. Several people chatted with her about "that amazing flight you did."

"Didn't think I'd see *you* here," said Colt Strickland, taking the seat beside her. "Figured you'd be long gone after you hijacked my tanker." He leaned in close. "Although crazy and risky, that was a total badass thing you did."

"Did what I had to. Lives were at stake," she said casually.

Tanner called the meeting to order. All conversation subsided as he began the briefing. "As most of you know, containment has reached 90%," he began, his deep voice carrying effortlessly across the room. "With the weather forecast holding steady, we expect to reach full containment within seventy-two hours." Tanner continued with operational updates and demobilization plans.

Ripley loved how he easily commanded everyone's attention. *Do I love him? Yes.*

So, what was it exactly that held her back from fully committing to him? She needed time to think about the *why*. With the frenetic schedule these past few weeks, she hadn't thought about anything except being in the present with him, refusing to worry about tomorrow until it got here.

Silva positioned his laptop on the table in front of him and connected it to a projector. "As you're aware, Marcus Reynolds and James Keller were apprehended four days ago, thanks to the efforts of many in this room. We've learned much during their interrogations."

He glanced up at the TV cameras and news reporters, then displayed two sets of photographs on the large screen behind him. Reynolds with his distinctive facial scar, and Keller with his military haircut. Beside each were mug shots.

Detective Martinez stood next to him. "Reynolds and Keller have been charged with multiple counts of arson, attempted murder of firefighting staff, and domestic terrorism," she explained. "Facing these charges, Reynolds has cooperated in exchange for consideration during sentencing."

Silva clicked to the next slide, showing a corporate logo Ripley recognized from news reports—Northstar Minerals Development.

"Initially, we suspected a corporate connection," Silva continued. "The evidence pointed to Northstar, potentially using fire to manipulate land values or bypass environmental regulations."

Silva pulled up the next slide, showing a woman's photo. "This is Margaret Reynolds, Marcus's sister. She was the Environmental Compliance Director at Northstar. However, she discovered evidence the company was falsifying environmental impact statements for several proposed developments."

Martinez continued. "Margaret Reynolds became a whistleblower, submitting evidence to federal regulators. Three weeks later, she died in what was ruled a single-vehicle accident on the Glenn Highway."

A chill ran through Ripley as the pieces began falling into place.

"Marcus Reynolds was convinced his sister was murdered to silence her," Silva explained. "His obsession with revenge consumed him. He connected with Keller, a former military demolitions expert with radical environmental views, through an online forum. They targeted areas Northstar had an interest in developing. By burning these areas, they believed they could prevent Northstar from profiting from their developments up and down the West Coast."

Silva clicked to another slide with a map. "The pattern of fires followed Northstar's development interests up the coast—Portland, Seattle, Vancouver, and Anchorage. Each fire grew more sophisticated, more dangerous."

"What about the attack on Captain Beecher's aircraft?" Ryan asked, drawing all eyes to Ripley.

"That was Keller's initiative," Silva replied grimly. "After Captain Beecher's drops thwarted their planned fire spread, he deliberately targeted her aircraft."

A stab of anger sliced through her as she listened to the confirmation of her suspicions. The crash that had nearly killed her and Loman hadn't been random bad luck. It was engineered by a man whose warped sense of justice had put countless lives at risk.

The briefing continued with details of the investigation, the evidence collected, and the pending legal proceedings. Ripley wrestled with her conflicting emotions, recalling the sensation of crashing and the destruction of her cherished Blazebuster.

When the meeting adjourned, Ripley remained seated, processing what she'd just heard.

Strickland leaned close, their shoulders touching, his face close to hers. "We haven't had the chance to catch up. Want to get together later?"

"No. I don't." She looked him squarely in the eye. "Didn't mind helping you in the air, but I'm not interested in any ground activity."

"Took balls to do what you did. So sexy." He slipped his arm around her. "Then again, that's what made you hot back in training. Every guy wanted you, but I'm the one who scored you for my girlfriend."

Ripley recoiled. "You scored nothing! I wasn't your freaking girlfriend, we were just—"

"Fuck buddies," he finished with a toothy smile. "How about picking up where we left off?"

She leveled her gaze. "Only after I stick a burning spruce up your ass!"

Strickland guffawed, and Tanner eyed him like a pissed-off eagle preparing to torpedo a gull for stealing his fish. For a second, she thought he'd be the one to drill a burning spruce up Strickland's ass.

"You're no fun anymore. But you still take unnecessary risks." Strickland rose and zipped up his leather jacket.

"I don't take risks. I do what it takes to get the job done," she snapped, now regretting having helped him. She'd never do it again, that's for sure.

Strickland only flashed her a wide grin and ambled out of the command center.

Tanner waggled his finger at her, and she made her way to the front, where he stood talking with Silva and Detective Martinez.

Silva closed his laptop. "I wanted you and Tanner to hear this firsthand, considering your involvement in this arson case. The FBI will take it from here, but they may call on you to testify later on."

"Do you think Reynolds is right?" Ripley asked suddenly. "About his sister being murdered?"

"One corporation's greed potentially led to a death, which led to acts of vengeance that threatened an entire city," Tanner summarized grimly. "Hard to find heroes in that story."

"No heroes," Silva replied. "Just people who made bad-guy choices, thinking it was the right thing to do. We'll keep you both posted on what happens from here."

Tanner thanked them, and after the room emptied, he turned to Ripley.

"What's the deal with Strickland?" His tone had an edge that made her shift uncomfortably. "Why was he all hands across America with you?"

She made a dismissive wave. "He thought we could pick up where we left off back in training. We were young, away from home, filling our lonely nights with..." She twirled her finger.

"Sex?" He said it matter-of-factly with a straight face.

Surprised by his blunt assessment, she rushed to explain. "That's all it was. I never had feelings for him. How could I, with an ego bigger than Alaska?"

"Didn't like his arm snaked around you like he was claiming you. Or was that for my benefit?" he said dryly.

She loved his reaction. "You're such a multitasker, juggling a meeting and jealousy at the same time."

He grimaced. "Yeah, okay, so I turned a little green."

"Aw, that's so sweet." She switched to business when the door opened, and some staffers came in. "What do you think about the arsonist's motives?"

"They're caught. That's all I care," replied Tanner.

"I thought about how Reynolds started with grief for his sister, then twisted it into something monstrous. How the line between what he thought was justifiable became deranged fanaticism."

Tanner nodded. "Except his road to hell was paved with good intentions, and it damn near torched a city."

"What's your motivation as a firefighter?" she asked. "Guess I haven't asked you that."

Tanner's jaw tightened slightly. "Protect lives and property. Not out of vengeance or ideology, but because some things deserve our protection." His tone invited no argument.

"Is that why you risked getting trapped at Hillside Haven?" she asked.

He chuckled. "Is that why you stole an air tanker and did the most insane maneuver I've ever seen?"

She tilted her head. "Told you why I did that, and why I always do what I do. Not for the glory, but because what I do from the air helps to protect what matters on the ground."

His face suddenly lit up. "Come to Montana, Ripley. When this is over. Just for a visit, to see how you like it."

Ripley blinked, caught off guard by the invitation.

"After we demobilize and you have your hearing, come to Montana." He held her gaze captive. "I don't mean to pressure you with everything you have on your plate. We'll get you through the hearings first, then we'll talk about it."

So much jangled in her brain she couldn't have decided anything right now if her life depended on it. Staying in the present was her safe place. The future was murky, and she wondered what she wanted from this relationship. She needed time to sort everything.

"If I agree to visit you in Montana, then we'll see if we have staying power," she said finally, running out of diversions.

"That's my girl." The smile that traveled across his face was worth every bit of fear she'd had to overcome so far. She had to continue this relationship on her own terms, taking baby steps.

After all, he'd said they were kindred spirits, and he had confidence they'd work things out, living and working in different states.

How can I argue with that?

Chapter 33

Tanner

"One hundred percent containment." Tanner stared at the words on the incident status report, letting them sink in before signing his name at the bottom. After thirty-one grueling days, countless close calls, and the combined efforts of over twelve hundred firefighters and support staff, the Elmore fire was officially contained.

Anchorage had been spared.

A universal cheer went up all over the ICC as everyone began the process of demobilization. Whiteboards were erased and the tactical maps that dominated the room were carefully rolled and put away. Frenetic radio chatter had lessened to the occasional routine check-in and coordination of mop-up operations by the hotshot crews.

"It's official?" Ryan asked, approaching with two cups of coffee.

Tanner accepted a cup. "Just signed off. We'll monitor the black for another forty-eight hours to make sure no hot spots remain. I informed the local media. The mayor is ecstatic."

Ryan raised his cup. "To surviving another one. This one was dicey."

"Here's to the crews who made it possible." Tanner clicked his cup against Ryan's. He took a sip, then added, "And to relationships forged in fire."

"Agreed." Ryan's knowing smile told Tanner he didn't need to elaborate.

Although Tanner's involvement with Ripley was no longer a secret, they stuck to their work boundaries. No one seemed to have a problem with it, so maybe she'd been overly paranoid. With fire operations wrapping up now, it no longer mattered.

"Ripley's disciplinary hearing is tomorrow morning," said Ryan. "Word is Doss is bringing in aviation fire bosses from the regional office."

"I plan to be there," replied Tanner. "Any predictions?"

Ryan shrugged. "Hard to say. What she did was unauthorized and dangerous as hell, but it also saved thirty-plus lives. That statistic tends to muddy disciplinary decisions."

Tanner's phone vibrated with a text from Ripley.

Heard the news about 100% containment! Dinner to celebrate?

He quickly typed back: *Have lots to wrap up. Meet at Glacier Brewhouse around seven?*

Perfect! See you then, she replied.

"Remember, your transition briefing with the local agencies is early tomorrow morning, so don't celebrate too hard," cautioned Ryan. "Happy for you, buddy. Good job as IC. I'll sing your praises everywhere."

"Thanks," Tanner replied, pocketing his phone. "Need to finish up some paperwork."

By the time Tanner left the ICC, the sun had cast long shadows across Anchorage. For the first time in a month, the city wasn't hazy with smoke. He drove to the hotel to shower and change before dinner. The extended-stay room had become a comfortable home over the past month. Tomorrow, he'd fly with

Ripley to the hearing in Fairbanks. The thought sobered him as he dressed in clean jeans and a button-down shirt.

Glacier Brewhouse was bustling with tourists and locals when Tanner arrived. Downtown Anchorage hummed with renewed energy as life began returning to normal. He spotted Ripley at a corner table, her hair loose around her shoulders instead of in its usual ponytail.

He blinked, noting she resembled a goddess in a blue sundress, displaying cleavage that swiveled many heads as he approached. He loved being with a woman everyone admired.

"You clean up nice, Commander Westlake." She smiled as he floated toward her. "Almost didn't recognize you in civvies without ash and your radio as accessories."

"Can't call me commander anymore. I've officially demobilized." His eyes took her in as he sat down. "I've rarely seen you in anything but Nomex and flight suits."

"Except when I've been naked in your room," she purred, beaming at him. "Found this little number at a nearby mall."

He cleared his throat and swallowed. "Looks great on you."

It didn't look great, it looked fan-freaking-tastic.

The server arrived with water and menus, took their drink orders, and left. He reached across the table for her hand. "How are you feeling about tomorrow?"

Her smile dimmed. "Nervous. Prepared for the worst and hoping for not so terrible."

The server appeared to take their order and a short time later, he delivered two plates of king salmon steaks. It didn't take long for either of them to finish their meals. After declining dessert, Ripley leaned back. "When's your flight to Montana?"

"In a day or two," he replied. "Assuming everything is wrapped up by then. Haven't checked flight schedules yet—"

"Tanner Westlake, is that you?" a familiar feminine voice cut in, slicing him like a knife.

His stomach flip-flopped at the buxom blonde approaching their table with a voracious smile.

"Melissa," he managed in an oh-hell tone. "What are you doing in Anchorage?"

His ex-wife beamed, ignoring his obvious surprise. "I decided to take a trip to Alaska with some girlfriends. When I heard you were here working on that god-awful fire, I thought, what perfect timing! I can't believe I ran into you!"

Glacier Brewhouse was popular, but not the only popular restaurant in Anchorage. This was too perfectly timed to be coincidental. His annoyance was off the charts, and he tried not to panic as his worlds collided.

"Melissa Nelson, this is Ripley Beecher." The words tasted like ash in his mouth. "She's a tanker pilot with the Alaska Fire Service."

"Melissa Westlake," his ex corrected, her gaze traveling to Ripley in a critical assessment. "I kept Tanner's name. Changing my professional credentials turned out to be too much of a hassle." Her overly sweet smile struck Ripley as entirely fake.

Ripley's smile was cordial. "Nice to meet you. Are you in medicine, then?"

He admired Ripley's calm and collected demeanor. His was anything but.

"Dermatology," replied Melissa, placing her hand on his shoulder. "Tanner and I met in Missoula when he came in for some nasty poison ivy after one of his jumps. Look at you, honey, still rushing into danger after all these years. Some things never change, do they?"

Her possessive touch made him tense, and he leaned away from her hand when he noticed Ripley staring at it.

"What a coincidence. You being here at the same time I am," he said coolly.

Melissa glossed over it. "I've been dying to see glaciers and everything else people rave about. Honestly, when I heard you were here, I thought it was a sign."

From the way Melissa eyed her competition, he wondered if she was threatened by Ripley's gorgeous looks.

Ripley must have sensed it, because she rested her forearms on the table and gave Melissa an easy smile. "Where have you toured in Alaska?"

"Here, there, all over, really," his ex prattled in response.

Tanner could always tell when Melissa was lying. She'd obviously shown up in Anchorage because she'd heard about Ripley, probably through the smokejumper rumor pipeline. She'd done this before, back home with other women he'd dated, always checking out her competition like they were still married.

His ex burbled on. "I've been meaning to get hold of you, anyway. But now that we both happen to be here, we need to talk about some things." She emphasized the word 'happen.'

"We have nothing to talk about." He glanced at Ripley. This was beyond awkward. "Please excuse us, we have business to discuss—"

"Oh, how rude of me. Forgive me, babe, I'll let you finish your dinner," Melissa interrupted. "I'm staying at the Captain Cook. Let's have breakfast tomorrow. I'll call you." She leaned in close to stage-whisper for Ripley's benefit. "We have so much to catch up on, honey." She offered Ripley a tight smile. "Lovely to meet you, Rebecca."

"Ripley," she corrected calmly.

"Of course. Ripley," Melissa replied with mock sincerity. "Enjoy your evening."

As Melissa sashayed away, Tanner blew out a stream of air. "Holy shit. I'm so sorry. Wasn't expecting that at all."

Ripley wore a puzzled expression. "Quite the coincidence."

Tanner dropped his napkin onto his plate. "Melissa has always had impeccable timing, down to the precise second. She has a sixth sense for ruining my day."

A corner of Ripley's mouth lifted. "So, I noticed."

He leaned forward, peering at her intently. "For the record, I have no intention of having breakfast, lunch, or anything else with her. That chapter of my life is long past closed."

Ripley nodded emphatically. "I believe you... babe." She batted her eyelashes at him.

This made him laugh, and Tanner was reminded why he'd been drawn to Ripley in the first place. Where Melissa thrived on pointless drama, Ripley thrived on purposeful action. She kept him anchored in the present, which had become his lifeline.

"Have I mentioned how much I appreciate you?"

"Once or twice," she replied, smiling.

They finished their dinner, both sensing a quiet tension after his ex-wife's grand entrance. He had enough on his plate and didn't need his ex-wife crashing their celebratory dinner. Afterward, they drove to their hotel.

"As much as I'd love to spend the night with you, we'd better get a good night's sleep before flying to Fairbanks in the morning," said Ripley, ever the practical one. "Plus, I want to be attentive for the hearing."

"Right," he begrudgingly agreed, wishing he could get her naked and make passionate love to her. "The Alaska Airlines flight is at 0700, but it's only a forty-minute flight to Fairbanks." He walked her to her room, and they hesitated outside her door.

She slid her arms around his neck. "I'm going to think positive things about tomorrow's hearing. No point in going all gloom and doom."

He needed to explain. "I'm sorry about the ex-wife barging in on us like that. She's done this before. Just never expected her to pop up in Alaska, of all places. I don't know what to say."

She put her finger to his lips. "Stop fretting. She obviously found out you were here and seized the opportunity. If she's here with girlfriends, she'll probably go off with them to tour around."

Unfortunately, he knew otherwise, and that's what bothered him. "I don't need her drama. As for the hearing, whatever happens, happens. Try not to worry and get some sleep."

She gave him a thoughtful look. "I'm curious about something. If you and Melissa live in the same town, why would she come all the way to Anchorage to talk to you?"

"Honestly, I think she heard about you and wanted to check you out. One time I was on a blind date a fellow smokejumper had set up. Melissa popped up out of the blue to size her up. I'm sure Ryan told the jumpers in Missoula about you, and one of them told her, since she stays in touch with them."

"Interesting," said Ripley. "She acted like she wants you back. How long since the divorce?"

"Three years." He shook his head. "Don't let her interference bother you. You still plan on coming to Montana, right?" Oddly, he needed reassurance with his ex now in the picture.

"Assuming they don't throw me into pilot jail. Though it sounds like we might have to go undercover in Montana to avoid your ex. But then, we're used to sneaking around." She playfully poked him in the chest.

"We won't hang around town. I'll take you to Glacier or Yellowstone Park, and there are resorts in the Flathead Valley." Tanner laughed. "If they sentence you to pilot jail, don't worry. I'll break you out."

She pulled him to her and planted a sensual kiss on his lips. He moaned when their kiss deepened, wanting badly to go inside her room.

"Are you sure I can't stay?" he whispered, pulling back.

"Nope. You'll keep me awake, and I need my wits about me tomorrow."

"In that case, good night, my lovely. Dream about flying unicorns pooping rainbows."

She laughed. "See you in the lobby, bright and early." She kissed the sea dragon tat on his neck. "Goodnight, Mizuchi. Watch over my man while he sleeps."

Her lips on his neck aroused Tanner so much, he headed for his cold shower. He couldn't wait to get this hearing over with so they could get on with their lives.

Chapter 34

Ripley

The next morning, as Ripley hurried to dress, she switched on the TV. The local news displayed a video clip of Tanner at yesterday's press conference. She loved his confident incident commander persona, fielding questions with his trademark calm authority. He was even hotter on camera, and she chuckled at the female reporter all but batting her eyelashes during the interview.

Despite Tanner's reassurances about the disciplinary hearing, apprehension rattled her. Not only about the consequences of her unauthorized flight, but about everything else: the distance between Alaska and Montana, the challenges of their demanding jobs, and now the troubling appearance of Tanner's ex-wife.

A knock at the door startled her. She evaluated herself quickly in the mirror, wearing her olive green Nomex pants and yellow shirt with the AFS pilot logo and her hair hanging loose around her shoulders.

She opened the door to Tanner, dressed casually in cargo pants and a smokejumper T-shirt with his IC baseball cap. He held a paper bag in his hand. "Thought you might want breakfast before we head to the airport. Donuts from a gourmet bakery down the street."

Ripley stepped aside to let him in, loving the familiar scent of his aftershave. "Is this your way of making sure I have comfort food before the hearing?"

He placed the bag on the table. "You skip meals when you're stressed."

"You noticed that?" She was both touched and unnerved by how well he knew her habits after only a month of working together.

"I've noticed lots of things about you," he replied, unpacking pastries and coffee. "Like how you squeeze your tongue between your teeth when you're super focused. And how you look to the east when you get up in the morning."

"Firefighter and pilot habit—always reading the skies. Dad taught me that. I'm a lot like him, I guess. Meticulous about flying and always calculating risks." She stopped short of saying anything more. "We'd better head to the airport. I'd really be screwed if I missed this flight."

Tanner drove his truck and parked in short-term parking, where they hurried through check-in and security. After boarding, Ripley let Tanner have the window so he could take in the breath-taking views on the way north, while she sat in the middle seat.

After buckling her seat belt, Ripley rested her head back. "Thanks so much for coming with me."

"Doss advised me to provide a statement as the incident commander," he replied.

"Something's been bothering me," said Ripley. "I keep thinking about how your ex-wife seemed surprised to see us last night. Especially you."

"Nothing about that encounter was accidental," he muttered.

Hearing Tanner say it brought a fresh wave of unease. "You think she came to Alaska because of you?"

"I know she did." His annoyance somewhat relieved her. "Got a text from her this morning asking to meet for coffee. I told her I wasn't interested in meeting up."

"She really is beautiful, you know." Ripley tried to sound casual, but she was anything but.

"Trust me, she knows that." Tanner rested his hand on her thigh. "Are you worried about it?"

Ripley hesitated, not wanting to sound insecure. "Not worried, just aware that you have a history with her, I guess."

"What Melissa and I had was based on physical attraction and convenience. Our marriage fell apart when she realized my job required spending time away from her." Tanner rubbed the back of his neck. "She wanted an attentive husband who was home every night, who attended hospital fundraisers and dinner parties with her colleagues. She liked the idea of being married to a smokejumper more than the reality of it."

"What happened that finally ended it?" Ripley realized how little she knew about his failed marriage.

"She found someone whose life aligned with hers. A pharmaceutical rep who worked regular hours and enjoyed her social life." He shrugged. "We wanted different things in life. Last I heard, he left her for someone else, so she's on the prowl again."

As the plane gathered speed and lifted, Ripley dozed off until Tanner elbowed her awake. "Look, there's Denali!" When she leaned across him, the blue and white massif with its jagged shadows filled the window on the left of the plane.

"Someday I'll fly you around it, up close and personal," she said dreamily. "Ever since coming to Alaska, I've wanted to do that."

"I would love that. It's a date."

When Denali faded from view, they descended into Fairbanks and came to a halt. Yawning, they exited and headed straight to ground transportation, as they hadn't checked bags. An Alaska Fire Service shuttle met them and drove them to Fort Wainwright.

THE HEARING HAD GONE better than either of them had dared hope. Tanner had weighed in with the lives she'd saved, and while Ripley received an official reprimand for her unauthorized flight, the board declined to suspend her pilot's license, citing the "extraordinary circumstances and life-saving outcome" of her actions. Her skills were in dire need, so her grounding was lifted, effective immediately. She was authorized to fly Blazebuster Two back up to Fairbanks, since Strickland had been dispatched to Canada to fly fires.

Afterward, she thanked Dave Doss and the others, and she and Tanner caught the return flight to Anchorage. She knew his final debriefing was scheduled for tomorrow morning, and afterward, he was free to go. Her stomach tightened at the thought of his leaving.

On the way to the hotel from the airport, Tanner stopped at Momma O's in Spenard for halibut sandwiches. Much to Ripley's delight, he drove to Westchester Lagoon, where he parked the truck and led her along the coastal trail to a comfortable hard-backed bench overlooking Cook Inlet.

Ripley bit into her sandwich and swallowed, relieved to have everything finally behind her. "Doss said I'll be dispatched to Canada. Their fire season is ramping up. I'll miss the hell out of you."

He lifted a brow. "Just keep your distance from Strickland. I don't trust that guy." He leaned into her. "I'm glad everything worked out for you to stay in the air. The city of Anchorage has arranged for a celebration tomorrow after our debriefing. It should be fun."

"As long as I'm with you, anything is fun." She refused to think about their parting, so instead she admired how the sun glimmered in his hair. She was relaxed, which she hadn't been in a long time.

A very long time.

Chapter 35

Tanner

The morning sun glinted off the polished brass of the Anchorage Fire Department's ceremonial axes as an honor guard posted the colors. Tanner watched as the city officials gathered on a makeshift stage erected at one end of the Delaney Park Strip in downtown Anchorage.

The community gathered to honor everyone who worked on the Elmore fire. Firefighters in dress uniforms mingled with hotshot crews in their laundered yellow Nomex. Pilots stood next to engine operators and law enforcement. Support staff chatted with homeowners they had helped evacuate. The mood was celebratory yet solemn, recognizing what had been lost and what had been saved.

Tanner waved at Ripley, standing next to Mel, along with the other fixed-wing and helicopter pilots. She wore her dark green flight suit, with the Alaska Fire Service patch displayed on the shoulder, looking every bit the capable pilot that she was.

As he watched her interact with her colleagues, Tanner noticed how much more at ease she was. Unbeknownst to Ripley, he'd talked to Doss before the hearing about retaining her pilot's license. Afterward, he was thankful the disciplinary board had agreed to it.

Ryan appeared at Tanner's side. "Quite a turnout." He nodded toward where Ripley stood. "You two figure out what happens next?"

Tanner hesitated, unsure how much to share since they hadn't figured out a plan, other than Ripley would visit him in Montana between wildfires. "We're working on it."

"Whatever you both decide, don't give up on your relationship, bro." Ryan clapped him on the shoulder. "I've never seen you this upbeat during a firefight. Because of Captain Beecher?"

Tanner raised his brows at his buddy's insightful analysis. "Guilty as charged."

The Mayor of Anchorage stepped to the microphone, calling the ceremony to order. The crowd quieted for his speeches, which expressed gratitude to the firefighters, recognition of the agencies involved, and the city's roller coaster ride for the better part of a month.

Tanner was summoned to the stage to receive a commendation on behalf of all incident command staff. Public recognition wasn't his thing, but as he accepted the plaque from the mayor, the cheers and applause from his staff and the citizens of Anchorage who were present overwhelmed him.

"Thank you, Mayor," he said into the microphone. "This belongs to every person who responded to the Elmore fire, from the municipal engine crews who first responded to the hotshot crews who built miles of line. And it belongs to the pilots who dropped water and slurry in impossible conditions. Some of you risked your lives and careers to protect this community. Your courage and sacrifice are what wildland firefighting is all about.

It's been my privilege to work with all of you." He fixed on Ripley's beaming face and winked.

The crowd applauded, and the ceremony concluded with the dedication of a memorial plaque to commemorate the Elmore fire and those who fought it. Afterward, everyone was in a party mood. Food trucks had lined the street next to the park, and a live band started playing popular country and rock tunes. Kids raced between activity booths set up by the different agencies. Smokey the Bear handed out stickers and candy from the Forest Service booth.

Tanner made his way through the crowd, talking with women who gushed at him and men who wanted to talk shop about the firefight. He shook hands and exchanged words with firefighters and homeowners who expressed gratitude for saving their homes.

He eyed Ripley interacting with her own fan club—young people who wanted to know what it was like to fly the big tankers. Tanner waited patiently while she tactfully answered questions.

She ambled over to him. "Splendid speech, Commander. How badass of you to mention my insubordinate rule-breaking."

"Couldn't resist." He grinned. "Figured 'pilots who flew in impossible conditions' sounded better than 'the one pilot who stole an air tanker and nearly gave us all heart attacks.'"

Mel sidled up to Ripley. "I break out in a cold sweat every time I recall that harrowing flight. But after seeing how you handled that tanker, I'll fly with you any day. If your dad were here, he'd say the same."

She laughed. "He would have pulled it off with more style. Dad wouldn't have kissed those treetops like I did."

Tara and some of her crew joined them. "From where we were, your masterful flying looked like *Batman* was piloting that plane."

"You all did the hard work on the ground." Ripley blushed.

Tanner loved her humility. Other pilots would brag about it, like Strickland, he thought sourly. He was glad that guy was out of the picture.

"Speaking of hard work." Tanner nodded toward the beer tent. "Let's grab a cold one. Word on the street is the Midnight Sun Brewery whipped up a Firefighter's Ale for the occasion."

The group drifted toward a long white table in the seating area, their easy camaraderie a welcome change after their shared ordeal. Tanner noticed how Ripley got along with the Aurora Hotshots as they shared stories about the fire and laughed at inside jokes.

When everyone was seated with a beer, Kenzie raised her red Solo cup. "Here's to surviving the odds. And to the flyboys and fly-women, who made it possible." She nodded at Mel and Ripley.

Tupa, the Samoan crew member from Anchorage, added, "And to the commanders and a certain pilot who knew when to throw protocol out the fricking window!"

Everyone laughed and clinked cups.

The oldest Aurora Crew member, Nick Rego, turned to Tanner and Ripley with an impish grin. "Are we going to toast the elephant in the room?"

Tanner raised an innocent eyebrow. "What elephant would that be?"

"The one where our IC and a certain hotshot tanker pilot have made googly eyes at each other ever since Big Lake," Rego replied bluntly. "We took bets on when you'd both own up to it."

Ripley stayed neutral as everyone turned toward her and Tanner.

He found her hand beneath the table and squeezed it. "I guess the elephant became obvious when Captain Beecher risked her life for us at Hillside Haven." He gave her a side-eyed grin.

"How about when you gushed all over the airwaves?" asked Tara with a broad smile.

"Does this mean you're staying in Alaska, Tanner?" asked Kenzie.

"Nope, I'm heading back to the Smokejumper Base in Missoula," he said. "You know how it goes. Distance isn't always the obstacle it seems."

"Especially not for someone who flies for a living," Mel added, elbowing Ripley.

As the celebration continued, Tanner had a desire to show Ripley what she meant to him, not only to their colleagues, but to the world at large. When the band started playing, he turned to her. "Dance with me?"

Her brows lifted. "In front of everyone?"

"Especially in front of everyone. Hold on a minute." He dashed over to the band and made a request.

The first strains of "Smoke Gets in Your Eyes" played as Tanner slipped his arm around her waist. He sensed several pairs of eyes following them, but none of it mattered anymore. What did matter was Ripley in his arms, moving with him to the slow rhythm of his favorite song. He drew her close, a quiet declaration to anyone watching that she was his.

"Everyone is watching," she murmured into his ear.

"Let them," he rumbled back. "I'm not ashamed of how I feel about you, Ripley. And no one can say anything about the boss-subordinate relationship because this incident is over."

"I jumped off that cliff when I stole the tanker, and you jumped off with me when you got mushy on the radio." A wide, joyful smile illuminated her face. "You might say we came out of the closet."

Most in the fire community were rooting for them, given how everything had played out. They were both returning to their home bases, where their relationship would face the real test. But now, with Ripley in his arms, he was certain their fire wouldn't be contained by distance or conventional boundaries. Their blaze burned too bright, too strong, to be extinguished.

Tanner did a double-take when he noticed Melissa standing in the crowd drilling a stare into both of them. He hadn't expected to see her there.

After he finished dancing with Ripley, Melissa made her way over. He let out a growl, wishing to hell this wasn't happening.

"There you are." Melissa rested her hand on his arm, flashing Ripley a smug look. "I was hoping to see you."

"What are you doing here?" He was losing patience with her intrusiveness.

"I ran into Ryan yesterday, and he told me about this picnic. So sweet of Anchorage to do this for all of you." Her attempt at diplomacy fell flat, along with his displeasure at seeing her.

"All right, Melissa." He folded his arms. "I give up. Tell me why you're *really* here? I have a tough time believing you showing up in Anchorage is a coincidence."

Melissa's smile dripped with sweetness, and he saw right through it. "Well, even though I'm here on vacation, we have things we need to discuss."

"Not after three years, we don't," he said emphatically.

Ripley moved up from behind and slid her arm around his waist. "Ready to go, hon?" Her tone was deliberately casual, but he swallowed a laugh at her sarcastic term of endearment.

"Absolutely." He dipped a curt nod at his ex. "Nothing to discuss, Melissa. Enjoy your vacation."

"We'll see about that, babe," she called after him as they walked away. "Bye-bye, Rebecca."

"Her name is Ripley!" he yelled over his shoulder, irritated as hell. He abruptly stopped, scooped Ripley into a passionate kiss, then put his arm around her, steering her toward his truck. He sensed his ex's death stare boring into them as Ripley chuckled at the exuberance of his kiss.

Only when they climbed into his truck did he allow himself to relax.

Ripley leaned across the console to brush his cheek. "I'm sorry she upset you. Has she told you what she wants?"

"No, but I have a pretty good idea." He switched on the engine and shifted into reverse to back out. "My income has increased since the divorce, so I'm sure that's part of it. Also, my mother left me her home in Arizona when she passed from cancer last year. I imagine Melissa would love to get her mitts on both."

"Oh, Tanner, I'm so sorry about your mom," she said quickly. "You must really miss her."

"She was a good woman. It was hard."

"No wonder Melissa is demanding your attention." In spite of it all, Ripley laughed.

Tanner laughed along with her as he drove down C Street. "She can plot all she wants. She's in my past, and that's where she's staying."

"I've always wondered about something," said Ripley, staring out the windshield. "When you love someone and break up with them, where does the love go? Does it transfer to the next person?"

Tanner braked for a light, giving her a quizzical look. "Deep thoughts, much? What made you say that?" The light changed, and he stepped on the gas.

"Isn't love like energy, where it can be neither created nor destroyed? Love doesn't die once it's created, does it?" Despite her sunglasses, he could tell she was staring into the distance.

"Well, I'm no expert, but I don't think the love you have for one person transfers to the next. Love is different with each new person," he reasoned.

"So, the love you had for Melissa, what happened to it?"

"It just... stopped. The love must have gone somewhere else in the universe because it sure left me." He thought about last night's conversation where he'd laid his cards on the table.

"I've told you how I feel, Ripley," he said in a serious tone. "You know where I stand. Whatever comes next with you, I'm all in."

The fleeting panic that crossed her face bothered him. "Ripley, you possess the courage to fly through amazingly hairy situations, yet you seem petrified of emotional commitment. Why is that?"

"I've told you before." She shifted in her seat. "I'm not good at relationships. I have a hard time trusting people."

"But you're good at taking calculated risks," he replied. "All I'm asking is that you apply some of that courage to us."

"I will." She hesitated, staring down at her lap. "I just have to do things on my own terms."

"Okay. I won't bug you about it." Tanner pulled into the hotel parking lot and killed the engine. He leaned across the console. "Come here and give us a kiss."

"Now *that* I can do," she said, meeting his lips with hers.

Chapter 36

ipley

R Ripley folded a T-shirt and tucked it into her duffel bag. As she lay the rest of her clothes on her bed to fold, she refused to think about parting from Tanner tomorrow afternoon when she flew the new air tanker back to Fairbanks.

Yesterday's community celebration had been a turning point for her, with their relationship finally out in the open. This was what she wanted, wasn't it? Wait until the fire was out so they could see where it all might lead? Still, she hesitated, her fear of commitment rearing its ugly head. Maybe she needed this separation from Tanner, so she'd have time to think.

A knock on the door interrupted her thoughts, and she opened it, delighted to see him with his dimpled smile.

"Hey, thought we could grab something to eat?"

She stepped back to let him in. "Sure. Almost done packing."

He moved to the window, looking out at the city. "I've been thinking about logistics."

"Oh, yeah?" she asked distractedly, folding a pair of pants. "What kind of logistics?"

"Like me doing more fire assignments in Alaska." Most men she'd dated had expected her to assimilate to their lives and what they wanted, not the other way around. This was a first.

"That would be great, but I couldn't guarantee I'd be here if they dispatched me to Canada or the lower forty-eight. Neither of us can predict where we'll be sent next, during any fire season. Or whether—" She stopped, the unspoken fear lodging in her throat.

"What is it that scares you, Ripley? What is it you're really afraid of?" He sounded perplexed, bordering on frustrated.

She racked her brain, wondering how the heck she could get him to understand. Time to come clean, as they say. And she trusted him. She took a deep breath. "I need to tell you something."

Tanner sat on the bed and patted the spot next to him. "Here, take a load off."

She sat next to him, fiddling with her fingers. "When I got into that tanker to make the drop on Hillside Haven, Mel said I was just like my father. He meant it in a good way, saying Dad would have been proud of the risks I took. But I saw it differently."

"How so?" He had her undivided attention.

"When Dad risked everything to save someone he loved, he lost his life in the Paradise fire in California. Do you remember what happened there?"

"How can any of us ever forget?" he said quietly. "The entire town burned."

She nodded slowly. "After I left for college, my parents moved to Paradise, and Dad flew tankers for Cal Fire." She shifted uncomfortably. "He dropped slurry on the Paradise fire. Everyone had evacuated except Mom, who was helping their next-door neighbor, Mrs. Parker, a woman in a wheelchair who couldn't find her cats."

"Where were you during all this?" he asked.

"Working on fires in Colorado." She paused. "By the time I heard about it, much of the town was in flames. I requested to demobe, but when I got there..." The images played in her mind like a nightmare as her voice caught in her throat, each word a tremor.

Tanner remained still, waiting.

"Dad panicked when he'd learned Mom hadn't evacuated." She swallowed to control the emotion. "He ignored direct orders and made a salvo drop on our house and Mrs. Parker's house. The slurry bought enough time for a fire crew to get Mom and Mrs. Parker out."

"Damn," he said, with a shuddering breath.

"After Dad released his load, something went wrong. Maybe mechanical failure, maybe the low altitude or the steep dive angle. They still don't know the exact reason. Dad crashed two blocks from where he'd saved my mother's life."

Tanner's fast intake of breath squeezed her heart. "I'm so sorry, Ripley."

She shook her head. "Mom never got over it. She survived, but knowing her husband died saving her eventually destroyed her. She drank heavily, then got onto pills. I took leave from my job to take care of her, but all she'd say was, 'I should have burned instead of your father.'"

A tear leaked down her cheek. "Guilt ate her alive. She died three years later from an overdose. Her last words to me were, 'Don't love anyone who works in wildland fire. It only brings heartbreak.'"

"And you became a tanker pilot." Tanner rose from the bed and moved toward her, but she held up a hand to stop him.

"Don't you understand?" she cried out. "When I hijacked the tanker for Hillside Haven, I did the same thing my father did. And you were in the same position my mother was. If I had crashed, if anything had gone wrong during that drop, you would have had that same survivor's guilt: that the person you loved chose your life over their own."

"But none of that happened—"

"I know it didn't! But it could have," she cried out fiercely. "If I allow myself to love you, and anything bad happens to you, it would destroy me. And if something were to happen to me, it would be the same for you. Loving people only leads to unbearable pain, just like Mom said. Now that I've fallen for you, I... I..." She couldn't finish, only stood there, trembling.

Never in her life had she been this terrified.

"Ripley, the entire human race goes through this. That's just the way it is." Tanner closed the distance, scooping her into his arms. She collapsed against him, and he held her while she wept, stroking her back.

"I'm so sorry," he murmured into her hair. "I had no idea. Mel mentioned you lost your dad, but he didn't say how."

"Everyone thinks my parents had this great love story," she choked out. "The heroic pilot who died saving his wife. They never saw what came after. They never saw my mother drink herself to death because she couldn't live with being the reason he would never come back to her."

"I can't imagine what you went through with all that." He wiped her tears with his thumb, then offered her a tissue from a box on the nightstand.

"That's not all." She took the tissue and wiped her nose. "I know. How could there be more, right? Two years after my mother passed, I lost my best friend, Allison. We met in flight school and applied to tanker training together. She was killed when someone ran into her small plane while she was landing in Colorado Springs to pick up her air tanker."

"Oh, man, that's terrible. I'm truly, truly sorry." Tanner tightened his embrace, and she felt as if an enormous load had lifted.

"I told you all this for a reason." She pulled back to look at him. "It's why I'm afraid to love again."

He opened his mouth to speak, but she cut him off.

"I know what you're going to say. That my parents' story doesn't have to be ours. That we're different."

"But we are different," he said. "Ripley, what you did for me and the rest—flying in those conditions, risking everything up at Hillside Haven—that *was* love, whether or not you say the words."

"That's what scares me," she blubbered. "I'm in so deep that I did exactly what my father did. Who's to say I won't do it again?"

He cupped her cheek. "I would have done the same. It's what people who care for each other do. If our positions had been reversed, I would have moved heaven and earth to save you."

They gazed at each other across a crevasse that separated past from present, between truly loving someone and accepting the consequences of that love in a dangerous, uncertain world.

Ripley's phone buzzed with a message reminder from Ryan, and she snapped back to the intrusion of present day responsibilities.

"I have to attend the Air Attack close-out meeting at the ICC," she said, collecting her keys. "Afterward, I'll bring you some sushi, and we'll have a quiet dinner. Sound good?" While the interruption had irritated her, she also needed some distance.

"Everything will be okay. Trust me." Tanner kissed her forehead. "Come up to my room when you get back." He moved to the door and let himself out.

When the door closed behind him, she took a minute to compose herself. She was emotionally drained but oddly relieved. She'd finally shared the fears that had shaped every relationship decision since losing the ones she loved.

Telling Tanner the truth was one thing but figuring out where to go from here was another. She wondered if love was always this complicated, this fraught with impossible choices. Or if she and Tanner were people whose careers made love more volatile.

As Ripley hurried to her truck, she was shocked to see Melissa, her big blonde hair bouncing as she clicked across the asphalt in her stilettos. After the come-to-Jesus conversation Ripley had just had with Tanner, the last thing she wanted was to bump into his ex-wife. She'd been surprised when the woman had popped up at yesterday's celebration.

"Hello, Rebecca," said Melissa, as if they hadn't been introduced twice already. "I was hoping to run into you, actually."

"Oh?" Ripley saw no point in correcting her when she did it to be mean, or whatever her intent was. Maybe it was jealousy.

Melissa stopped in front of her. "I thought you should know that Tanner and I have been talking."

Ripley tensed. She didn't need this right now, with her emotions already simmering on high. "What does that have to do with me?"

"Oh, he didn't mention it?" Melissa's eyes gleamed with apparent satisfaction. "We met for coffee this morning. We had unresolved matters to discuss."

"So, you came all the way to Alaska to discuss what you could easily talk about back in Missoula? That makes zero sense." Ripley drilled a stare into the shorter woman in her tight jeans, low tank top, and stilettos. She was out of place here, with all the firefighters coming and going.

"I'd already planned this vacation, plus I was curious to see who my husband was running with," she smirked.

"Running with?" Ripley swallowed a guffaw. "We didn't run anywhere. We worked together."

"When I heard Tanner was here and had a new girlfriend, I naturally became concerned. I still care about his happiness, you understand. And considering what I've encountered..." She made a disparaging gesture toward Ripley. "I thought it was an opportune time to discuss some things with my husband."

"Tanner has just finished commanding a thirty-day-plus siege on a catastrophic fire. I doubt he has the energy for such discussions," Ripley said bluntly.

Melissa gave her a sharp look. "What do you know about my husband's energy levels? Maybe *you* are the one depleting them." She pursed her lips with a head-to-toe innuendo Ripley did not appreciate.

Ripley took a menacing step. "I don't like what you're implying. And he isn't your husband anymore. He's your ex-husband."

Melissa stepped closer. "And you need to understand my husband and I are discussing reconciliation, so you need to stay out of his life. I don't need a skank complicating things."

Ripley's hands automatically curled into fists as she fought to control her temper. "I don't know you. You have no right to call me that. Take it back," she said evenly.

"Or what? Is that a threat?" Melissa said with fake sweetness.

"It's a warning." Ripley straightened to her full height, glaring down at her.

Melissa glanced at her baseball cap. "Captain Beecher, huh? Yes, I heard you were a tanker pilot. No matter, since we're getting back together. I'm on my way to talk to him right now, as a matter of fact." She shot Ripley a smug smile. "He told me to stop by to discuss it."

"Yeah, right. Sure, he did," retorted Ripley, rolling her eyes. "If Tanner wanted you back, he would have told me."

"No, he wouldn't. He wouldn't tell you because he enjoys having a special lay on every fire he works." Melissa laughed. "He's been doing it for years! He's only toying with you, using you. Why do you think our marriage ended? Anyway, nice chatting with you." Melissa brushed past her, clicking her stilettos across the asphalt and disappearing into the hotel.

For a minute, Ripley thought about going after her.

And do what? Give her a piece of my mind?

She thought about calling Tanner to warn him. She still had the burner phone Silva had given her. That was another thing on her to do list: get a new phone when she got home to Fairbanks. She decided against calling Tanner since she was already late for the Air Attack meeting.

As she drove to the ICC, Melissa's words echoed. Tanner wouldn't lie about reconciling with his ex, would he? And had he really met her for coffee this morning? Surely, he would have mentioned it. Hard to tell if the woman was lying. It bothered her that Melissa was heading up to see Tanner, but there wasn't much she could do about it.

After all, it was none of her business, anyway.

THE ELEVATOR DINGED as it reached the fourth floor, and Ripley shifted the takeout bags in her arms, a smile tugging at her lips. She'd ordered Tanner's favorite from the sushi place they'd frequented for a quiet dinner alone. This was their last evening in Anchorage before they'd go their separate ways.

The elevator doors slid open, and Ripley's world tilted sideways. She watched in frozen horror as Melissa—barefoot, stilettos in hand—pulled Tanner down for a slow, deliberate kiss in the hallway just outside of his room. His hands rested on her arms.

He wasn't fighting her off.

Ripley's heart thundered so violently her fingertips pulsed. The takeout bags slipped from her fingers, landing with a thud on the elevator floor. What the hell was going on?

Melissa was barefoot. Coming out of Tanner's room. Barefoot!

Heat flooded Ripley's cheeks, followed by a crushing wave of pain in her chest that made it hard to breathe. All those promises about being over his ex-wife, all those sweet words about wanting a future together—had it all been lies like Melissa said?

Before either of them could see her, Ripley abandoned the dropped food on the elevator floor and beelined for the stairway. She flung open the door and took the steps two at a time down to the second floor, her vision blurring with tears she refused to let fall. Not until she was safely behind the door to her room.

Her hands shook as she fumbled with her key card, swiping it several times before the light turned green. Once inside her room, she slumped against the door and let the hot, angry tears roll out, burning tracks down her cheeks.

How could she have been so stupid?

She'd known better. Men always said what they thought she wanted to hear, made promises they never intended to keep. But Tanner had seemed different. The way he'd looked at her, held her, reassured her when she needed it—he'd won her over where no other could. And now he'd ripped her heart in half.

Her phone buzzed with a text. Then another. She ignored them, tossing her duffel bag onto her bed and stuffing clothes into it with jerky, violent movements. She had to get out of here. Needed to get as far away from Tanner Westlake as possible before she did something really stupid, like march up to his room and say things she might regret.

What explanation could there be? I saw what I saw.

With trembling fingers, she dialed Ryan's number.

"Ripley? What's up?"

"I need to fly the tanker back to Fairbanks tonight." Her words sounded strangely hollow.

Ryan paused. "But AFS isn't expecting you until late tomorrow afternoon. You said you were going to spend the day with Tanner before he flies out tomorrow evening."

She was so furious she couldn't think straight. "Plans changed. I need to get back and report for duty."

"What happened?" asked Ryan. "You sound—"

"Nothing happened," she cut in, the lie tasting bitter on her tongue. "I just need to get back to work. Can you please have the ground crew get my bird ready to fly?"

"Everyone's off duty now. How about tomorrow morning, around ten? Did something happen?" He paused. "I know Tanner's ex is here. Oh, man, I shouldn't have told her about the picnic. I know you and Tanner have something good going on."

Something good? Right.

Her throat constricted. "Not anymore. Do *not* tell Tanner I'm leaving in the morning. Got it?" Her demand had him hesitating. "Promise me."

"All right, I promise."

"Thanks, Ryan." She ended the call.

Ripley finished packing with mechanical efficiency, ignoring the constant buzz of Tanner's calls and texts. She grabbed her belongings, checked out at the front desk, and fled to her truck. After peeling from the parking lot, she checked into an airport hotel. Only then did she read Tanner's messages.

Are you still at the meeting? It's going on three hours. I'm hungry!

Then another: *Your truck still isn't in the parking lot. Is everything okay?*

And finally: *Ripley, please call me! I'm worried.*

Each notification felt like a fresh knife wound. How could she tell him that after pouring her heart out about her fears, she'd discovered he was keeping secrets about his ex-wife? Her phone buzzed with more texts. She powered the phone off and shoved it into her daypack.

She sank onto the bed, her thoughts churning. Even if Melissa was lying about reconciliation, their little kissing encounter had exposed the fundamental truth Ripley had been trying to ignore: she was already in too deep. The pattern was repeating—she was becoming her mother, loving someone whose choices would destroy her. The only difference: she could escape before it was too late.

The sight of them together had shattered her. Tanner, who'd convinced Ripley she was worth fighting for, had been kissing a woman he supposedly no longer loved. Tomorrow, he would board a plane for Montana, returning to his life—a life that included a woman who wanted him back. Ripley would return to Fairbanks and bury herself in her job as a skilled aerial firefighter. End of story.

Safer this way. Cleaner. Less complicated.

Tomorrow she'd be back home in Fairbanks, back to the familiar rhythm of fire calls, slurry drops, and sleeping in her own bed. Back to the life she'd built for herself... and back to being alone. Her emotions spun around her exposed underbelly, laid bare by her afternoon confession, the sharp pain of Melissa's revelations, and seeing Tanner kissing her.

How could he do that after everything we've been through together?

It made no sense.

As she stared out at the blinking runway lights, Ripley convinced herself it was better this way. She'd dodged a bullet, discovering Tanner's true nature. No matter how hard she tried, the image of Melissa's arms around his neck wouldn't leave her mind. What hurt most was that he hadn't pulled away.

She would forget that Tanner Westlake ever existed.

The lie was as empty as her heart.

Chapter 37

Tanner

The argument with Melissa rang in his ears after making the mistake of letting her into his hotel room. She'd tried getting him into bed, but only got as far as taking off her heels before Tanner clutched her elbow and escorted her to the door.

He handed her the stilettoes. "Your tactics don't work. You need to go *now*. I'm expecting Ripley." He opened the door, gently pushed her through it, then stood in the doorway, waiting for her to leave.

"That skanky pilot slut?" she shot back, whirling to face him. "Come on, babe, you know you want me." She stepped in close and pulled his head to her with one hand and kissed him, her insistent tongue trying to pry his lips open.

He shoved her away from the kiss she forced on him. "Are you out of your damn mind? We're not getting back together. We will *never* get back together. I love someone else."

"No, you don't! You just think you do. You still love *me!*" Melissa tried her manipulative tears, the ones that had crumbled him years ago. But no more. "We were so good together once. We could be again. Your little fling with that pilot—"

"Stop right there." It was all he could do to hold his temper. "What Ripley and I have isn't a fling. You traveling up here to break us up is the lowest thing you've ever done. She outclasses you, and you can't handle it. I know you, Melissa. The minute you heard about Ripley Beecher, you set out to prove you were better than her."

"Tanner, you don't understand—"

He cut in. "I understand plenty. You don't compare to her. She has more class, more integrity, more honesty in her pinky toe than you'll ever dream of having. This is over, Melissa. We're done. Go back home."

She delivered a parting shot. "Don't worry, you'll come crawling back to me when she leaves you high and dry for someone else, because that's what skanks do!" He backed her into the hallway so he could close the door. Once he did, he cussed up a blue streak, shaking his head at her audacity.

His anger switched to concern when he couldn't get hold of Ripley. She wasn't opening his texts, and his calls went straight to voicemail. Something was wrong. Maybe she was in the shower, or maybe her phone had died. There had to be a reasonable explanation for why she wasn't answering.

Tanner grabbed his truck keys and headed for the elevator, jabbing the button for the second floor. When the door opened, he looked down to see two bags of sushi takeout. Now he knew something was wrong. Instinctively, he suspected what it was.

He knocked on Ripley's door, gently at first, then insistently. "Ripley? I need to talk to you." Nothing. He pressed his ear to the door, listening for any sound from inside. Silence.

Icy dread seeped inside him as he rode the elevator back down to the lobby. "Excuse me," he said to the desk clerk. "I'm looking for Ripley Beecher in room 237. She's not answering her phone or her door."

The clerk's fingers clicked across her keyboard. "She checked out half an hour ago."

This wasn't making sense. "Checked out? Are you sure?"

"Yes, sir." The young woman paused. "Is everything all right?"

Tanner stared at her, his mind calculating the timing. Thirty minutes ago. Close to the time Melissa had been in his room. "Did she leave a message? Anything at all?"

"No, sir. She told me to send her bill to the Alaska Fire Service in Fairbanks, then she left."

Tanner walked out to the parking lot in a daze. Sure enough, Ripley's truck was gone. He retrieved his phone and tried calling her again, his fingers fumbling the numbers as he tapped. Straight to voicemail. He left another message.

"Ripley, it's me. I don't know where you are or why you left, but please call me back. Something happened tonight that I need to explain. Please, just call me back."

He stood staring at his phone, willing it to ring. When it remained stubbornly silent, he wandered back inside and up to his room, his mind working through what may have happened.

Had Ripley seen Melissa leaving his room? Was that why she'd disappeared? Even if she had, why wouldn't she give him a chance to explain? They'd been through too much together for her to just vanish without a word.

Unless...Tanner sank onto the edge of his bed, tugging at his eyebrow. Unless Ripley had seen exactly what Melissa wanted her to see. His ex-wife was cunning, and she'd made it clear she had no intention of letting him move on with someone else.

I told her Ripley was coming to my room. She kissed me in the hallway, hoping Ripley would see. Dammit to hell!

And he bet she had. How could he be so stupid? He tried calling Ripley again. And again. Each time, his call went to voicemail. She must be ignoring his calls.

The realization hit him like a sledgehammer. Whatever had happened, whatever Ripley thought she'd seen or heard, she wanted nothing to do with him. The woman who'd fought many a raging fire without balking was running from him.

Tanner lay back on the bed fully clothed, staring at the ceiling as the hours crawled by. Sleep was impossible. Every time he closed his eyes, he saw Ripley's face—the trust in her eyes when she'd said yes to trying to make their relationship work. Had he destroyed all of that? Had Melissa's vicious intent won out?

His phone remained silent on the nightstand, mocking him with its lack of incoming calls or messages. He had no idea how to find her, much less how to make her listen to the truth.

The woman he loved was gone, and he didn't know where to look.

EARLY THE NEXT MORNING, Tanner decided it was time to stop playing it safe and live a little more dangerously. He grabbed Mel, and they checked out of the hotel, tossing their gear into the truck. Then they made a mad dash to downtown Anchorage to a jewelry store Mel found online, waiting impatiently for it to open. They were the first customers of the day.

"You look like you'd rather be jumping into a fire without a parachute," Mel observed with amusement, perusing watches in a nearby counter.

"At least I'd know what to expect," admitted Tanner. "This is terrain I've never jumped into. When I married Melissa, she picked out the ring. Never thought I'd be in the market for another engagement ring."

"There's a second time for everything," grinned Mel, rolling his toothpick to the other side of his mouth.

"Still haven't heard from Ripley." Tanner glanced at his phone for the twentieth time. "It's not like her to ignore my messages."

He'd grown increasingly concerned as the night wore on without hearing from her. That morning he'd banged on Mel's door, hoping Mel could shed some light on her sudden avoidance.

Mel had offered him a suggestion. "If you're serious about her, prove it. Show her you're all in. No half measures."

"How do I do that?" Tanner had asked him.

"She's been running scared for so long, you need to up the ante. Be ready to put everything on the line. That means a symbol of commitment. The permanent kind," explained Mel.

Tanner had given him a deer-in-the-headlights look. "You mean... like a... like an engagement ring? We've only known each other for—" he'd sputtered.

"How long you've known each other doesn't mean squat in the wildland fire business," Mel had pointed out. "We live fast and love hard because we never know what tomorrow will bring. You think Ryan waited years to propose to Tara? Ask Cohen when he asked for Raynie's hand. When you know, you know. Carpe diem, my friend."

Desperate times called for desperate measures, which was how Tanner had landed in this jewelry store in downtown Anchorage, shopping for an engagement ring before he flew back to Montana. The only problem was, his future fiancée was MIA.

The display cases gleamed under carefully positioned lights, rows of rings blurring together. Tanner rubbed his neck, overwhelmed by options that seemed too flashy, too plain, too traditional, or too modern—none quite right.

"Tell me more about what you're looking for," the jeweler prompted, an older woman with kind eyes and the patience of someone who'd guided countless indecisive men through this process.

"Something that fits who she is," Tanner replied, struggling to articulate what he wanted. "She's a tanker pilot—practical, no-nonsense. She needs a ring that won't snag on equipment or get in the way when she's wearing gloves in the cockpit."

"But also, something special," added Mel. "Ripley's not your average pilot."

The jeweler held up a finger. "Let me show you something from our custom collection. It might be just what you're looking for."

She disappeared into the back room and returned with a small velvet box. Inside was a ring unlike the ones in the display cases—it was a band of polished titanium inlaid with a line of deep blue sapphires that caught the light like stars in a night sky.

"Titanium is extremely durable," the jeweler explained. "It's used in aircraft construction for its strength-to-weight ratio.

And the sapphires are set completely flush—no protrusions to catch on equipment or gloves. Perfect for an airplane pilot."

Tanner tilted the ring for the sapphires to catch the light. It was practical, distinctive, and captured Ripley's essence: strong and resilient.

"She'll love this," he said with certainty. "I'll take it."

Mel nodded approvingly. "Suits her perfectly. You can size it later to fit her."

As the jeweler prepared the purchase, Tanner turned to Mel about a gnawing concern. "One minor detail: what if she says no?"

Mel shrugged. "She might. And you'd best prepare for that."

The jeweler returned with his purchase. "All set. I hope it brings you both much happiness."

Tanner chuckled. "First, I have to find the woman who's going to wear it."

When the jeweler gave him a quizzical look, Tanner said, "Long story."

"Always is, honey. Good luck," she said, handing him the black velvet box.

He eyed the receipt. "Guess I better keep this in case I have to return it, huh?"

"Think positive," said Mel, slapping him on the back. "You have to find her first. Now give me a ride to Merrill Field so I can fly Juliet back up to Fairbanks."

"Sure. I owe you for helping me out this morning," said Tanner as he and Mel headed to his truck, parked on 5th Avenue, across the street. As Tanner pulled into Merrill Field, his cell sounded. He tapped it right away, hoping it was Ripley.

"Hey Tanner, are you anywhere close to the airport?" asked Ryan.

Tanner's brows drew together. "I'm dropping Mel off at Merrill Field. Why?"

"I have something to tell you that I'm not supposed to tell you," said Ryan. "But Tara told me if I didn't tell you, she'd never speak to me again."

Tanner braced himself for bad news. "Does it have anything to do with Ripley?"

Temporary silence on the other end. "You could say that. I'll tell you when you get here. Make it quick," Ryan said mysteriously, and Tanner ended the call.

"Sorry to cut and run, but no time to explain. Ryan needs me at the airport." Tanner shook Mel's hand. "See you, buddy. Glad I got to know you. Hope to see you sooner than later."

"Sure thing. Good working with you," said Mel, then he turned to get his bird ready to fly.

While Tanner waited for traffic to clear before turning toward the airport, he watched Mel climb into Juliet and crank up the rotors. Once he was back on the road, he sped down 5th Avenue, wound up on Minnesota Drive, then hung a right on Northern Lights Boulevard, gunning it the rest of the way to Ted Stevens Anchorage International Airport.

He thanked the traffic gods for all the green lights.

Chapter 38

R*ipley*
The morning air at Ted Stevens Anchorage International Airport carried the familiar scent of jet fuel and adventure, two things that normally lifted Ripley's spirits. Except today. She moved through her pre-flight routine, her mind whirring with thoughts of Tanner and what she'd seen last night.

"You sure you're good to fly?" asked Ryan, eyeing her with concern as she completed her inspection of the tanker. "You look like you didn't sleep much."

"I'm fine," Ripley nodded absently, focusing on her checklist.

Sleep had been elusive, filled with replays of Melissa's bare feet and that kiss that had shattered everything she'd believed about her and Tanner. A solo flight to Fairbanks was exactly what she needed. Time alone to sort through her battered emotions.

"I have a fire boss who needs a ride to Fairbanks, and you have an empty seat." Ryan handed her a clipboard with the manifest. "He'll be here in a few minutes. He's running late. Help yourself to rolls and coffee." He nodded toward the operations office.

"I guess coffee will help." But she hadn't the energy or willpower to act on it.

Dammit. She'd looked forward to having time alone in the boundless skies, where she could think clearly without interruption. She wasn't in the mood for idle conversation with some guy who would drone on and on about fire.

She stood on the tarmac, filling out a flight data form on a clipboard, when footsteps approached. Without looking up, she said, "You the fire boss heading to Fairbanks?"

"Yep," came a clipped reply.

Out of the corner of her eye, she noted he wore full flight gear: standard issue flight suit, helmet with visor down, gloves, the works, so she couldn't make out any features. She chuckled to herself. Another nervous flier who took his safety protocols seriously. She finished scribbling and handed off the clipboard to the ground crew, then turned to face the fire boss.

"I'm Captain Beecher, your pilot for this morning's scenic tour of interior Alaska," she said, attempting humor with forced cheerfulness.

"Sam Smith." His voice sounded strained as he dipped a quick nod. Chatty guy.

"Climb aboard, Sam Smith. The co-pilot seat is all yours. Wheels up in five minutes." She hoisted herself into the pilot's seat and cycled through her pre-flight checklist.

He gave her a curt nod, clearly not in the mood for chatter. Fine by her. She had enough on her mind without making small talk. He buckled in, folded his hands on his chest like he planned to nap, and seemed comfortable enough. Good, no nervous passenger to wrangle.

Ripley put on her aviation helmet and turned on the plane's intercom system for communication, positioning her hot mic in front of her lips.

The tower cleared them for takeoff, and Ripley guided Blazebuster Two down the runway, loving the familiar surge of power as she lifted the air tanker into the morning sky. Anchorage fell away and faded into the distance, along with the broken heart she left behind. She climbed skyward, the hum of the plane engine drowning out the bittersweet ache inside of her.

They climbed steadily, passing through ten thousand feet, then fifteen thousand. The landscape below transformed from urban sprawl to wilderness, vast stretches of forest broken by ponds, lakes, and rivers, gleaming like silver ribbons in the morning light.

"Beautiful country to match a beautiful woman." The deep voice rumbled into her ears, and she damn near choked; she knew that voice like the back of her hand.

The blood drained from her face as she swiveled her head to the co-pilot's seat, nearly giving herself whiplash. The mystery man lifted his helmet visor and smiled.

"What the—what the...?" she stuttered into her hot mic. She was one hundred percent irrevocably rendered speechless.

"Tanner Westlake? How the hell did you sneak onto my aircraft?" she spluttered.

"Ryan arranged it," said Tanner in his sexy drawl. "And don't get mad at him for telling me. Tara made him do it. When I couldn't get your attention on the ground, I figured you couldn't avoid me up here." He spread his arms, motioning at the cockpit. "Unless you have a parachute. But that's my thing, not yours, isn't it? You said you don't jump out of perfectly good airplanes."

The words exploded out of her. "What the hell do you think you're doing?"

"Finally getting your attention," he replied, relaxing in his seat like he belonged there. "You weren't answering your phone, and you checked out of the hotel."

"So, you hijacked a ride in my aircraft?" Ripley's voice climbed an octave. "You impersonated a fire boss. Do you have any idea how many regulations you just broke?"

"I *am* a fire boss. And may I remind you: pot, kettle, black on you following regulations and hijacking this very aircraft, I might add," he lobbed back. "Guess Ryan forgot to tell you who was on your manifest."

Ripley stared at him in disbelief, then at the altimeter reading twenty-two thousand feet. They were well and truly airborne now, with nowhere to deposit one sneaky, manipulative, infuriating incident commander. Despite her fury, her treacherous heart did a little flip.

"I should toss you out without a parachute," she muttered, hating to admit it was a clever maneuver.

"That would be murder." He glanced out the passenger side window. "Think of the paperwork."

"Then I should toss you out with a load of slurry. At least that way, you'd make a colorful splat when you hit the ground."

"That would still be murder." His tone was light, but she noted the tense lines around his eyes, like he hadn't slept. "We need to talk."

"NOW you want to talk? Funny how you didn't want to talk last night when your ex-wife had her tongue down your throat with her shoes off!" The words tore from her throat, raw with hurt.

Understanding dawned, and his expression changed. "I knew it! You did see that."

"Aha, you admit it! Hard to miss when you knew I'd be coming to your hotel room." She focused on the instrument panel, not trusting herself to look at him. "Saw her come out of your room barefoot and then kiss you. And you weren't exactly fighting her off."

"Ripley, look at me."

"I'm flying a mother-effing air tanker, Tanner," she snapped. "Looking at you isn't a priority right now. Did you sleep with her? Did you have sex?" Since he admitted kissing her, she was determined to get to the bottom of this little shit show.

"Melissa forced that kiss on me. I was standing in my doorway, telling her to get the hell out of my life, when she pulled me down and planted one on me. I was so shocked, I couldn't react fast enough to push her away."

"Oh, you *poor baby*!" she shouted, her grip tightening on the controls. "Why did you let her inside your room in the first place? To chat about the weather?"

"She ambushed me. Showed up claiming she wanted to talk about us, which should have been my first clue to slam the door in her face. I tried to be civil, tried to explain that there was no 'us' and never would be again."

"Oh, an *ambush!*" she guffawed, widening her eyes in fake wonder. "And she was barefoot during this civilized conversation? Do tell!"

The plane hit minor turbulence, and she focused on her instrument panel. "Stop distracting me. I have a plane to fly."

"You can fly this plane with your eyes closed. Listen to me, Ripley. Yes, Melissa kicked off her heels because she wanted to get me into bed. But I didn't sleep with her. Nothing happened." He gestured his arms like a baseball umpire, calling a runner safe.

Much as she wanted him to spend the rest of the flight outside clinging to a wing, his explanation sounded somewhat plausible. It was exactly the kind of manipulation Melissa would use to win back her ex-husband.

"Why didn't you call me to explain what happened?"

"I tried, but you weren't answering. When I went to your room, the desk clerk said you'd checked out. I spent the entire night wondering where you'd gone."

She was too stubborn to speak, knowing he waited for her response. They flew in silence, only the drone of engines filling the chasm between them. Below, the Alaska Range stretched endlessly, peaks dusted with summer snow.

She couldn't stand it any longer. "You know what the worst part was? For just a second back there in Anchorage, I thought maybe I could have this. Maybe I could have someone who wouldn't abandon me and let me down." Her voice broke on the last word.

"You *can* have it," he countered. "We both can."

She gestured at the vast wilderness below them. "Look where we are, Tanner. Look at what we do. You live in Montana; I live in Alaska. We chase fires all over the country, never staying in one place for more than a few weeks. How is this supposed to work?"

"We'll *make* it work." His thick words rolled across the cockpit.

"You always say that, but it's not a plan," she countered. "It's a hope and a prayer."

"Don't you mean a wing and a prayer? Like in the movie, *Always?*"

She shook her head. "The tanker pilot dies in that story, remember? I already know what grief looks like. I don't need reminders. I don't want to be Dorinda in the white dress dancing with the love of her life, who's a ghost."

"But he came back as a ghost to help the air tanker pilot his fianceé would fall in love with," explained Tanner. "It killed him having to help the guy—no pun intended—but he did it because he wanted the woman he loved to be happy. Even if it meant loving someone else. That was the clincher."

She gave him a side-eye. "What does all that have to do with us? Just because the movie is about aerial firefighting?"

"Shit, Beecher! You honestly don't know?" He shot her an incredulous look. "I've fallen so hard for you that your happiness matters to me, even if I'm not the guy for you. I hope I am, but sometimes a wing and a prayer are all we need. Be brave enough to take a leap of faith for cripes' sake. I should strap a parachute on you and force you to jump from this plane just to prove my point."

"You couldn't land it without me!" she quipped.

"Want to make a bet?" He leaned forward and flipped on the autopilot switch.

Her jaw dropped. "You smokejumpers think you're so damn smart. Newsflash! I've taken leaps before. I've cared about people and wound up losing them—" Her voice was almost childlike.

"I'm not your dad, and I'm not Allison," he interrupted. "I'm not going anywhere."

The old wounds crept in. "People always say that and then they fucking leave!"

Frustration leaked into his voice. "You're so scared of being hurt, you're willing to miss out on all the love out there that's waiting for you. Love doesn't come with guarantees, but that doesn't mean it's not worth fighting for."

Ahead of them, Denali emerged from the morning haze, its massive bulk dominating the landscape. At over twenty thousand feet, it was a spectacular sight. Ripley switched off the autopilot and adjusted their course for a closer view.

"There you go. Don't say I never gave you anything."

"Would you look at that," Tanner breathed, distracted by the mountain's majesty.

"Twenty thousand plus feet of pure Alaska," she said benignly. "On a clear day like this, you can see it from two hundred miles away."

They flew closer until the mountain filled their field of vision, a towering tribute to the wild, untamed beauty of Alaska. In the shadow of this mighty mountain, their problems seemed insignificant. It was almost as if Denali was hinting at them to work things out.

He gazed out at the magnificent mountain range. "Puts things into perspective, doesn't it? Here we are next to Denali, arguing about staying together. What will it take to convince you we should?" His breathing changed. "Ripley, I have something to ask you."

She glanced at him, fidgeting with his hands. "What is it?"

"I know this is insane. I know we've only known each other for a short time, and I know you think I'm an impulsive jerk for hijacking your flight—"

"You aren't an impulsive jerk," she mumbled, softening a little.

"I also know what you and I have doesn't happen often. Maybe it never will again." He opened his hand, revealing a small black box.

Time suspended, and her heart stuttered as he opened it. "Captain Ripley Beecher, will you marry me?"

Her world narrowed to the ring, the mountain, and the question hanging in the air like the plane. Denali loomed beside them, bearing witness to the most unexpected proposal in aviation history.

"Are you out of your mind, Westlake?"

"Yeah, but that's not an answer."

She glimpsed the sparkling ring, astounded at the leap of faith he was asking her to take. Want grappled with fear, and she backpedaled, stalling for time.

She stared out the windshield, avoiding his gaze. "I need to think about it."

It was the best she could do after he'd caught her off guard by sneaking onto her flight, and then... *popping the question?* It was so romantic, but that was the problem.

"That wasn't a yes," he said quietly.

"It wasn't a no, either." She avoided looking at the ring, despite her fingers itching to reach for it. She loathed herself for spoiling this moment, but springing this on her was too much.

He snapped the box shut; the sound punctuated with finality. He stuck it in his pocket. "You're still pissed at me."

"Your ex called me a skank!" she spat out, a stark contrast to the calm voice of air traffic control guiding her descent into Fairbanks. The insult stung like a festering wound.

"And that's my fault, how?" He truly sounded surprised. "You talked to her? Oh damn, I can imagine what she said to you," he groaned out.

"I just—I just need to think about things." She touched down on a runway at the Alaska Fire Service, the landing smooth and anticlimactic after their drama in the air. As she shut down the engines and completed her post-flight checklist, she was thrown off her game by Tanner, sitting quietly beside her, the ring box tucked in his pocket.

As they climbed from the aircraft, she asked, "Where are you staying?" She longed to invite him to her cozy rental, and her heart ached with the words she couldn't bring herself to say.

"I'll hit Mel up when he gets to town. He's on his way, and will be here in a couple of hours." Tanner replied, shouldering his gear bag.

She was hurt that Tanner hadn't asked to stay with her. Despite the emotional roller coaster of the last twenty-four hours, she wanted to make up for her jibe. "Even if I don't agree to marry you, maybe I'll keep that ring for a birthday present."

Tanner stopped walking, his face lit with surprise. "Wait—it's your birthday?"

"I almost forgot about it," she said flippantly. "See what you do to me?"

"Why didn't you tell me?" he asked. "How old are you, or am I not supposed to ask?"

They hadn't gotten around to discussing her age. "Forty. A big fat round number that screams my youthful days are behind me." Every one of those years suddenly weighed heavily on her.

A grin lifted his face, like the sun breaking through storm clouds. "Well then, Captain, we have some serious birthday planning to do."

"I don't celebrate birthdays." She didn't say it as an affront to Tanner, but after her noncommittal answer to his proposal, she didn't deserve a celebration.

"Maybe you don't, but I do," he said cheerfully. She was envious of his ability to always turn lemons into lemonade. Some people had a knack for it, and Tanner was one of them.

As they reached the hangar for the air tankers, she stole glances at the man who'd just hijacked her flight just to talk to her. He'd broken through every piece of armor she'd thrown up to him without giving up. Yet marriage was the mother of monumental steps. Wasn't it too soon? Shouldn't they know each other longer than a month?

Their silent tension was as thick as the smoke had been around Anchorage. Tanner's eyes were on her, but she couldn't bring herself to meet his gaze.

"I have an AFS shuttle that's taking me to my house in town." A pang of guilt stabbed her for not inviting him to stay with her. "You're welcome to stay at my place if you like. Nothing fancy, but it's clean. How long do you plan to stay in Fairbanks?"

"Since I didn't plan to be here, I'll probably catch a flight tomorrow for Missoula," he said. "Thanks for the invite, but I'd feel awkward staying at your place after, well, not accepting my proposal."

"I said I'd think about it," she returned quickly. "I didn't say I wouldn't accept it."

He gave her a lopsided smile. "I'll grab some lunch at the mess hall, then wait for Mel to arrive. Think it's better that way."

"Tanner, I just need some time and some space. I need time to think." She was being as honest with him as she could.

"I refuse to leave you alone for your birthday, though," he said.

She swore he looked forlorn, and she wanted to fling herself into his arms. But she really needed time to think. "I won't be alone. Mel texted and invited me to his house for dinner. Maybe I'll see you there later." She hurried to the shuttle van that had pulled up.

What am I doing, leaving him standing there? But I didn't ask him to come to Fairbanks! Right, keep telling yourself that, Beecher.

She tossed her gear in the back of the van and hopped in, forcing herself not to look at Tanner, standing there with his fire pack and duffel. Secretly, she was glad he'd be staying with Mel, and she'd see him later.

But right now, she needed alone time and was relieved when the shuttle dropped her off and she was inside her modest little rental. She heaved out a sigh and went straight to the fridge to get a sparkling water. She sank onto her couch, put her feet up on the coffee table, and closed her eyes.

What a birthday present: the love of her life showing up on her flight, with a ring and a proposal, no less. Who could say they'd had a marriage proposal while piloting an air tanker? She chuckled out loud at the thought.

She hadn't said yes to Tanner's proposal because she had to be sure. And how could she be absolutely sure after knowing him for only four weeks? After all the people that had come and gone from her life, in a few short weeks along comes a person who'd spun her world into cartwheels... and she couldn't stop the spinning. The weight of the decision pressed down on her like the big Alaskan sky.

Maybe a shake of the dice or a flip of the coin would tell her what to do. She reached into her pocket, pulled out a quarter, and tossed it. Heads, she should marry him. Tails, she shouldn't. She called heads...no, wait... tails! No, heads, tails, heads, tails...

The quarter spun through the air, then landed on the hardwood floor, spinning on its side for what seemed forever, until it wobbled and finally tipped to the floor. She stared at it in disbelief while the universe held its collective breath.

"You've got to be kidding me!" she hollered at the top of her lungs.

Chapter 39

T*anner*

After eating a hearty lunch at the Alaska Fire Service mess hall, Tanner lingered to chat with some firefighters, to kill time, waiting for Mel to arrive. He figured it would take Mel three hours to fly Juliet up from Anchorage. When the time came, Tanner moseyed over to the heliport to wait. When Mel arrived, he was more than surprised to see Tanner waiting for him. Mel told him to hold his explanation of what happened until they had cold beers in their hands once they relaxed at his home on the Chena River.

Mel's log cabin was exactly what Tanner had expected from a veteran pilot—rustic, spacious, and filled with aviation memorabilia showing a lifetime spent in the sky. Model aircraft hung from the ceiling beams, vintage aviation posters covered the walls, and a massive stone fireplace dominated one end of the great room.

A total bachelor pad. He felt instantly at home.

"Beer in the fridge. Help yourself," Mel called out as Tanner dropped his gear in a corner. "You look like you need one."

That was an understatement. Between his restless night worrying about Ripley and the intensity of their aerial confrontation, Tanner felt like he'd been stuck on the frappe setting of a blender. He could use some liquid comfort.

"Thanks for letting me crash here for tonight," Tanner reached in to grab a bottle of Alaskan Amber. "I wasn't exactly planning on staying in Fairbanks. And after what happened with Ripley, I knew she needed some space."

"Yeah, about that." Mel relaxed into his favorite chair, a well-worn leather recliner positioned to take in a view of the Chena River. "Don't keep me in suspense. Tell me what happened after you dropped me off and arrived at the Anchorage airport."

Tanner explained the whole thing, starting with Ryan's suggestion that he get Tanner on her flight, and ending with his asking her to marry him. "She said she'd think about it. I wasn't expecting that answer," he concluded, taking a pull on his beer.

"You caught her off guard. Your covert sneak-up onto her flight was an automatic strike against you, though I thought it was a clever ploy," said Mel, sipping his beer. "However, I know a way you could score some points back."

"How would I do that?"

"You've got it bad for our girl Ripley, and she's based here in Fairbanks. Meaning, you'd have to commute from Montana like a long-distance Romeo. That's not sustainable, in my opinion."

"It's complicated—" started Tanner.

Mel held up his forefinger. "Not really. If you want to be with her, you need to be where she is. Like all the time. End of story."

"I've thought about it." Tanner picked at the beer label, considering. The idea had been lurking in the back of his mind since he'd realized how serious his feelings for Ripley had become, but hearing Mel say it out loud made it a possibility.

"The Alaska Fire Service is always looking for experienced incident commanders," Mel continued. "Especially one with your WUE track record. My guess is, Dave Doss would hire you in an Anchorage minute. He was impressed with your handling of the Elmore fire. You should talk to him."

"Oh, yeah?" said Tanner, pleased with the compliment. "I suppose I could."

"No time like the present," said Mel, tossing Tanner the keys to the van. "You do that, and Ripley will know you mean what you say."

AN HOUR LATER, TANNER sat across from Dave Doss in his office in the Alaska Fire Service building at Fort Wainwright. The older man's white hair made him look like he'd fought fire long before the turn of the century.

"So, you're interested in a transfer," Dave Doss said stated, looking at Tanner over wire-rimmed glasses. "I must say, I was pretty impressed with how you handled the fire down in Anchorage. Give me a verbal resume."

Tanner offered him the condensed version—his experience, qualifications, and reasons for wanting to move to Alaska. He left out the part about proposing to one of Doss's contract pilots at twenty-five thousand feet that morning.

"Your reputation precedes you," Doss said when he finished. "I've worked with folks in Montana who spoke highly of you. We could use someone with your specialized expertise up here, and we'd share you with the lower forty-eight when necessary."

"I appreciate that. I'm definitely interested."

Doss leaned back in his chair, cleaning his glasses with a lens cloth. "This wouldn't have anything to do with Captain Ripley Beecher, would it?"

Heat crept up Tanner's neck. "Was it that obvious?"

"Son, half the fire community's been watching you two circle each other like a couple of hawks. The other half's been taking bets on when you'd finally make a move. You pretty much outed yourself on the radio down there." He chuckled.

"I'm working on it." Tanner gave him a lopsided grin.

"Smart of you to wait until you were no longer her boss. Ripley's a hell of a pilot and a fine woman, but she strikes me as having more stone walls around her than a moated castle. Risk-taker in the air but plays it safe on the ground."

"That pretty much sums it up," replied Tanner, impressed with Doss' insight.

"Well, if anyone can crack that nut, it's probably you." Doss stood and extended his hand. "I'll make some calls, see what I can do about fast-tracking a transfer. Might take a bit. Another pay period or two."

"Thanks, Dave." Tanner's mind whirled a mile a minute at what he had to do.

If at first you don't succeed, try, try again.

AS TANNER DROVE BACK to Mel's cabin, his phone buzzed with a text from Ryan.

Aurora Hotshots demob'ed from the Elmore fire and have arrived in Fairbanks on an Alaska Airlines flight. Party time before the next fire call!

By the time Tanner reached the cabin, two AFS vans were pulling into the driveway. The Aurora Crew had arrived—Tara, Kenzie, Tupa, Rego, and others he'd worked with in Anchorage. They spilled out of their vehicles with the easy camaraderie of people who'd been through hell and back together and came out the other side.

"Well, look who's here!" Tara called out, grinning at Tanner. "Heard you pulled quite the stunt this morning, hijacking Ripley's air tanker."

"Word travels fast," he replied, accepting handshakes and back-slaps from the crew.

"In this business? Everyone in the Milky Way galaxy knew by the time you guys landed." Kenzie glanced around. "Speaking of which, where is our fearless pilot?"

"She's avoiding me," Tanner admitted. "I may have overwhelmed her."

"I told Ryan to tell you she was flying up this morning. But it wasn't my idea for you to sneak onto her flight," said Tara, laughing. "That was Ryan's idea."

Tanner grinned. "That was a clever idea, actually."

"So, what happened that caused her to avoid you?" pressed Tara, everyone stopping to listen.

"Yeah, what'd you do, brah?" Tupa asked suspiciously.

Tanner glanced around at the people who'd become his friends over the past month and who'd rooted for his growing relationship with Ripley.

"I asked her to marry me," he said, shrugging.

The reaction was immediate and explosive. Tara let out a whoop. Kenzie grinned like an idiot, and everyone talked at once.

"About damn time! We've been watching you two dance around each other for weeks," said Tara.

"What'd she say?" Kenzie wanted to know.

"She said she'd think about it."

A sudden silence hung in the room. Tanner could have heard a mosquito cough.

"Well, that's not a no," Tupa pointed out optimistically.

"It's not a yes either," Tanner replied glumly.

"Give her time," Tara said. "Ripley's an independent spirit, and this is a big step for her. She needs to trust that you're serious about this."

He shrugged. "How much more serious can I get? I proposed!"

"Right, after knowing her for what, a month?" Tara shook her head. "It didn't help when your ex-wife showed up wanting you back."

Tanner blew out air. "Tell me about it. I took care of that problem."

"Make sure Ripley knows your ex is out of the picture, buddy," Mel chimed in.

"She knows. I told her," said Tanner. "Also, today is Ripley's fortieth birthday. That's a milestone that deserves celebrating."

"Let's throw her a surprise party!" suggested Kenzie, appearing from behind a van with an armload of gear. "Something special."

"I already invited her to dinner at my place, so let's do it here," offered Mel. "Plenty of space and a splendid view of the river. In fact, we can set everything up on my big party deck."

The idea took on a life of its own, with everyone chiming in with suggestions. Within minutes, they had a plan that dazzled Tanner. They approached this like they did building fire lines.

"We'll need decorations," Tara said, pulling out her phone to tap out a list.

"And lots of food," added Kenzie. "Burgers and brats. Maybe a few steaks?"

"I'll handle the grill," volunteered Tupa.

"We need to delay Ripley coming over without her suspecting anything," said Mel. "I'll text her and make up a reason."

"We can help take care of that," Tara said with a mischievous grin. "Kenzie and I will take her out for a celebratory pitcher of beer. While we're gone, you guys will transform this place into party central."

As the crew scattered to do the preparations, Tanner talked with Mel on his sunny deck. They leaned on the railing, watching ducks ride the river current.

"Nervous?" Mel asked.

"You could say that," admitted Tanner, sipping another bottle of Amber. "What if she runs again?"

Mel laughed. "Ha, the runaway pilot. At least you'll know where you stand. She'll come around once she knows you mean what you say."

"Doss is transferring me," he said. "So, I'll be going back to Missoula to move my stuff up here. Not going to sell my mini-ranch in the Bitterroot, though. My jumper buddies will be happy to rent it."

"You can stay here until you find a place." Mel lowered his Ray-Bans. "Or you can bunk at the barracks at AFS, but you'd have a roommate."

"No thanks," said Tanner, laughing. "I'll take you up on your offer."

"Wait a second. I have an idea." Mel disappeared inside, then returned carrying a model aircraft, a perfect replica of the Dash 8-400AT air tanker that Ripley piloted, painted in the distinctive red and white colors of the StormAir planes.

"This is my pride and joy." Mel held up the model. "Took six months to build and get every detail perfect. I've been waiting to give it to Ripley for a special occasion. Looks like today is the day." He held it out. "Only now, I want you to give it to her."

Tanner took hold of it, examining the intricate craftsmanship, admiring every component that was true to the real thing. "Oh, Mel, I can't do that. You made it. *You* should give it to her."

He shook his head. "Give her this, along with that ring that's burning a hole in your pocket. Show her you understand who she is, and what matters to her. You do that, and you'll win her heart forever. Trust me."

Tanner gazed at the model tanker, thinking about the woman who flew the real one with skill and courage. The woman who'd saved lives, risking everything for others, and had captured his heart when others had tried and failed.

"All right. Thanks, Mel. Thanks for everything. I really mean that."

"Don't thank me yet." The older pilot gave him a man slap on the back. "Thank me when she says yes."

As the party preparations took shape, Tanner thought about what Tara said. Ripley needed proof that he was serious about his proposal, that theirs wasn't a relationship of convenience just because they had easy access to each other working in wildland fire.

He decided it was time to show her just how serious he really was.

Chapter 40

R*ipley* "Explain to me again why we're celebrating my birthday when I specifically said I don't do birthdays?" asked Ripley, sliding into a booth across from Tara and Kenzie.

"Because you're forty! That's a milestone," Tara replied, flagging down their server. "Besides, when was the last time you actually celebrated anything that wasn't work-related?"

Ripley considered this while scanning the Tundra Tropicana's drinks menu. "Good point. I think the last birthday party I attended was my dad's fiftieth, and only because he threatened to ground me from flying with him if I didn't show up."

"Crikey, you're long overdue." Kenzie grinned. "A pitcher of Alaskan Amber please," she told the server, before turning back to Ripley. "Tell us what happened this morning. Ryan said you and Tanner had quite the flight."

Ripley's cheeks warmed. "He told you about that?"

"Honey, the entire fire community knows." Tara laughed. "Tanner sneaking onto your flight isn't the sort of thing that stays quiet up in this neck of the woods."

"I still can't believe he did that." Ripley shook her head, swallowing a smile. "That guy has no sense of boundaries."

"Maybe that's what you need," suggested Kenzie. "A guy who won't let you hide behind barricades."

"I don't hide—"

Tara held up her forefinger. "Ripley, I've known you for over a month now, and in that time, I've seen you risk your life for complete strangers without hesitation. But the minute things get personal, you bolt. You're the bravest coward I've ever met."

The words stung her because they were true. "Emotional investments are painful. That's why I enjoy flying planes. Planes never hurt you like people do, well, unless they fall out of the sky. I feel safer on a plane than I do in a love relationship."

Kenzie leaned forward. "Look, we get it. This job doesn't exactly encourage long-term relationships. We're always moving, always focused on the next fire, the next crisis. But when someone comes along who makes our chaos worth it... you should think twice before letting him go."

Their pitcher arrived, and Ripley filled her glass and took a long sip.

"You want to know what scares me most?" she said finally. "Not the flying, not the fires, not even the possibility of getting injured for life. It's letting someone matter so damn much that losing them would annihilate me."

"Like your dad," Tara said softly.

Ripley's voice caught. "My life took a bizarre trajectory after the deaths of three loved ones in the blink of an eye. The loss of love from my life was real. I abandoned companionship for solitude and became an expert at self-sufficiency and self-reliance. Then along comes Tanner, who does his damndest to charm me into letting go of my one-woman show."

"And that's bad because...?" said Tara, sipping from her glass.

Ripley paused as an epiphany dawned. "He has me wanting things I didn't know I needed."

"Such as?" posed Kenzie.

"Someone to talk with about my day. Someone who understands this crazy lifestyle of ours." Ripley laughed. "And who sneaks onto my flight to Fairbanks just to have a conversation with me. Tanner wants things I'm not sure I could give him. I've never figured out what men want in a relationship." She downed the rest of her glass and filled it.

Kenzie piped up. "Here's what I know. After working with mostly guys on these fires, I've learned a thing or two. What most men have told me is, they want a woman who he can show his soft side to without worrying she'll think less of him for it. Someone with good humor who doesn't take everything seriously. And a woman who'll have his back in the tough times, and who believes in him."

"Also, a woman with her own life and interests, not someone who loses herself in the relationship," intoned Tara, sipping her beer.

Ripley pondered the words of wisdom with these new friends who seemed to get her. She hadn't found easy connections with many women outside of her fire world and was grateful for their perspectives.

"I've never seen a man more terrified than Tanner was when you made that drop on Hillside Haven," said Tara. "When he thought you might not make it out..." She shook her head.

Ripley's eyes flicked to hers. "What did he do?"

"The man was beside himself and paced like a crazed, overwrought grizzly." Tara smiled. "That's not the reaction of someone who is just having a fling. He knew the risks of you flying so low that you might not pull out of it. But when you did,

I thought Tanner would pass out from relief. You should have seen the grin on his face."

Ripley let all of that sink in as she weighed her Big Decision. "Tara, how did you and Ryan deal with the professional distance thing when you became involved?"

Tara groaned. "When I transferred to Alaska from Montana, he wound up being my training instructor. Talk about awkward. Here I was, trying to prove myself, and then I went and fell for the guy who was evaluating my work performance."

"Then what?" asked Ripley.

"We waited for training to end, after dancing around it for the longest time. We were worried that getting involved would ruin our careers. Then we figured out how to build a life together, and we took the leap."

She recalled how Tanner had used those same words.

"When you know, you know," added Tara. "And from where I'm sitting, Captain Beecher, you know."

Ripley stared into her beer, replaying Tanner's proposal and the way he'd looked at her when she told him she'd think about it. And the way he'd blindsided her by sneaking onto her flight like a covert romantic ninja, asking her to marry him at twenty-five thousand feet. He'd literally exploded her brain, not to mention her heart.

"Tanner asked me to marry him. I said I'd think about it," she finally confessed.

The women stayed silent until Tara spoke up. "Tanner told us."

Ripley wasn't upset about it, since things like this had a way of becoming viral the second they happened. "When I got home, I tossed a coin to see if I should say yes or no to Tanner's proposal." She glanced at their expectant faces, enjoying the suspense.

"What did you call?" asked Tara, her eyes wide.

"Heads." Ripley laughed and rolled her eyes. "Then I freaked out and kept flipping back and forth until it landed."

Kenzie made a hurry-up-and-tell-us gesture with her hand. "And it landed on?"

"Tails!" said Ripley, perplexed.

Everyone gave her an oh-no look.

"You can ask a Ouija board, a fortune-teller, or a psychic, and you still won't know," said Kenzie. "Beecher, you're a flipping pilot, mate. Making critical decisions is part of your DNA. So, make a damn decision!"

Everyone burst out laughing at Kenzie's pragmatic Aussie philosophy. They finished their pitcher of beer, and by the time they paid the check, a burden had lifted from Ripley's shoulders.

"All right, ladies," Tara said as they climbed into her Subaru. "Time we go to Mel's for dinner. I don't know about you, but I'm famished."

Twenty minutes later, Tara pulled into Mel's driveway. Several vehicles were parked along the gravel drive, and Ripley knew something was up. Especially when the cabin seemed unusually quiet for having so many vehicles outside. Tara opened the front door and motioned for Ripley to go first.

"SURPRISE!"

The word erupted from most of the Aurora Crew, crowding Mel's great room along with streamers, balloons, and a cake on a table in the center, with "Happy 40th, Ripley!" in sky blue frosting with a little plane outlined on it.

"You guys," Ripley breathed, her face heating at her new friends gathered on her behalf. "You didn't have to—"

"Yes, we did," interrupted Kenzie, pulling her into a bear hug. "Family celebrates family."

Family. These people—this crazy, brave, wonderful group of firefighters—had become her Alaskan family without her even realizing it. Because that's the way it worked here.

Before Ripley could say another word, the crowd parted to show Tanner standing next to the massive fireplace. He appeared somewhat nervous, which was unusual for him, looking absolutely perfect in blue jeans and a henley shirt with the sleeves pushed up. He combed his hair back with his fingers and walked torturously slow, as he moved toward her in a pair of dark cowboy boots. He stopped in front of her and dropped to one knee.

Oh, God...

Her insides somersaulted as the room fell silent. She'd never seen firefighters this quiet.

"Ripley Beecher." Tanner's voice rumbled through the hushed space. "This morning, at twenty-five thousand feet, I asked you to marry me. You said you'd think about it. Well, I've thought about it. A lot."

The small black box appeared in his hands, and he opened it to reveal the ring she'd avoided looking at before—it was uniquely beautiful, but it blurred as she blinked back tears.

"I won't spend another second wondering 'what if' when we can build a life together." Tanner removed the ring and held it up to her. "I love your courage, your skill, and yes, your morbid sense of humor, despite the fact you're a rule breaker."

The tears wouldn't stay back, but she no longer cared. All she cared about right now was never letting go of Tanner Westlake... for as long as they both shall live.

"In our line of work, nothing is guaranteed except the present. It's all we really have. So... I'm asking you again, in front of all these people—not that there's peer pressure or anything..." He slanted her a grin. "Will you marry me?"

The room held its collective breath as Ripley gazed at this man who'd stormed into her life, convincing her that loving each other justified the risk.

She brushed the hair away from his forehead, noting a faint glimmer of humor in his eyes. "I love you, Tanner the Wolfman. And yes, I will marry you."

"Feels damn good to hear you say that, Beecher." Tanner slipped the ring on her finger and stood to scoop her up in a kiss. The room erupted in cheers and congratulations.

Everything was perfect: the ring, this moment, and being surrounded by people who loved them both. She couldn't remember ever being this happy.

Mel whistled to quiet everyone. "Tanner has something else to say, don't you, Tanner?" He gave him a wide grin.

Tanner chuckled. "Oh, yeah, that's right. I put in for a transfer to the Alaska Fire Service. Dave Doss is making it happen."

Ripley stared at him in shock. "You what?"

"If we're going to do this, we should probably live in the same state. Plus, Alaska can always use another incident commander."

"Tanner, you're uprooting your entire life for me?"

"I'm not uprooting it," he said firmly. "Just planting it somewhere else. Somewhere with you. Oh, and I have another present." He offered her a small, gift-wrapped box and waited for her to open it.

She lifted out a new cell phone and smiled. "Is this so you can keep tabs on me?" she teased, throwing her arms around his neck in a bear hug.

He backed away and lifted Mel's model plane from a nearby table. "Another token of appreciation for helping me, not only on the fire, but in keeping me grounded." Everyone laughed at the irony of his pun.

"This is Mel's creation, but he wanted me to give it to you." He held it out to her. "Happy Birthday, Ripley."

The beautiful tanker model took her breath away, and she rushed over to Mel to envelop him in another bear hug. "Thank you, dear friend," she whispered in his ear.

"This is from your dad," he whispered back. "I know he'd be proud."

And she knew it, too. Life had a way of bringing everything full circle, Ripley thought, as everyone surrounded her to admire the ring and the beautiful tanker model Mel had crafted. She adored the gifts from her future husband. Destiny fulfilled.

She was the luckiest woman in the world.

WHEN THE LAST GUEST had gone home and the cabin was quiet except for the gentle sound of the Chena River flowing past, Ripley and Tanner were finally alone in the guest room Mel had prepared for them. The celebration had been perfect, but now she wanted her new fiancé all to herself.

"Come here," he said softly, reaching for her hand.

She moved to him, suddenly shy despite everything they'd been through together. He drew her close, his hands framing her face to gaze into her eyes. She kissed him, pouring all her love and certainty into him. Her desire for him was endless, boundless. His arms came around her as if he'd been waiting his whole life to hold her.

They savored each touch, each kiss. His hands were gentle as they traveled the lines of her face and neck, as if to memorize every detail. He kissed where his hands had been, and she rested her head back to give him access to whatever he wanted. When he lifted her shirt over her head, his eyes became hooded.

She wanted him. Badly.

"You're beautiful." The way he said it made her believe it. Right now, she'd believe him if he said the Martians had invited him onto their spaceship.

Ripley's fingers found the buttons of his shirt, working them open with trembling hands. When she spread her palms across his chest, she loved the feel of him and how perfectly they fit together.

They undressed each other, taking time to appreciate what they were sharing. Every kiss was a promise, every caress a claim on each other. Tanner laid her back on the bed with tender, sincere kisses.

"I love you so much," he murmured against her throat.

"Love you more," she breathed, the words rolling out easily, buoyed by her no-fear resolve in choosing to commit herself to him with everything in her soul. She knew her parents and best friend Allison would be proud.

They joined together, their hearts synchronizing their beats as they reveled in one another. The outside world faded until there was nothing but the love that had grown between them, despite all odds. They made slow and gentle love, taking their time after moving at the speed of light for the past month.

Afterward, they lay entwined, neither wanting to break the spell of intimacy. She rested her cheek on his collarbone, relishing the rapid thrum of his heartbeat.

"I can't believe you did all this for me," she murmured. "I can't believe this is real."

"Oh, it's real," he assured her, kissing her bare shoulder. "Very real."

"I was so scared," Ripley admitted. "I thought I'd lost you before I'd even really had you."

"You'll never lose me. Ever. And that's a promise."

She lifted her head to look at him. "I've loved you all my life, you know—the promise of you long before I heard you on my radio at Big Lake. And when you spoke to me on the radio, it felt like you were calling me to you. I couldn't believe it when you showed up at the Palmer air base after I'd landed."

"I *was* calling to you. I had to meet the woman who flew that tanker," he said, pulling her up for a kiss.

"The weirdest thing," she said. "When I met you, it was like everything in my life suddenly came into focus—like everything was going to be okay—and now it is."

"You sure know how to make a guy feel good." He pressed her tighter against him. "I wish we'd met sooner, because the split second I met you, I knew you were the one."

"Yeah, right, you say that to all the women." She poked him.

"But you're the only one I want to spend the rest of my life with," he rumbled out.

"You've become a wolf," she purred. "And I love it." She reached for him again for another round.

Outside, the Alaska summer night stretched endlessly, the sky never quite dark even at midnight. Somewhere in the distance, a loon called across the water, its haunting cry echoing off the trees.

She thought about the journey that brought her here: the losses that had shaped her, the fears that had defined her, and the unexpected love that changed everything. She thought about the risks they'd each taken, both in the air and on the ground, and the trust they'd built in each other along the way.

Tomorrow would bring new challenges. New fires to fight, new dangers to face. But tonight, wrapped in Tanner's arms with her engagement ring catching the midnight sun streaming through the window, she felt something she hadn't felt in years.

A profound sense of peace.

And for a woman who'd spent her life flying from place to place, never settling, never staying, this was the greatest reward... the greatest adventure of all.

Her leap of faith.

Thanks so much for reading Alaska Firestorm! If you enjoyed this book, please tell your friends and family, and please post a review

on Amazon. Reviews make an huge difference in my success as a writer and help other readers discover the story!

Author's Note

Aerial firefighting pilots have given their lives in the line of duty. Here are some recent deaths of aerial firefighters:

Pilot James B. Maxwell: The pilot of a single-engine air tanker crashed in Grant County, Oregon on July 25, 2024, after dropping a load of retardant on the Parasol Fire in Grant County, north of the Falls Fire. He was returning to Burns to reload.

Pilot Juliana Turchetti: Juliana Turchetti, a pilot with Dauntless Air, died on July 10, 2024, while battling the Horse Gulch Fire in Montana. She was described as losing control of the aircraft during an in-flight maneuver to scoop water.

Amentum employees: Two individuals with Amentum, an aviation company contracted to CAL FIRE, died in a plane crash in California on July 23, 2024, while en route to repair a CAL FIRE helicopter. They were identified as pilot Gabe Kulp and mechanic Thomas Smith.

In 2024, the United States saw eleven firefighter fatalities in the United States, including three air tanker pilots.

On July 10, 2021, the U.S. Bureau of Land Management in Arizona faced a tragic aviation accident that resulted in the loss of two individuals who were battling the Cedar Basin Fire on the Colorado River District. Pilot Matthew Miller and Air Tactical Group Supervisor Jeff Piechura were on board an aerial supervision platform, conducting visual reconnaissance and aviation command and control over the fire, when the tragic accident occurred. These dedicated firefighters embodied the true spirit of their profession through their unwavering commitment and remarkable bravery.

PLEASE PRAY FOR THE safety of all wildland firefighters and structural firefighters who risk their lives to protect people, property, and natural resources from the destructive force of fire in North America and overseas. This series is dedicated to each one of them.

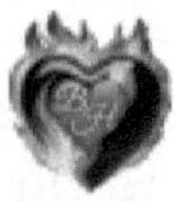

Bonus Content!
Does Ripley become a runaway bride, or does she follow through with her promise to marry Tanner? Download the bonus story from Bookfunnel and join my VIP Readers List to find out! Insert this address into your browser.
https://dl.bookfunnel.com/eukul4q7qm

Acknowledgements

I'm grateful to all who helped make this book happen by helping me with the story and providing moral support. First, I want to thank my readers who have been with me since the beginning and the ones who have picked up to read any of my books. I love writing these stories for you, and it is a thrill when you say you enjoy them and tell others about my series. I'm especially grateful as this book was a departure in creating Ripley, who I did not want to leave when I finished her story. I wanted to keep flying with her! I'm also grateful to the people who talked about what it's like to fly these amazing planes and helicopters to fight our nation's and Canada's wildfires.

A huge thank you to former logger, commercial fisherman, educator, and Montana wildland firefighter, Marc Simenson, who helped me plot this story. You're a fantastic business manager and all-around good guy. I think I'll keep you.

Kudos and thanks go to my wonderful editor at Evil Commas, Judy McCrary, who helped me improve this story.

An enormous round of thanks to Steve Stripling and Mike Ford of the *Big Alaska Show*, on KFQD radio in Anchorage. They have supported me from the very beginning, back in 2020, when I wrote my first novel, *Alaska Spark*. They've had me on as a guest several times since, and we laugh so much it's hard to stay on track. I'm grateful to them for telling me another Alaska Tall

Tale, and as a tribute, I named my first officer co-pilot Nubs from Moose Pass, Alaska.

A special thank you to the late Henri Bisson, former Director of the U.S. Bureau of Land Management, Alaska State Office, for having supported every book I've written in this series. He suggested I include those who have lost their lives in the line of duty, as a tribute to the brave women and men who protect lives and property. Rest in peace, Henri. You are sorely missed.

Grateful to my former employers and the public information staff at the U.S. Bureau of Land Management, Alaska Fire Service in Fairbanks, AK, and other agency resources: U.S. Forest Service, Chugach National Forest; Municipality of Anchorage Office of Emergency Management; Chugach Electric, The Weather Service, State of Alaska Division of Forestry & Fire Protection, Anchorage Fire Department's Wildland Fire Division and Fire Marshal's Office; and AFD Wildfire Community Town Hall Meeting, May 19, 2025, in Anchorage, Alaska.

Last but not least, I'm grateful for my furry besties, the Mandy Lorian and Rooby Doo, my superstar goldens, who promised not to toss their balls onto my keyboard while I wrote this novel (as long as I bribed them with treats). They didn't always honor their promise, so if you've found typos, I'm blaming them. Thank goodness their balls didn't land on my 'delete' button!

Also By LoLo Paige

Want more firefighter stories? Check out my other books in the
Blazing Hearts Wildfire Series
Alaska Spark – Book One Alaska Inferno – Book Two
Alaska Blaze – Book Three
Alaska Firestorm – Book Four
Alaska Flame – Novella
Blazing Hearts Montana Fire
Montana Blaze
Montana Smoke
Montana Flame

Check Out LoLo's Romantic Comedies and Other Books!
The Wandering Hearts Series
Hello Spain, Goodbye Heart
Irish Thunder
The Polar Paired Series
Cupid's Kerfuffle
Everybody Loves Polar Bears
Flights, Fights, and Christmas Lights
Historical Fiction as Lois Paige
The Butte Girl's Club

FREE Series Prequel! Alaska Spark's Ryan and Tara had their
own journeys that led them to the Land of the Midnight Sun.

Why did Ryan leave everything behind and how did Tara get her second chance at love? Join my reader community to download this free series prequel only available at *www.lolopaige.com*[1]

---

1. *http://www.lolopaige.com*

About the Author

LOLO PAIGE IS AN AWARD-winning, multi-genre author, publishing independently and traditionally, with the Wild Rose Press. Her books have received several awards, including the Eric Hoffer and Kindle Book Review awards for best indie romance. Her romantic comedies, *Everybody Loves Polar Bears, Hello Spain: Goodbye Heart,* and *Irish Thunder* are all based on personal experiences in and out of Alaska. She also has a coming-of-age, historical fiction novel coming out in August 2025, *The Butte Girls' Club,* under the pen name Lois Paige.

LoLo's romantic suspense books about wildland firefighting have topped Amazon Bestseller Lists in the U.S., Canada, and Australia, and *Publishers Weekly* has featured her books from the *Blazing Hearts Wildfire Series* in their Booklife section. As a former wildland firefighter, her true story in The Anchorage Press about escaping wildfire in Alaska won an Alaska Press Club award, which led to her debut novel, *Alaska Spark.* Cherry Adair and Kat Martin have both endorsed her romantic suspense fire series.

Follow me on Amazon, Facebook and Instagram!